Red Mass

**Other Novels by Rosemary Aubert
in the Ellis Portal Mystery Series**

Free Reign
The Feast of Stephen
The Ferryman Will Be There
Leave Me By Dying

Red Mass

AN ELLIS PORTAL MYSTERY

Rosemary Aubert

BRIDGE WORKS PUBLISHING COMPANY

Lanham • New York • Boulder • Toronto • Oxford

Published by Bridge Works Publishing Company, Lanham,
Maryland, an imprint of The Rowman & Littlefield Publishing Group, Inc.

Distributed in the United States by National Book Network, Lanham,
Maryland. For descriptions of this and other Bridge Works books, visit the
National Book Network website at
www.nbnbooks.com.

FIRST EDITION

The characters and events in this book are fictitious. Any
similarity to actual persons, living or dead, is coincidental and not intended
by the author.

Library of Congress Cataloging-in-Publication Data

Aubert, Rosemary.
  Red mass : an Ellis Portal mystery / Rosemary Aubert—1st ed.
    p. cm.
  ISBN 1-882593-96-0 (cloth : alk. paper)
  ISBN 1-882593-95-2 (pbk. : alk. paper)
  1. Portal, Ellis (Fictitious character)—Fiction. 2. Private investigators—
Ontario—Toronto—Fiction. 3. Toronto (Ont.)—Fiction. I. Title.

PR9199.3.A9R43 2005
813'.54—dc22   2005001237

10 9 8 7 6 5 4 3 2 1

For Barbara and Warren Phillips

Red Mass

Chapter 1

At Michaelmas in the autumn of the year, Canadian judges in black silk robes, red woolen sashes and starched white-linen collar tabs gather like red-winged blackbirds to celebrate the Red Mass. I often observe red-winged blackbirds in their natural habitat and have never seen two males on the same branch. Ordinarily, you would not have caught me and Supreme Court Justice John Stoughton-Melville in the same room, either, even a room as large as the nave of St. Michael's Cathedral. This day of the Red Mass, knowing I was in Stow's presence made me conceal myself from his sight.

At sixty years old, I am a man living out my last chance. I don't draw attention to myself. I don't sit where people can see me unless I mean them to. I sat in the back of the cathedral among law students and the general public, where my eyes could scan the crowd who had come to celebrate the archaic practice of opening the courts with a church service.

Crimson vestments adorned the seven celebrants of the mass. Rank upon rank of judges, red-jacketed Mounties and even the cap of the cardinal added to the color of the occasion. Of all who were present, only the cardinal and the chief justice outranked Justice Stoughton-Melville. I saw Stow shift nervously in the pew, glance over one shoulder then the other, clearly a man ill at ease. Did he find it demeaning to be a third-ranking dignitary behind the cardinal and the Chief Justice of the Supreme Court? Or— harder to imagine—was he afraid of something? I was glad I was too far away for him to notice me.

"Supreme Court Chief Justice Amanda Welsh-Martine. Supreme Court Justice Puisne John Stoughton-Melville. Justice F. Robert McKenzie of the Ontario Superior Court of Justice . . ."

As the archbishop honored the respected attendees by reading out their names, I strained my neck to get a better view of Stow's escort. On either side of him stood an exceptionally tall young man in a scarlet tunic trimmed in gold. So he traveled with his own Mounties! How impressive. How like Stow to waste the taxpayers' money instead of his own.

He fidgeted again, and I glanced quickly away, which would have been the reason I wasn't looking when, just as the choirboys rose to sing the opening hymn, the huge cathedral echoed with a small sharp sound that had nothing to do with Gregorian chant.

Without actually seeing them move, I realized that the two Mounties flanking Stow had just made him their prisoner.

I'd been a judge myself the first time I'd felt the cold steel bands of the law around my own wrists. Still, I was shocked to see Stow arrested. I experienced that curious slowing of time that happens when some life-altering occurrence plays itself out before one's eyes. I saw Stow's shoulders stiffen. Even beneath the absurd red robe with its white fur-trimmed cape, the muscles of his back became visibly rigid. Years on the bench—and on the skids, too—had taught me the difference between a man who stands up straight when he faces defeat and one who slumps. Stow did not slump.

"Hosanna in the highest . . ."

Who had planned this horrific display of punishment—and why and how? Fortunately, Stow was spared the disgrace of having to crawl past someone else on his way out of the pew. He and his guards were on the aisle.

But they were on the center aisle, and in order to remove their prisoner from the church, the police were going to have to march him, Supreme Court robes and all, right down the middle of the hundreds of dignitaries, only a few of whom seemed to be gaping at the tall man in red walking in step with the red-coated officers.

"Blessed is he who comes in the name of the Lord."

I, too, sat on the aisle. Was there any reason for Stow to think I would be present at the Red Mass? I never would have come without prodding. Not even in the old days when I might have expected my own name to be called out. I preferred to stay away, even before bitterness, shame, regret and longing had attached itself to anything that had to do with me and the court. Vainly, I tried to hunker down behind the tall student in front of me. Even though Stow was the one being hauled off, I was the one who'd be embarrassed if he saw me.

"Hosanna in the highest."

As Stow passed by the assembled judges, men and women possessed of professional—indeed legendary—calm, no head turned.

The same was not true of the heads of the lawyers, including mine. Lawyers were always welcome at the Red

Mass—but as spectators. Unlike the judges, we welcomed the opportunity to gawk at our betters.

When I turned, Stow's eye caught mine.

I winced and dropped my gaze.

But not before I saw, at the very back in the deep shadows at the rear of the church, a slender female figure who, as if by prearrangement, slipped out behind Stow and the Mounties and disappeared from my view into the bright sunlight outside the cathedral.

My instinct was to follow, too, but I fought the urge. Stow had been my friend once, but that had been a long time ago. If I owed him anything, the debt had been cancelled by time. And by distance, too. The distance between an outlaw and a potentate of the court.

"What in God's name is going on?"

"Shut up, Nicky," I whispered to the young man sitting beside me. "Pay attention to the service."

Like most of the hundreds of other officers of the court present at the Red Mass, I turned my attention back to the officiating archbishop and pretended not to have seen what I so clearly had.

What could Stow have done to merit being taken into custody? Were it anyone else, I would automatically have assumed that criminal charges had been laid. To assume such a thing of a Supreme Court Justice, let alone a pillar of the community like Stow, was inconceivable. Had he, then, been arrested for his own protection? It is one of the duties of the Royal Canadian Mounted Police to protect important public figures. But not to handcuff them. Not to drag them off in full view of the public they are pledged to serve.

The rest of the Red Mass passed in a blur. I imagine there was the usual homily, the usual reminder to all present of the power and majesty of the court, of the supremacy of law, of the honor of service to one's country and Queen. I heard not a word.

I'm speeding through the streets, stone sober despite the booze and the coke. It's raining and I can barely see, but I feel like the Pope or the Queen—as if anybody who cared to could see me. What have I done? How have I let go so quickly and so thoroughly? There is no need to ask why. There is no why. There is only the fact that I have tried to kill a woman by choking her in the middle of a crowd of people in the Eaton shopping center. I have been driven around this city by chauffeurs for years now. But though this car is unmarked, anybody would know it is a police cruiser. Impulsively my eyes seek a means of release. But there is no door handle. And even if there were, how could I open the door with cuffed hands? The steel grates against my wrist. Do I care more about my skin or about my Cartier watch?

"Coming back to the Barristers' Dining Room, Ellis?"

"What?"

I started at the whispered question, looked up to see the procession of dignitaries, led by a police honor guard, slowly making its way out of the church.

"You're back in the profession now. You gotta get out more. Personally, I wouldn't miss the reception for the world. Watching stuffed shirts stuff themselves. What could be more fun?"

"Oh, Nicky!"

Nickel McPhail IV, named for his great-great-grandfather who had made a fortune in the mines of northern Ontario, was a few decades younger than me—thirty to my sixty. But he had "adopted" me on the first day I'd returned to law school after so many years in disgrace. It embarrassed me to think that Nicky was my teacher and not the other way around. It flattered me that he nevertheless followed me around like a puppy, asking questions about what he teasingly called "the golden days of our calling."

5

Nicky was possessed of the astonishing sense of personal ease that comes only from generations of great wealth. The standing joke was that he could afford to be a fun guy because he had been born with a nickel spoon in his mouth, but to my mind, his personality had nothing to do with luck. Nickel was simply a decent, positive, honest, civil man.

"No, Nicky, I'm not going," I whispered back. One of the judges in the procession heard my whisper and cast me a warning glance. It's not wise to forget that a judge's livelihood depends on his hearing.

"I wouldn't be welcome," I said more loudly. One of the things Nicky had taught me—as if I needed to learn—was never to show that one was intimidated by a judge.

"Don't be ridiculous, Ellis, even the lackeys are invited." He nodded toward the four judge's deputies at the very rear of the grand procession—two women and two men who escorted judges when they were robed. Each of them was middle-aged, trim, alert. I never referred to court service officers as lackeys myself, especially since I'd done a stint as one. But even a basically friendly guy like Nicky sometimes showed contempt for the nearly invisible underlings of the system.

"I have no desire to stand among judges and fellow lawyers eating tiny sandwiches and trying to think of clever retorts, Nicky."

"I keep telling you, Ellis, you need reality training. You've been away for a long time, and you've spent the last six months with your nose glued to a laptop. It's time to reclaim your place among your peers."

I glanced up at his earnest, handsome face. The McPhails were tall men. I'd seen a full-length portrait of Nicky's father in the lobby of Osgoode Hall among the portraits of the other Chief Justices. "Listen, kid," I said, "I'm interested in cases and causes, not gossip and pretense."

"You're interested in what's going on with your old pal John Stoughton-Melville," Nicky replied. "You don't fool me with your righteous routine. But if you know what's good for you, you'll stay out of it. Come on, you old relic, get with the program and get on the bus."

He wasn't speaking metaphorically. There *was* a bus waiting outside the iron gate of the fence that surrounded St. Mike's Cathedral. As I followed Nicky toward it, grumbling as I went, I suddenly remembered something that had happened at least twenty years before. The Pope had come to Toronto and, I seemed to recall, had said mass at St. Mike's. The mass had been for clergy, but hundreds of laypeople had stood outside the fence, hoping to catch a glimpse of the Pontiff. I stood in the crowd with my mother. When the Pope appeared, she crossed herself and pressed closer to the fence. I tried to pull her back, afraid she'd be crushed in the crowd, but she resisted. I turned to see if there was a way out, an opening through which I could drag her if it became necessary. I looked around, and then I looked up. Across the street from the cathedral, the roofs of all the buildings were lined with military snipers, their long-barreled guns outlined against the afternoon sky like a crown of thorns. I glanced around.

"Watch where you're going, Ellis; you'll fall on your face . . ." Nicky gave my shoulder the sort of little push that makes a man feel old, and I realized we were next in line to board the bus back to Osgoode Hall and the Red Mass reception. Like my mother on the day of the Pope's visit, I was up against it. There was no turning back, no choice except to follow Nicky onto the bus.

"Most unfortunate. Quite surprising. One never knows what to expect these days, does one?"

Once I got to the reception, I sidled up beside a cluster of the more senior judges, hoping to overhear some snatch of conversation that would give me a clue about Stow. But their conversation was so guarded, so general and vague, that I couldn't tell whether they were discussing the arrest of the Supreme Court judge or the latest verdict in a criminal case.

Across the room, the four "lackeys" huddled beside an eight-foot fern in a corner. Against the brocade-upholstered chairs, the deep blue carpet, the long white window treatments, they looked uncomfortable and eager to escape. Like me.

"Hi," I said to them.

The deputies nodded and smiled, but I could see my presence put them slightly on guard, as if they expected me to ask them to fetch something, good minions that they were.

"It's a shame what happened at the mass, isn't it?" I prodded.

To no effect. "It was lovely as always," one of the officers said.

"What are *you* doing here, Portal?"

Ignoring the deputies entirely, a large, elderly man with dark craggy brows and a thatch of wild white hair pushed himself between me and them as if his judge's robes exempted him from ordinary civility. "I wouldn't have thought you'd have the gall," he said.

Out of the corner of my eye, I saw one of the male minions glance quickly from the old man's face to mine. Clearly the deputy knew who both of us were. "You may have returned to the bar, Portal, but rest assured you've no hope of regaining the bench."

"Thank you, Your Lordship," I replied. Always thank a judge even if he screws you. That was Nicky's advice. Good idea but not new. I'd taught it myself in years gone by. "It's a pleasure to know that Your Lordship has paid such close attention to my career."

"You were a troublemaker when you were young, Portal," he growled, "and now you're an old troublemaker. You'd be best advised to be of good character and keep the peace."

This insulting legal warning, often given to people on bail, was a veiled reference to my criminal record, now permanently sealed by a pardon. But if the old coot thought he was shocking me, he was wrong. I made no secret of my past.

I nodded good day to the pompous ass, threaded my way through the crowd and out into the lobby. The Byzantine mosaic of the floor amplified the sound of my hurrying steps, and the portraits of stern old former Chief Justices of Ontario stared in disapproval as I rushed toward the front door. I had to get outside. I was suffocating.

In the late afternoon sun, the formal gardens in front of Osgoode Hall bloomed with an exuberance that was almost embarrassing. Mounds of impatiens—red, flaming pink and orange—spilled out past symmetrical borders and over the deep green lushness of the grass. Purple, rust and yellow mums vied for attention with the feathery flower heads of tall, exotic grasses. A real red-winged blackbird, having strayed, no doubt, from the river valley or the harbor islands or the lakeshore, clung tenaciously to a thick stalk and kept his eye on the door of Osgoode as if waiting for his impersonators to come out.

Still unable to get the image of the handcuffed justice out of my mind, I decided to walk for a while along Queen Street in order to clear my thoughts.

As soon as I left Osgoode, I passed "new" City Hall, built in the 1960s when I had been a law student the first time. Forty years had not diminished the startle effect of its spaceship-like architecture.

Across Bay Street to the east rose Old City Hall, a Gothic mass of dark pink stone built by immigrant masons when Toronto was an outpost of Queen Victoria's empire. It had long been a courthouse. In fact, years before, Judge B. Sheldrake Tuppin, my mentor, had reigned in its upper reaches. I, too, had been a legend there. First as a champion of the downtrodden and then as one of them.

In the basement of Old City Hall, as in the basement of most courthouses, there were cells. Such a cell might be nothing but an enclosure built of cinderblock painted white so that graffiti would not easily adhere to it. In the middle might be a partial wall about three feet high, just high enough to give a man a little privacy while he squatted to use the stainless-steel toilet that had no seat.

Stow was a marble man, unveined snow Carrara his preference. I couldn't imagine how cinderblock and stainless steel would strike him, though I could remember the cold steel edge of the toilet against my own once-pampered bottom.

I continued east. Past the Eaton Center, now, as always, full of tourists and shoppers. Past construction at the corner of Queen and Yonge. The odor of fresh cement filled my nostrils, bringing instantly to mind, as it always did, memories of my father, the *muratore*, the *brickière*.

I walked past St. Michael's Hospital, then the "United Church Cathedral" on the grounds of which the indigent lounged in the cooling air. Past the pawnshops of Church Street, past Moss Park with its armory and arena, outside of which there was always a pile of snow, even on the hottest day. Queen Street East, like much of downtown

Toronto, was getting more upscale as the years went by. The greasy spoons, dingy bars, dusty secondhand furniture stores and run-down used-car lots were being replaced by art galleries, antique sellers, chic little bistros, car dealers for European imports. The day would soon come when no seedy stretch of downtown would be comfortable for the panhandlers, hustlers and hookers who had kept streets like Queen alive for a couple of hundred years.

At the corner of Parliament and Queen sat the building I hadn't realized I was headed for: Harmony Circle Health Center, which everybody called "the clinic."

"She ain't here," I was informed when I got within a few feet of the door. Three men of indeterminate age were sprawled on the sidewalk with their backs up against the wall of the storefront. They had the tough, weather-beaten, dark red skin of "bush Nish," as they liked to call themselves. "Bush" meant they lived outside, most likely in one of the many wild ravines that cut through the city. "Nish" meant Anishawbe, "the People," native North Americans.

"Thanks," I said as I stepped past them and tried the door. It sprang open to my touch.

"She's not here," a pretty young receptionist told me. She wore a white smock like a nurse's uniform, but embroidered on the front was a circle divided into quarters: white, black, red, yellow. All the races of the earth.

"Did she go home?" I asked, surprised. Since returning to Toronto from nursing school in her hometown, the Cree settlement of Moosonee on James Bay, my dear friend Queenie Johnson spent nearly every waking hour at the clinic. Not only was she the chief nurse practitioner at the health center, she was also its administrator. When she wasn't treating patients, she was chairing meetings where prominent members of the community planned projects to assist the homeless and the otherwise disadvantaged of the inner city. "I hope she's not sick?"

"Mr. Portal," the young woman answered, "you know as well as I do that Queenie probably wouldn't stop working if she was sick. But, thank goodness, she's not. No, she's down at Tent City."

"Tent City? Is it still up by the marsh near the Bloor Viaduct?"

The receptionist shook her head. Like so many of the workers at the clinic, she was a person Queenie had rescued. I didn't know the girl's past. Perhaps she'd been a prostitute or an addict, or both. But now, she glowed with health, and her thick black hair shone with blue highlights in the fluorescent light of the white office. "No. They had to move again."

"Can you tell me where?"

She looked up at me and smiled. "Of course I can, Your Honor," she said.

It had been my street name when both Queenie and I had been on the skids. Nobody called me "Your Honor" anymore except the people at this clinic—including Queenie, and recently, I realized with confusion, as a term of endearment.

"They're down before Broadview Avenue on the east side of the river above the Toshiba sign."

"Thanks," I said.

"Are you going down there?"

"Yes. Why? Do you have a message for Queenie?"

The girl laughed. "I don't need to send her a smoke signal, Your Honor. She's got her cell phone. I can call her if I need to. You want me to tell her you're on your way?"

I toyed with the idea of going back on the streetcar to retrieve my car near Osgoode, but Broadview was less than a fifteen-minute walk, and I wanted to talk to Queenie as soon as I could. It would be best to get down to Tent City before dark.

"No need to call her," I answered.

"Okay." She hesitated. "You have any reason to be concerned about the police?"

"No," I answered, surprised at the question, though I was certain it was one that was often asked at the clinic. "Why?"

"I think there's plainclothes guys down there."

"I'd be amazed if there weren't," I told her. "Those officers are everywhere. There's one sitting outside right now. He told me Queenie wasn't here."

"Yeah," she said. "That's Constable Moran. He looks pretty authentic, doesn't he?"

"Listen," I answered, "he's been working plainclothes for so many years that if he ever went back into uniform, he'd get arrested within the hour for trying to impersonate an officer."

The sinking sun was warm on my back as I walked toward the bridge over the lower Don River at Queen Street just west of Broadview. Spanning the bridge was an arch and across it, in wrought-iron letters, a quotation from the ancient philosopher Heraclitus: "This river I step in is not the river I stand in." It meant that everything changes.

I glanced north to where the river flowed down from a massive ridge separating the city from the sprawling suburbs. I had more in common with bush Nish than most people. I'd lived rough myself, up there in the wild ravines.

To the south, I spotted the massive electronic sign advertising Toshiba. Nearer, the steel skeleton of a former factory rose against the sky with eerie emptiness. I could see construction equipment beside it. Soon it would become some sparkling new dealership for expensive foreign cars, like the buildings already rising out of the industrial ruins on the other side of the river.

"You think you know everything since you been to that damn government college, but I'm telling you, you got more cops and reporters around than our people—and if you think there's any native down here except yourself, you're as much of a fool as you was when you was a stinkin' drunk."

I heard the belligerent voice before I spotted the camp strung along the riverbank, but I couldn't see the speaker, nor the person being spoken to.

I half ran, half slid down from the embankment beside the roadway to a narrow stretch of land squeezed between the brown waters of the stream and the concrete-and-metal abutment of the Don Valley Parkway off-ramp.

A scattering of dirty white canvas tents, wooden packing crates, cardboard boxes and pup tents made from blue plastic tarpaulins lined the eastern shore, so near to the water that the bottoms of some of the wooden crates were wet. I couldn't imagine who had suggested such a precarious site for an encampment. I could see from the way most of the packing crates were nailed together that these people lacked the skills necessary to live comfortably in the wild. Screws are far better than nails, and wooden pegs, if you know how to choose the right twig and have the strength and the patience to whittle it, are the best of all.

"Your Honor, what are you doing here? I thought you were with the judges at St. Mike's."

A slender figure emerged from the shadows beneath the poplar trees and stepped into the rays of the low-lying sun. I reached out to keep her from tripping over a man prone on the ground before her feet. Her fingers were warm to my touch, and instinctively, I gave her hand a squeeze. She squeezed back. Queenie would never tell me how old she was, but she had to be over fifty. The first time I remembered seeing her, over a decade before, she'd looked like an old woman with dull matted hair, broken teeth and nails, bulky with too many clothes, awkward with the gait of a drunkard.

All was different now. Her straight silver hair was shiny, her slim figure unhidden by the snug jeans she wore with a fringed leather jacket that hugged her waist. The jacket was partly unzipped, and beneath it, I could see a tee-shirt with the circle symbol of the clinic.

"I'm interrupting you in your work," I said with a sudden stab of guilt. "I should have phoned you . . ."

She smiled a little. In the old days, I used to think Queenie didn't know how to smile. "It wouldn't have done you any good, Your Honor. I forgot my cell phone. I left in a hurry because we . . ."

"He don't need a report," interrupted the belligerent voice I'd heard before. A ragged figure stepped out from behind Queenie. Little had changed in his appearance since the last time I'd set eyes on him. The same filthy long hair, the same dirty face and blue jeans and denim jacket, the same shoes held together by gray-beige plastic packing tape. It all looked too authentic to be real, and if I hadn't known better, I would have taken him to be one of the plainclothes cops.

"Johnny," I said, trying to hide my distaste at meeting him face-to-face. "I saw your picture in the paper."

He smiled. His teeth were brown and cracked, but they were still whiter than his face and seemed to glow in the rapidly failing light. I could tell he was genuinely pleased that I had paid enough attention to him to mention the news photo. "I'm doin' what I can for my fellow man," he said with apparent sincerity.

Queenie smiled again. Her white teeth were perfect. "Johnny's standing up for everybody on the street," she said. "He's better at giving speeches than anybody would have thought."

Not so. Johnny Dirt, as he had been known on the street all his adult life, was one of the biggest purveyors of claptrap I'd ever encountered. Johnny and Queenie had some history between them. He had once left her daughter for dead on the street. Queenie was a churchgoer, a devout Anglican. She had forgiven him. The same did not apply to me.

"Queenie," I said, taking her by the elbow and moving her away to a spot farther down the river where we could talk privately. "What's going on down here? I thought this encampment was up by the Bloor Viaduct. I thought you had helpers coming down and a service to bring people up to the clinic."

She stared across the water. Queenie was pure Cree. Her profile against the gold-toned river was sharply etched. She was one of those women who become more rather than less beautiful as the years pass by. And she was reticent—always had been.

A mallard skidded across the metallic surface of the water, leaving a necklace of ripples in its wake. Queenie waited for the bird to fold its wings and settle into a swim before she said, "Everybody in the city wants these poor people out of the valley. I'm doing all I can, but this is my problem, not yours. You, Your Honor, have a different problem."

"What?"

She turned her face toward mine as she spoke, but I couldn't look her in the eye. I had the feeling she was going to tell me something I didn't want to hear.

"Justice Stoughton-Melville—the one you always call Stow? He wants you. And he wants you now. You've got to find him, and you've got to get him out of this trouble he got into today."

"But Queenie . . ." She didn't know Stow, had never met him. So how did she know more about my friend than I knew myself?

Before I could question her, the man we'd almost tripped over found us. Without saying anything, he sat down on the ground at Queenie's feet. She lowered herself and made him more comfortable by helping him to lean against a slimy black rock. I couldn't tell whether it was covered with old moss or new pollution, but the man made no objection to using it as a backrest.

She pulled a small but very powerful flashlight out of the pocket of her jacket and asked me if I'd hold it.

The wool shirt the old man wore was wretched, but Queenie rolled back its sleeve with the amount of careful attention another person would have expended on new silk. Beneath the sleeve lay a bright white patch of surgical gauze secured by clean strips of adhesive tape. The center of the square of gauze was stained dark red, surrounded by a vile shade of green, the sight of which made the back of my throat lock.

"Let's see how you're doin' tonight," Queenie said.

I could see the man's effort to hide his pain when Queenie, with one swift, practiced move, ripped the bandage from his arm. A laceration the size of a two-dollar coin, oozing with blood and pus and ringed by puffy scarlet skin, festered on the limb of the old man.

Remarkably, Queenie seemed cheered by this gruesome sight. "Much better than yesterday," she said with satisfaction.

The patient looked pleased with himself, as though he'd accomplished a difficult feat and earned the approval of a beloved mother.

Chapter 2

"Queenie—?"

When she finished with her patient, she glanced at me, but I could read nothing in her eyes, at least in part because darkness had begun to descend. "Excuse me," she said simply and moved away toward a small knot of women who had been waiting for her.

I slipped into the shadows and watched the scene unfolding in front of me. In the flickering campfires of falling night, shadows flitted across the face of the dispossessed, revealing them to be as various as the faces of the lawyers, judges and deputies at the Osgoode reception. I saw young people with the premature look of age that life on the street dispenses. And I also saw the blank look of innocence on the faces of older men and women whose minds had been wiped clean of thought by years of abuse: drugs, alcohol, tobacco, sex and the most powerful of all abusers of humans—poverty.

Not knowing that I watched, Queenie moved among the outcasts, her lithe figure smoothly bending in the firelight to administer a drink here, a pill there, even, in one instance, a hypodermic. She was quiet and gentle among these vagabonds, but she was confident and knowledgeable, too. She was one of them, one, I mean, of us.

When I was sure I would not be interrupting her, I called her name softly and stepped into yellowish light that filtered down from the roadway above. "Can you take a little break?" I asked.

She was startled to see me still about, but her face registered obvious pleasure. "Can you stay for supper?"

"Stay. We ain't eatin' like yer fancy friends, but we ain't eatin' rat neither."

I fought something I hadn't felt in a long time: the urge to punch Johnny Dirt in the face. "I know a rat when I see one," I answered.

"The Good Hand food bank van came around this afternoon," Queenie said, ignoring us both. "We've got beef and mushrooms cooked over the open fire—and also a lot of hot dogs, potato chips and lentil soup. And day-old brownies and bruised bananas for dessert."

"It sounds like a feast, Queenie," I said, "but I think I'll head back home. I left my car at Osgoode."

She reached out and took my hand again. Her warm skin brushed the cool gold of the figured ring on the third finger of my right hand. Queenie was as familiar with that ring as I was by now. She knew it had been a gift from Stow more than thirty years before. "You came down here tonight because you're feelin' bad about him, ain't you?"

Since graduating from nursing school, Queenie could speak perfect English, but sometimes she reverted to ungrammatical language to make the street people feel more at ease. When she spoke that way with me, I felt she was being intimate, that she was alluding to the rough past we shared.

"Queenie," I said, squatting down close to the fire and gently pulling her down beside me, "if I thought that Stow were using you in any way . . ." I shook my head, not wanting to remind her of the days when violent anger had ruled me. "I won't go there, but I need you to remember that no matter what favors he's done for me, he's never let me forget that I'm his inferior. I've paid dearly for everything he ever gave me. Why would he send a message to me through you? He's perfectly free to say anything he wants to anybody. And, I don't need to add, free to pay anybody he wants for whatever he needs. He can do what he likes."

She kept perfectly still beside me as if she had to think about what I'd said. Then she shook her own head slowly. "I don't think so, Your Honor," she said. "I don't really think so."

"Tell me why he used you to get to me."

A sudden cold breeze blew up from the river, and Queenie stiffened as if to brace herself against the coming coldness of the autumn night.

"Nobody uses me."

For a moment we seemed unable to say anything more to each other. Into the silence between us came the sound of the Tent City dwellers spreading their bedding, some beneath the sky, others in the boxes and lean-tos and under the tarps. One young girl unwittingly set up too close between two old men, both of whom, I knew, would "accidentally" roll on top of her in the night. *What business is it of mine?*

"If you care about somebody," Queenie said softly, "you don't need to ask yourself why. You just go with the caring, and you help them. You don't ask what they owe you, and you don't stop at what you owe them."

"Are you talking about Stow?" I asked in alarm. "Do you owe him something?"

"Yes," she said. "I owe him the client's privilege of confidentiality. Don't ask me why I know he needs you." She leaned closer and kissed my cheek. "Go back to your fancy car and get home, Your Honor. You're getting too old and too soft to squat by the river in the light of the moon."

"There's no moon out, old woman."

"There will be by the time you get home."

She was right. It took me half an hour to make my way back up to the roadway because a number of people stopped me to tell me how glad they were to see me back down in the river valley. They said it was nice to know a man who didn't forget where he came from—as if anybody came from the skids. They also seemed to think I had friends at City Hall and that I would tell these friends to leave Tent City alone.

It took me another hour to get back to Osgoode, retrieve my car and make my way home to my apartment, which overlooked a treed ravine of the river valley in a neighborhood north of the downtown core. When I opened the door, the whole living room was flooded with the silver-blue light of the full moon rising over the valley. Deep within the shadows of the ravine, the creatures of night moved in that blue radiance, and if any of them envied me far above them in a warm room beneath a solid roof, they were only partly right about my state being more fortunate than their own.

I am a man whose struggle with God has been no easier than his struggle with the law. That Sunday I went to church for the christening of Sally Alice Portal, my second

22

grandchild, daughter of my son Jeffrey and his wife Tootie. On the morning I entered St. Jerome's, a thoroughly modern church on a thoroughly colorless street in the eastern suburbs, I'd not been to church twice in the same week in nearly three decades. Considering the disturbing episode I'd witnessed earlier in the week at the Red Mass, it's not surprising that I hesitated before stepping into St. Jerome's, even though I was late.

Time had changed Queenie's fortunes, and it had changed mine, too. Once I had lived in secret in the Don River valley. Now I owned an apartment building on the edge of it. I indulged in the occasional Armani, like the dark silk suit and pale linen shirt that I trusted were appropriate for this event. Since my rehabilitation, I'd reconciled with most of the members of my family, but I wasn't used to being with all of them together.

To avoid making a spectacle of myself, I sneaked in at the back of St. Jerome's and chose a seat behind everybody else. The church's architecture was comforting, resembling somewhat the belly of a white-oak whale.

Former Goth Princess Tootie Beats and her architect husband, my son Jeffrey, seemed to have switched personal appearances. Tootie, who had once dressed exclusively in garments becoming only to vampires, now wore a pink suit and a little gray hat with a white rose perched on top. Jeffrey, whose wildest excesses in the old days hadn't even extended to tee-shirts, was now dressed in a black collarless shirt, narrow black leather slacks, a bottle-green jacket and very shiny black boots. He also sported earrings in both ears. His blond hair, I was shocked to notice, had suddenly become long enough to be held at his nape in a ponytail. Had not the happiness of these two positively shone from them as they cooed over their baby, I would have feared that their fashion confusion marked a rift. Jeffrey turned, saw me, offered an awkward little wave, which I returned.

Behind them were two older couples whom I had seen only sporadically over the years. My sister Arletta and her husband. My brother Michele and his wife. They shared the pew with Ellen, my daughter, her husband and their child. And with, I suddenly realized, the same mysterious person who had slipped out of St. Mike's cathedral behind the captive Stow a few days before.

I could now see only the back of this person, so that it took me a minute to understand who she had to be. She was, like Queenie, slim, but there the resemblance ended. This woman was wealthy, and always had been. Her navy blue suit was impeccably cut to reveal her pleasingly broad shoulders, her narrow waist and softly flaring hips. No one with posture like hers had learned it anywhere except at a fine school—the kind that used to be called "finishing school."

Her ice-blond hair was pulled back in a small chignon, old-fashioned but refreshingly new at the same time. From her navy straw hat, a small dotted veil descended to cover her eyes. I couldn't see her face, but I could make out the line of her jaw, curved firmly and set with what seemed like pride. She looked like an exceptionally well-turned-out grandmother.

Which she was: Anne, my ex-wife, the woman whose life I'd ruined first by neglect, then by shame. The woman whose forgiveness I believed I'd won, if only by my having stayed away from her for more than ten years.

I felt that if I studied her for one second longer, she would feel my eyes on her. I forced myself to concentrate on the christening.

The priest prayed and anointed baby Sally Alice, who let out a scream that ricocheted off the false buttress of St.

Jerome's as if to let the world know that another of my descendants was making her presence known.

Last in, first out. Or so I'd hoped, but it didn't turn out quite that way. I was called over by Ellen to say hello to her uncle, my brother. A clumsy promise to "catch up," an uneasy vow to "get together." Would I ever be at ease with these people again? I tried once more to make my escape, but before I got to the door of the church, a small hand slipped into mine and I looked down to see the bespectacled face of my namesake and protégé, Angelo Portalese Bradley Mills, my eight-year-old grandson. Given my birth name by his loving mother, who chose to remember her roots. "Grandpa," he said, "are you coming back with us to the house?"

"Of course he is." The sweet warm autumn afternoon suddenly smelled of Chanel No. 19.

I awaken beside her wondering whether she knows that I have been home for only one hour. She always looks so clean that I cannot come into her bed without scouring myself. Not because of her but because of the people I have been with instead of her. Lately I find that I am thankful that I no longer smell of booze when I come to her. I've graduated. She can't smell cocaine on me. She doesn't know that smell.

Unavoidably, I held out my hand. "Thank you, Anne," I said, sounding far more confident than I felt, "but I . . ."

She smiled and took the offered hand with the perfect equanimity she had always possessed. She looked forty-five. Had there been many consultations with the best surgeons, weeks spent recovering in spas and resorts?

"I saw you at the Red Mass," she said smoothly, "I understand you've been readmitted to the bar."

"Yes."

"Dad! I'm so glad you could come." Jeffrey was suddenly beside me, imposing himself between his mother and me almost as he had done when he was a child determined to patch up our continuous quarrels.

"Son—congratulations! It's an important day, isn't it?" I felt tongue-tied. I was never good at small talk. Especially with Jeffrey.

He grinned, also struggling to think of something else to say. Mercifully, Tootie arrived at the door of the church with her baby in her arms, and he hurried to join her.

"Come with us, Grandpa. I want to tell you a secret," Angelo insisted. He, my ex-wife and I stood for a moment on the top step. I glanced around, trying to remember where I'd put my car, eager to get away. A crowd of young people surrounded the happy parents. Everyone else from our family seemed to have disappeared, though vehicles still jammed the vast circular drive in front of the church.

"I'd love to talk to you about what you're doing these days," Anne said. When I didn't answer, she hesitated, "and I'd like to ask your opinion about Stow."

"Stow?" Had he gotten to her, too? "What about Stow?"

"Ellis," she said, putting her hand on my arm in a gesture of surprising urgency, "I know that it must come as a shock for you to see us again."

I thought she meant her and my family. I nodded. I was growing more uncomfortable by the minute. Anne was lovely, more beautiful in her ice-queen way than I would ever have expected her to be at the age of nearly sixty. But she was part of my past. I couldn't bear to hear about the "us" of our family anymore.

Perhaps she sensed this. "By 'us,'" she explained, "I meant Stow and me."

"Stow and you? What does that mean?"

I forgot that little Angelo was still glued to my hand like a barnacle. And he was all ears all the time.

"Ellis," Anne whispered, "Stow is an old friend in a lot of trouble, but even if he did what the law suspects him of doing, I'm telling you, matters are not what they seem."

I wanted to vent my growing anger. What the devil was Stow up to? First approaching Queenie and now Anne? But Angelo was staring at me with his intensely curious gaze. My ex-wife noticed it, too.

"Can we have some private time together, Ellis?" she asked me. "We have so much catching up to do. Dinner?"

"Sure," I answered, not meaning it, only saying it so I could get out of there.

But when she called me two days later, I said, "Sure," again. And this time I was stuck.

"The children have kept me informed of your progress, Ellis," she said pretty much the moment we sat down, "so you needn't feel it necessary to speak about the past at all."

I smiled and nodded, in lieu of actually responding to this charitable remark. We'd chosen a new restaurant. Not only the restaurant, but also the whole neighborhood hadn't existed when Anne and I had been married. The place was on a piece of reclaimed harbor land, and the building jutted out over the water, so that one ate suspended in air with no visible support. Quite an appropriate choice for us, I reflected.

I couldn't think of a word to say at first. When the cocktail hostess and the sommelier failed to appear at our table, I speculated that the children had reminded Anne that I had long since gone from embarrassing lush to total abstainer. Or maybe she'd figured that out for herself. By the time the butternut squash soufflé with parsley pesto toast rounds had appeared, the silence had ruined my appetite. I stared out over the dark waters of Lake Ontario, wishing they might fold over me.

When I turned my attention back to Anne, I saw that there were tears in her surgically perfected eyes. "Ellis," she said, "love doesn't go away because of tragedy. When I married you, I intended to be with you forever."

"Anne," I said, reaching across the table to where her hand rested on the cloth, "we shouldn't have come here. This is foolish."

A waiter came and slid a bowl of orange tomato bisque in front of me. The bowl was the size of an egg cup and the price was fourteen dollars. There was no spoon. I looked at Anne who frowned down at the ridiculous dish and laughed. "Sometimes," she said, "I still make the soup your mother taught me." She lifted the tiny bowl and took a sip. "What do you do for food?" she said.

"I cook it," I replied.

"What do you do for sex?"

I was so shocked by the question that I choked and had to move quickly to keep a stream of orange glop from running down my chin.

"The answer would be more shocking than the question," I said.

Both of us burst out laughing.

It was midnight when I drove along Queen Street and past the clinic. Up on the third floor, Queenie's light was still on. Queenie had a small house somewhere in town, but I'd never been there. From the amount of time she spent at work, maybe she'd never been there, either.

I didn't ring, which would have caused her to climb down three flights of stairs. Instead, I used the key she had given me for emergencies, let myself in and made my way past the examination rooms and offices, all of which were closed up for the night.

When I got to the second-floor landing, I heard Queenie's voice. Before she'd gone back to nursing school, she had been unable to remember any of the Cree that had been her first language. Now, she could speak it fluently. However, I heard neither Cree nor street slang, but educated English. Then I heard my name mentioned. I inched up the stairs.

"Maybe you think you can get Ellis to do the things you want, but you could be dead wrong. I think you should . . . Hello? Hello?"

Obviously she'd been on the phone. I waited for her to redial and start talking again. Or for the phone to ring, indicating that the other party had taken steps to resume the conversation, but I heard nothing. After a wait of several minutes, I decided the decent thing to do was to let Queenie know I was there, but before I had a chance to call out, I heard her say, "Who's there?"

There was fear in her voice, and I was instantly sorry that I'd been so stupid as to listen to her call.

"It's only me, Queenie. It's Ellis."

I heard a chair scrape the floor, and in a moment she was standing at the top of the stairs, back lighted by the red glow of the Exit sign.

"You shouldn't be in this neighborhood by yourself at this hour," I warned her.

"Neither should you," she answered. "How was your dinner?" She seemed remarkably unflustered by having just been discussing me with somebody else.

I told her about the flying restaurant and the appetizer and the soup and the entrée and the creamed chestnut parfait dessert and the fact that Anne at sixty was lovelier than she'd ever been and that our grandchildren were so smart and adorable that they made an old man proud. And the more I talked, the quieter Queenie became, which, with Queenie, was as quiet as a stone in a frozen pond.

"You would have liked the restaurant," I repeated. "Everything on the menu seemed to have some connection with autumn—designed to celebrate the harvest." Until the words were out of my mouth, I didn't realize how insulting this would sound to a native woman who had deep respect for rituals welcoming each season.

But she smiled. I could see how exhausted she was. "Queenie," I said, "let me help you."

"Help me with what? Are you a doctor now—or a social worker?"

"Let me help you with some of the work you have to do here. I could do community liaison. I've been known to attend a meeting or two in my time."

"Your Honor," she said, briefly touching my wrist with her cool fingers, "I don't need help attending meetings."

"Well maybe I could assist you with correspondence or . . ."

"Why? Do you think I can't write?" She turned toward the window of her tiny office and glanced down onto Queen Street. I couldn't see what was going on out there, but I heard angry shouting in the alley beside the building. Queenie studied the scene below her, shook her head, turned her gaze back toward the center of the room where I stood. "You've got your hands full already," she said. "You and your son have your apartment building to run, and now that you're back being a lawyer, you'll be getting a job."

"I will always have time for you," I said, taking a step toward her.

She moved away, nearer to her desk. She picked up a piece of paper. From where I stood, it looked blank, but she seemed to read it for quite a while before she said, "They were glad to see you down in Tent City. They asked if your being down there meant that you'd taken an interest in their problems."

"Legal problems? I'd be very happy to help any of your clients with routine matters—wills, leases, small claims or traffic court, that sort of thing."

She looked surprised. "I don't think you'll find many people who need to make a will around here," she said.

"Queenie," I responded, "I don't know what's the matter with me. I don't mean to insult you. I'm sorry. I know how concerned you are about the tenters."

"They're fine now," she said, her eyes straying to a pile of files on her desk, "but everything is so temporary."

"Everything, Queenie?"

She looked up at me. For a moment, it seemed she had something to say in answer to my query, but the moment passed, and we each kept our separate peace for an embarrassingly long time.

"It's nice of you to offer to help," she finally said. "There *is* one thing you can do."

"Anything."

"You can get your butt out of this neighborhood so I can go home and get to sleep without worrying about you getting mugged."

Touched by her concern, I stepped closer to give her a kiss on the cheek, but she moved abruptly, and absurdly my lips brushed the empty air.

When I got home, I found a letter from the Attorney General of Ontario in my mailbox. I felt afraid. Why was the minister in charge of the justice system of the whole province writing to me? Could I be in trouble again? For what?

When I got upstairs and turned over the envelope, I saw it was actually from the Deputy Attorney General, Bailey

Knowlton Black, Q.C. This was no doubt a less important matter—an invitation to a cocktail party or some other formality marking the beginning of the legal season. I could deal with it in the morning. Within the half hour, I was sound asleep, dreaming about blue plastic tarps and butternut squash soufflés.

The next morning I made myself a coffee and sat down to enjoy it beside the floor-to-ceiling window that I had installed in the kitchen of my fourth-floor apartment. Beneath me was spread a hundred acres of forest, though I was in the center of the city and could see high-rise apartment buildings in the near distance.

I tore open my mysterious letter, taking perverse pleasure in ripping the Attorney General's elaborately embossed red coat of arms in half.

My eyes fell on the letter's single line and took it in at once. It was a request for me to come to see the Deputy Attorney General at my earliest convenience.

My convenience?

Maybe getting back into lawyering wasn't such a bad idea after all. I had no clients yet, but already things were looking up.

"Ellis," the Deputy said, "I'm delighted that you were able to see me on such short notice. Have a seat. Can we get you a coffee? A cup of tea?"

Bailey Black was one of the few remaining men bearing the title "Queen's Counsel," an honor reserved for the most distinguished lawyers and conferring the privilege of wearing silk gowns, a privilege usually reserved for judges. He looked about two years older than I, the sort of man I'd have been if I'd not relinquished my good name to ambition and violence. "Can I do something for you?" I asked.

"Sorry," he said, "I'm sure you're a busy man." He motioned toward a large chair upholstered in red leather fastened to its oak frame by gold tacks. "Ellis, your name has been submitted for consideration for an innovative judicial appointment that we expect to be made in about a year's time."

"Judicial appointment?" I gasped.

Bailey Black smiled his wide politician's smile.

"You seem somewhat surprised, Portal."

No kidding.

"Deputy, allow me to speak frankly," I told him when I had a chance to catch my breath. "It's been years since I was on the bench, and it's no secret where I've been in the meantime. I was only readmitted to the bar a few months ago."

"Portal, this administration has been accused of hardheartedness, of putting people last. The Minister, the Premier and, of course, I myself don't want us to appear to be the sort of government that is uncaring about the needs of people—especially our most vulnerable citizens." He paused and looked at me as if I were supposed to know what he was talking about.

"I'm speaking of children, of course," he said, "vulnerable, poverty-stricken children."

"I don't know anything about children," I protested.

He ignored me. "The Attorney General is about to announce that he is setting up a special judiciary appointment that will exclusively serve the legal needs of children, both civil and criminal. The posting will recapture the use of an old and honorable legal title, the Judge of Orphans. At present we have four nominees for this position. Because of your previous contributions on the bench and your personal knowledge of the needs of the marginalized on our city streets, you have been made one of our distinguished candidates.

"The other candidates are a nun who founded a children's legal crisis center, a social worker who saved the lives of several orphaned girls and a prominent professor at one of our universities. All of you are lawyers. All of you have served the city and the people long and well. May the best of you win, Portal."

He extended his hand, and I shook it, just as if I believed every word. When I left his office, I had but a single plan for the future use of my exceptional abilities, and that was to find a way to pull as good a trick on my friend Nickel McPhail as he had just tried to pull on me. Surely this meeting was a practical joke. Why would a man who'd already disgraced himself once as a judge have a chance to do it again?

Jeffrey was waiting for me when I got back home. I found him in the parking lot of our building, gazing out over the ravine, which looked as though it had burst into flame. Both my son and I loved to come out here in the evening after a day downtown, to breathe the scent of tree-filled air, to hear the jays and cardinals call to their kin across the expanse of forest. The Don River valley was glorious in all seasons, but autumn was Jeffrey's favorite.

"Want to go for a walk, Dad?"

I nodded, and in silence we descended the treed slope that led to the river far below. When we reached the shore, Jeffrey said, "I put in a call today to the broker who negotiated our purchase of the apartment building."

"Yes?"

"I told him I might be interested in a parcel of land on the west side of the river."

"The undeveloped section where the river takes that turn toward the southwest?"

"A little farther in," Jeffrey said.

I'm afraid. Someone is following me. My camp has been vandalized, and I have no idea why or by whom. I take only what I can carry in my hands. I ford the river on foot at its most shallow point. I set up again. At night the trains roar by. The sound reminds me that I am safer than I was but not safe enough.

"Good idea, son."

If Jeffrey was pleased by my approval, he didn't show it. "The broker promised to keep us posted. The City is liquidating quite a bit of its real estate holdings these days . . ."

We walked on until Jeffrey stopped at a point where the stream riffled over rocks, forming shallow rapids. A half dozen little whirlpools twisted in the green stream. I reached down and swirled my fingers in the cool water, as if washing away the dust of the city and the day. The flaming leaves of the trees danced in the moving waters. Jeffrey bent down toward the river, too. "Dad," he said, "a long time ago, you told me the story that goes with that ring you wear." He gestured toward the embossed gold signet on my right hand. "I remember about the symbols there, the scales of justice and the blind goddess, but I can't remember the other part of it."

"Other part of what?" I stalled. I knew what he meant.

"Something about a promise?"

I drew a deep breath. The air was cool, as though the temperature had suddenly fallen. I decided to keep it short.

"John Stoughton-Melville—Stow—has always been a man given to the dramatic gesture," I began. "The day that he, his wife Harpur, I and two other friends became lawyers, he gave me this ring as a symbol of our friendship. He maintained that friends should be willing to sacrifice all for each other. To that end, he asked me to promise him—and Harpur, too—that once in our lives, each of us could ask one favor of another, a favor that could not be refused, regardless of the consequences."

"And you promised?"

"Yes."

Jeffrey looked up toward the deep blue sky as though he were addressing it instead of me. "Is that why you and Stow are still friends despite all the trouble that's gone down between you?"

I thought about that for a moment. "Maybe not friends, exactly, but acquaintances. Yes."

"And is that why you used to visit Harpur at the hospital?"

"Partly," I admitted.

She lies so still. I don't want to wake her. Nor do I need to. Sleep, my old love, sleep.

"Dad, are you still with me?"

"Son," I said, "Stow, Harpur and I went back a long way. The night she died, it was as if an old alliance were broken. Stow was angry with me for a long time after."

"What happened that night?" he asked.

But I couldn't answer. We walked on through the autumn wood, pausing to study the trees, the lay of the land, the twist of the river in its green and bubbling course. It was many minutes before we spoke again, and then only to guide each other toward the path that led up and out.

When we got to Jeffrey's apartment, he knocked, and Tootie answered with Sally Alice, "Sal," in her arms. The six-month-old giggled and held out her chubby hands, which I held to my rough face. She giggled again and squirmed to be held by me. Flattered, I took her and stepped inside.

But I nearly dropped the baby because I was suddenly grabbed around the knees. Angelo was there, visiting. "Grandpa," he shouted. "My secret isn't secret anymore."

"What?"

"Remember I told you that I had a secret? Well, now it's in the paper so I can tell anybody I want."

"Okay," I said, sitting down with the baby on my knee and Angelo leaning against me. "What's the secret that isn't a secret now?"

"I went to Mommy's work yesterday. I went to court."

I patted him on the head. "That's nice, Angelo. What did you see? Did you see Mommy in her black robe?"

"Sure. And you know what else?"

"What else?"

"I saw Chief Justice Stoughton-Melville. They got him for first-degree murder."

I stared at the boy, speechless. Finally I said, "I don't think you know what you're talking about, Angelo."

"Yes, I do, Grandpa. Look."

He ran over to the kitchen table and came back with the *Toronto Daily World*. Stow, in handcuffs, was on the front page.

Chapter 3

"I thought you were my friend."

"Don't be ridiculous, Your Honor. Mostly I've been your only friend. I haven't done anything wrong."

"Queenie," I insisted, "you should have told me."

"Told you what? I can't tell a person something I don't even know myself, can I?"

I felt guilty confronting Queenie at nine o'clock in the morning when the waiting room of her clinic was jammed full of patients, but I wanted some answers.

"You knew Stow was charged with murder, didn't you? And you must also know who he's accused of killing."

"No!" she said with such assertiveness that I jumped. I wasn't used to Queenie putting her foot down—not with me, anyway. "What difference does it make now? It's all over the papers that he's a suspect in a cold case. All I know is that he is trying to talk to you. He called me a couple of times. He asked me where you live, and I said I didn't know the address, which is true." She paused, flipped through her calendar. "I'm really busy right now, Your Honor. Maybe you could come back another time."

"Is he bribing you somehow? Is he giving you money?"

"What the hell do you mean?"

"For the clinic . . ." I choked out. At her look of shock, words froze in my throat. I didn't intend to accuse her of wrongdoing—just of going too far in the interest of her clients. "Maybe he offered you a donation if you would help him get to me." She ignored me. She turned to her computer and studied the screen as it sprang to life. I couldn't bear to have her angry at me. Not over Stow.

"Listen, Queenie," I said, coming up behind her. She clicked, and whatever was on the screen disappeared. "I'm just shocked that he would be accused of killing his wife. She's been dead for more than five years. Seems ridiculous to me."

"He wants to talk to you, that's all. He needs a lawyer. You're a lawyer."

"But—"

"I don't want to discuss this anymore." She rose and moved toward the door. I reached out and took her by the arm. She glared up at me, and I couldn't figure out why suddenly everything I did seemed to annoy her.

"Let me help you."

Her dark eyes harbored a sadness that never left. She could be laughing—or singing or celebrating—but that sadness was always there, like a scar.

"I don't need a lawyer," she said, deliberately misunderstanding me. "I'm not in trouble. And as for my clients, anybody could help with their legal problems."

"Anybody?"

"They got no money, no property, no relatives. If they do something that lands them in jail, they're sure of a warm place to sleep and regular meals. In is as good as out to a lot of them."

"I didn't buy that when I was on the street, and I don't buy it now."

She smiled. "Your big friend Justice Stoughton-Melville isn't bribing me, and you aren't bribing me either. Get out of here. I'll be your pal—like always. You don't need to do me any favors."

Her dismissal wounded me despite the forced lightness of her tone. I reached for her hand, but she evaded my touch.

"I could help them get ready for winter," I offered.

"Get ready for winter? What do you mean?"

I hesitated before I answered. "Do you remember all the things I used to do when I lived in the valley so that I wouldn't starve or freeze to death? Remember how you used to laugh at me and tell me that if I'd just submit myself to the social workers at the shelter, I could save myself so much trouble?"

"Your Honor," she said softly, "I can't bear to think about those days."

Touched by the emotion in her voice, I tried to hide my own feelings. "Sure you can," I answered heartily. "Especially if remembering helps other people to get through the worst days of the year."

"What exactly would you do?"

I pulled Queenie to me by trying—and this time succeeding—to take her fingers in mine. She dropped my hand, but she stayed close to the chair in which I sat. "I'd show the people down there in Tent City how to stay far enough away from the river and from each other, for starters. And I'd teach about card-board."

"What about cardboard?" she said, wrinkling her nose.

"You can't tell me you never stole a good piece of cardboard to sleep on," I teased her.

"From the garbage only," she answered. "Never from anybody else."

"You lie," I said, but the bitter memories of our time together on the street made me stop the teasing. "Anyhow, I'd teach them where to find what they need to keep warm. You know, just what kind of Styrofoam and bubble wrap is best for lining the inside of huts and crates. Not too thick or it'll make them feel claustrophobic. Not too thin or they'll freeze their sorry butts."

She frowned.

"I'm only kidding. I'm sure your clients don't have sorry butts."

"You don't either now, do you?"

"Not unless Stow gets hold of me."

It was meant as a joke, but Queenie shivered. I tried speaking more seriously. "I can teach them how to catch a Canada goose and wring its neck and remove its feathers and cook it over a fire. I can teach them how to tell a good mushroom from poison, how to keep butter from freezing, how to sew a . . . Queenie," I said, clasping her hand tighter. "I don't know what it is you need that Stow can offer, but I don't want you to talk to him. I want you to let me be the one you turn to."

"I'm not turning to anybody," she said. "I can take care of myself. And as far as my clients go, all your fine ideas won't work unless you're right down there with them, Your Honor."

The thought of spending time under a bridge near the Toshiba sign was so far from what I had envisioned for my renewed life that I cringed.

"What's wrong?" Queenie asked. "You have trouble with a hands-on approach? It's not the sort of volunteer work you had in mind, maybe. But it's what we need."

"And it's what you'll have," I stoutly declared. "Leave it to me."

I glanced at her. She wore her uniform of white slacks and white tunic with the circle symbol emblazoned near her shoulder. Her sleek, straight, pewter-colored hair swung at the level of her firm chin. Her skin was smooth and so perfectly toned that I was reminded of the golden leaves of the Don valley. She was small, but compact and strong.

And yet, by some trick of memory, there was suddenly superimposed upon this vision of health and strength another view altogether. It was as if I were looking at one of those spirit paintings in which the ghosts of the past are standing among the living. I saw a hunched, broken-toothed, dirty-haired hag so bundled up in ragged pieces of denim and wool that you couldn't tell how old she was or what sort of body she had under those trash-bin clothes. And beside this miserable pile, I saw *me*, her male counterpart. A reminder that it doesn't matter where you started from; it only matters where you end up.

"I've got a meeting, Your Honor," Queenie said, apparently failing to notice that I'd been staring into space. "And I'm already late. But if you're thinking about old times, you ought to remember that Stow helped when *you* were in trouble."

The phone rang. She picked it up. I relished this chance to escape before she tried again to talk me into helping Stow. I had fought hard to work my own way back from disgraced judge to respectable lawyer. It would not be to my advantage to help another loser.

But if I thought I could get away from Queenie that easily, I was mistaken. She grabbed my wrist and held it captive the whole time she was on the phone negotiating for a shipment of syringes. When she finally let go, I realized I had not really tried to free myself.

"For heaven's sake, Queenie," I said.

"Exactly."

"What?"

"For heaven's sake. That's why we help each other, isn't it? That's why you are going down to Tent City to show people how to survive the winter. And it's also why you are going up to Fernhope to talk to your old pal, Stow."

Smack in the middle of Fernhope maximum-security prison, a hundred miles north of Toronto, is a hunk of the Canadian Shield, a geological formation that has been in that place since before the laws of man were dreamed of. I'm not sure what the designers of the prison had in mind when they centered the complex on this mammoth hunk of rock, but the inmates say a prison with a heart of stone is an honest place to live.

I hadn't decided whether it was fear or friendship that was leading me to Stow, but I found my resolve weakening with every mile. In the city, autumn was at its early November peak, but the leaves thinned with the traffic and the buildings until I was passing farmers' fields, then cottages, then rock outcroppings crowned with spruce and pine. When I was quite sure the same spruce and pine had crossed my vision a number of times, I gave myself up for lost and reached for my cell phone.

"Nicky, I can't find the place. Didn't you do some work up here last year? Where is it, anyhow?"

"Where are you now, old man? Do you have any idea?"

"Jones Road. Does that ring a bell?"

"If you're not headed toward Bracebridge, cross the highway," Nicky advised.

I watched with dismay as a seemingly unending line of vans and pickups whizzed by. My heart in my mouth, I zipped across to a chorus of horns and squealing brakes.

"Now what, McPhail?"

"The turnoff to the prison is unmarked, but if you make the first sharp left, you'll be headed in the right direction. Just keep going until somebody tries to stop you."

The phone went dead, and I went on for a few miles. I started to notice that the road was narrowing. On either side, the rough-hewn rock had posts driven into it. A triple strand of razor wire was strung from pole to pole.

Not for the first time, I wondered whether Queenie had made a mistake concerning Stow's whereabouts. What was he doing in a federal prison before he'd even gone to trial? Why was he detained at all? He had money and connections. Was he dangerous? He had certainly not acted like a homicidal maniac the day he was hauled out of the Red Mass. As a man once accused of being a homicidal maniac myself, I felt qualified to judge Stow's appearance.

"Stop!"

Four officers in gray uniforms with fur-collared black leather jackets and Smokey-the-Bear hats approached, signaling for me to lower my window. Two cruisers blocked my way in front and behind.

I'm facedown on the floor, the terrazzo cool against my cheek. Harpur is screaming and screaming. I want to tell her how sorry I am, but there is a weight in the middle of my back. If I move, it will break me.

"Going for a little drive in the country, are we?"

A good-looking man the size of a buck deer leaned toward me in a maneuver designed to search the inside of the car. He was inches from my face, and any quick move-ment on my part wasn't wise.

"I have clearance to visit an inmate," I said, keeping my voice level and low.

"Produce it," he growled.

He watched me steadily as I slowly reached into my pocket. When I finally held the envelope toward him, he refused to touch it. "Remove the contents please, and hand them to me."

I did as he requested. He studied the document without the least change in expression. He seemed to be able to read without moving his eyes. I'd used the same trick when I was a judge, and later on the street, and I admired his skill.

"Remove your keys from the ignition and hand them to me."

Puzzled at his instructions, I nonetheless complied. He jingled the keys a little as he walked a few steps away and handed my paper to a second officer. The other two moved closer to me.

Without turning around, I tried to see through my rear mirror what the two with my authorization were doing, but they had moved to a blind spot.

It seemed to take forever for them to come back. "Sir," one of them said, "this is a fax."

I fought the urge to be sarcastic, because I really wanted the sidearms to stay put. "Yes, sir," I said, "it is."

"We can't accept a facsimile authorization." Without making any move to return the fax to me, he ordered, "Put these keys back in the ignition. Wait for us to pull over. Then slowly turn around and proceed back to the highway."

"No," I said.

A look of surprise flickered across his eyes.

"I want to talk to the warden," I insisted. "I'm a lawyer visiting a potential client. Check your list. You have his name and you have mine. I want you to call Visitors and Communication and confirm that authorization."

He studied the paper, making a big point of glaring at Stow's name, which was printed in large letters smack in the middle of the page. "There's no one by this name in this institution, sir."

It occurred to me that what he was saying was technically true. It was against every regulation in the book for an individual who has not been sentenced to be detained in a federal correctional facility. Therefore, Stow was not officially inside these prison walls.

But physically he was there, and I, who only hours before had not wanted anything to do with him, was now bound and determined to see him.

"I have authorization, and I demand to be allowed to enter."

"Stay there," the officer barked at me. He took his time sauntering over to confer with his fellow officers, then slid into his cruiser. Through the open door, I could see him clicking away at his computer. He used his radio and his phone, too. Quite an impressive little display of thoroughness.

"All right," he commanded when he got back to my car, "proceed to the prison gate."

The road got narrower and the razor wire thicker the closer I got to the gate, which, after a couple more miles, loomed ahead of me. I was surprised when it lifted automatically to let me into the parking lot. I felt fearful already, as if I had committed a crime, surrounded as I was by stout guard towers and high multibank light standards.

Around here, night would be much brighter than day. Two trucks making endless loops circled the grounds from opposite directions. I figured they'd pass each other twice an hour. When they did pass, I saw that no one in either truck acknowledged the presence of fellow officers. The drivers' eyes were trained only on the never-ending circle of the road, and the guard in the passenger seat kept his eyes glued to the razor-wired, two-story-high fence. The regulations of a maximum-security prison would make a terrorist pause.

I tried to imagine Stow in this environment instead of hobnobbing with the power players on Parliament Hill or sitting in his red robe on the highest bench in the land.

"Remove all metal objects from your person and step through the scanner."

"Place your wallet and other personal belongings in this wire basket."

"Show me the bottom of your feet. Right foot first. I said *right* foot . . ."

"Enter that door."

I did as I was told and entered a metal and wire-reinforced glass enclosure. A heavy metal door crashed closed behind me. Before me another metal door stayed resolutely shut.

More fear and more than a little claustrophobia gripped me. The tight little room started to spin. Dark blotches seemed to obscure my vision, and then the door before me cracked in half and fell away, and I found myself staring into a brilliantly lit room containing a small wooden table and two empty chairs.

"Put your hands palms up on the table. Put your feet flat on the floor."

I did what the disembodied voice from the overhead speaker ordered, thinking of Orwell and Kafka, too. The mechanized inhumanity made me pity the wretches incarcerated in this forbidding place.

"Counsel, thank you for coming," I heard from somewhere behind me. The voice sounded human.

I fought against making any gesture of self-protectiveness. I hadn't heard Stow's voice since he'd publicly cursed me at his wife Harpur's funeral five years earlier.

"Turn around, Portal."

I carefully twisted until I could see him. I don't know what I expected. I guess I'd pictured him as a prisoner, maybe like the prisoners who'd been inside with me, men down on their luck but surprised at how far down.

He wore a sweater that must have cost a couple of thousand dollars. Its gray-blue cashmere perfectly matched his eyes and set off the silver-blondness of his hair, which looked as though it had recently been cut. This alone, among all that I observed of Stow that day, did not surprise me. I knew that barbering was one of the skills taught to prisoners and that some were as good at it as Stow's hundred-dollar haircutter.

I had not expected the designer clothes, the black Gucci loafers, the Cartier watch, the air of complete control and command. Obviously Stow was not being housed anywhere near other prisoners, nor was he subject to even the most rudimentary rules of detainment. He was even wearing a belt.

Also obvious was that Stow's ingrained arrogance had not changed one bit despite his present circumstances and the fact that he seemed to be begging for my help.

"What are you doing here, Stow, and why summon me?"

He made me wait for an answer. He took his time walking around my back and toward the empty chair. I expected the guards to be keeping a close watch on him, and perhaps they were. One was near the door; the other had positioned himself to be simultaneously between Stow and the door and between Stow and me.

But I couldn't tell whether Stow presented unusual danger to one and all of us or whether the guards positioned themselves in the same way regardless of who the prisoner might be.

Stow slid his lanky figure into the chair opposite me. Blond men don't age well unless they have the best food, drink, toiletries, vacations and doctors, all of which Stow had. He looked almost robust, his lean frame lithe and muscular, his smooth skin lightly tanned. "What am I doing here, you ask? Is that a suitable question for my counsel of record?"

His counsel of record? His official lawyer? What was he talking about? I had not been retained by this man.

As if reading my thoughts, he said, "You might want to check in a day or two to see whether the retainer has been deposited in your account. You may rest assured that you'll not be held up at V & C. I've registered your name."

"You've informed the prison's Visitors and Communication office that I'm your lawyer?" I almost yelled.

"Surely you didn't think you'd get into this secure area using that fax from the warden? Anybody can fake one of those."

"How do you know so much about faking documents?"

He laughed. "Easy, Portal. Easy. All will be revealed."

I felt as I had in my youth when John Stoughton-Melville had laughed at my innocence, my lack of sophistication, my stupidity. As a result, I protested vigorously. "I'll need a court order to remove myself from the record."

"Removed from my case? I doubt it, Portal," he taunted. "I'm your first client in how many years? You'd look like a fool having but a single client and unable even to get along with him!"

"Stow, you bastard . . ." I forgot about the palms-and-feet rule. I rose a couple of inches from my chair.

A look of alarm passed across Stow's aristocratic features. I wasn't impressed. He was perfectly capable of feigning fear or any other emotion he cared to display. "Ellis," he said, "I advise you not to show feelings of any sort in here. Not only would you face certain ejection, you might cause me to have to be moved to a far less comfortable situation. Do you take my meaning?"

Yes, I took his meaning. Somehow he had contrived to make me his lawyer without my consent. I glanced at the guards.

Stow lowered his voice. "I want you to conduct this conversation as though it had no emotional content whatsoever. I want you to listen and I want you to respond. But I do not want those guards to know that there is any tension between us. Do you understand?"

"Patronizing me as always, Stow," I said. "You seem to forget that I can walk out of here at any moment. You can't keep me."

"We'll see about that," he said amicably, with a perfect imitation of his best smile. "We may soon learn that I can certainly keep you, as you so quaintly put it."

"I'm no longer in a position to fear you, Stow," I responded with more assurance than I felt, "so I suggest you forget about my helping you."

"Why did you come up here if you're unwilling to help me?" he asked.

"You got to Queenie somehow. I don't know what you promised her, but I want her to have everything she needs. I came because of her. But now I see that was stupid. I

51

don't know what you want, but I can't help. You need an experienced lawyer, not one who's been away from the bar as long as I have."

"You were the best, Ellis," he said, "and I assume you'll return to being so."

This was such patent nonsense. At my age? I would have laughed in his face had I not taken to heart his warning about the guards. "You never found me to be a good lawyer, Stow. And you were shocked when I was elevated to the bench."

"That's only your perception, Ellis," he said, moving his hands in a small gesture that could be perceived as lightly dismissing some harmless comment. Still, the guards did not move. "Your own sense of inadequacy caused you to believe that I undervalued your worth." He smiled pleasantly.

I smiled pleasantly, too, and continued to speak evenly and conversationally. "You're a hypocrite and a liar, Stow. The last time I saw you, you threatened my life. You humiliated me at Harpur's funeral."

The mention of the funeral was cruel, and I regretted it. I saw Stow's jaw tighten. He looked as though he were fighting tears. Much as I detested him, I was reminded that once he had felt pity for me.

"Look, Stow, as I said, I came here today because Queenie Johnson reminded me that when I needed help, you came through for me. I don't know how you got to her— or how you got to Anne, either."

At the mention of my ex-wife's name, I thought I saw him flinch, but I could have been mistaken.

"If you really expect me to help you," I said, "you're going to have to tell me in detail what's going on, Stow. How did you figure that Queenie would talk me into seeing you? And most importantly, what have you done? How can you possibly be accused of murder?"

When I realized what I had just said, I felt a jolt of alarm, and my eyes shot toward the guard who stood nearest the table. His eyes met mine and in them I saw boredom. How many conversations between supposed killers and their lawyers had he heard? He wasn't a young man. Like most people who get a government job, he'd probably worked in the prison the better part of his life. This was all old news to him, even if the client was as distinguished as Stow.

I plunged ahead. "I'm asking you again, Stow. What are you doing here?"

He took a deep breath, stagy and prolonged. "I'm here because no other facility had the security necessary to protect a Supreme Court judge," he said. "I'm not really under the jurisdiction of the Feds. I'm really on a provincial remand. My being here is a courtesy the federal correctional system is extending to the court."

Even though I hadn't practiced law in a long time, I was used to this sort of conversation. I was used to clients taking what my young friend Nicky called "the long way in."

"Stow," I said, "interesting as I find these technicalities, that is not what I'm asking about. I want to know . . ."

"Why I'm detained at all? Because I choose to be detained. I choose to be in custody so that the ridiculousness of the accusation against me can be made evident. And so that the charges will be dealt with as expeditiously as possible."

I took a deep breath myself. "Stow," I said, "Harpur's death was from natural causes. We all know that. We . . ."

I couldn't go on. The night she had died, I'd held her frail body in my own arms. She'd been failing for days. The thought of anyone murdering her was absurd.

"Ellis, you're the only one who can understand all this. You've got to get me off."

"Get you off? You sound like a common crook."

"You've got to!"

He reached across the table, grabbed my hand and touched the gold ring I wore.

It was then that the guards sprang into action and dragged him out of my sight.

Chapter 4

Back in the city, I checked my bank account and discovered that the balance was twenty thousand dollars more than it had been the last time I'd looked. I didn't know what the going retainer for a murder case was, so I had no opinion about the appropriateness of the amount. But I considered complaining to the bank manager about allowing access to the account without my approval. And I also considered sending a blistering letter to Stow objecting to his audacious assumptions.

Then I thought, the hell with it.

Not far from the courthouse at 361 University Avenue, I'd seen a sign in the window of a walk-up on Queen Street West. For rent was a tiny two-room office space above a store in one of the few remaining early twentieth-century buildings on the street. Unlike Queen Street East, where Queenie had her clinic, Queen Street West had been a haven for artists for decades. The Art Gallery of Ontario and the Ontario College of Art and Design were at Dundas and McCaul. Queen itself was thick with clubs and cafés and bookstores. As Tootie likes to say, "It rocks."

I gave the young man who was the landlord of the building the whole twenty thousand from Stow in cash, and in return, he gave me a paid-up one-year lease on my new office. I felt absurdly happy at having a law office again. I sat on the old wooden floor, its planks roughened by time, and stared at the peeling walls, planning what I might do with the place, until daylight faded and it was time to go downstairs for some supper.

A man who once lived for five years in the wilderness with no roof over his head except what he could construct out of found material can function in basic accommodations more easily than other men, and he also knows how to make just about any space habitable. Over the next few days, I cleaned the rooms and furnished them—rather too grandly for their situation, I must admit—from one of the most expensive furniture stores in town.

When my interior decoration was complete, I realized I had pretty much re-created the judicial chambers of my hero and mentor, B. Sheldrake Tuppin. When I was in law school the first time and he reigned atop Old City Hall, his chambers had been furnished in standard 1960s government-issue chairs, desk and bookcases. Reproductions of these objects were now called "heritage replications," and each piece had cost me about what Magistrate Tuppin had earned in a year.

My office was cozy, quaint and conducive to the task I now set myself, which was to research Stow's case. Fortuitously, my place was within easy walking distance of the law library at Osgoode Hall.

Which is where I was returning from on a late November afternoon when I opened the street door to find someone waiting for me in the shadows at the bottom of the stairs.

I thought it was a homeless person, and I felt first annoyance, then guilt, then a stab of recollection. I hadn't helped Queenie's clients get ready for winter as I had promised. Had the reprehensible Johnny Dirt searched me out to threaten me? I knew he was capable of violence. I steeled myself.

"Who are you and what are you doing here?" I demanded.

I heard a low rippling laugh, and simultaneously, I realized that the hallway was filled not with the acrid reek of unwashed hair and flesh, but with sweet citrus, a scent that teased my nostrils with some vague remembrance of another life.

"So sorry," a female voice breathed. "Didn't mean to scare you. Your neighbor downstairs said I could wait here. Couldn't find the light switch . . ."

By the time these words were uttered, *I* had found the switch. I hit it, and the narrow old hallway with its single flight of stairs sprang into golden light. Softly illuminated in the glow was a person whom I had completely forgotten in the years since I'd climbed out of the river valley and made my way slowly back into a life of respectability.

"Aliana," I said, "you look sensational! What are you doing here? I thought you were in the Middle East."

"Was. Now I'm back. Are you glad to see me?"

I should have been. Aliana Caterina, now in her forties, seemed to be at the peak of the lush Italianate loveliness she'd possessed all her life: thick black hair, olive skin, full lips meant for kissing. It seemed to me that she had been perfect from the first time I'd seen her when she was just a kid helping her father, Vincenzo Caterina, my father's assistant in the construction trade.

"Sure," I said. "Want to come upstairs?"

Within minutes, she was cradling a tall dark drink in her long fingers. It was cola. Aliana knew I was no longer a drinker. It seemed everybody knew. "I thought you loved being a foreign correspondent for the *Daily World*."

She shrugged. "It was okay. Exciting. Dangerous. *The* place to be. But a few things went sour, and I asked to be transferred home."

I could have asked exactly what had gone sour, but I didn't want to. Besides, there was a mark on Aliana's ring finger that four or five years of wearing a wedding ring might have left. I asked her again. "What are you doing down here? Nosing out terrorists?"

"I came to find you, Ellis," she said. She leaned back and crossed her long legs with a slow ease that made her beauty seem like a cliché against the backdrop of the old furniture.

"To find me?"

"Yeah. Because of your nomination. I thought maybe you'd grant me an exclusive—for old times' sake."

"Old times?" I smiled. "You *were* good to me, Aliana. If you hadn't written those articles about me ten years ago, nobody would have thought that an old judge who'd lost it and turned to drugs deserved any sympathy at all. I admit I owe you, but . . ."

"But what?" A drop of liquid had settled on her wide bottom lip. She ran her tongue along the curves of her mouth. Kissing Aliana had once been a rich fantasy.

"But I think you better tell Nicky to lay off the practical jokes. I'm on to him."

She looked confused. "Nicky? Nicky who? Do you mean I'm too late for an exclusive? You gave somebody else the first interview?"

58

"Aliana, cut it. You know as well as I do that Nicky McPhail got the Deputy A-G to send me a fake letter and even take a meeting with me, as if he were really considering me for an appointment. It was amusing, but enough is enough. Go back to Nicky and tell him to quit fooling around."

Aliana stared at me. "Ellis," she said, "what are you talking about? I never heard of Nicky McPhail, and nobody sent me here. I've been chasing you around town for a couple of days." She reached down into the depths of her Fendi bag and extracted a slim leather portfolio. From it she took a newspaper clipping. It was a column wide and a few inches long. I could tell from the crispness of the paper that it was recent. When Aliana handed it to me, my name jumped out as if written in neon.

"This is an announcement from the A-G's office," I sputtered.

"Yes. Yes, it is. Accompanied by a nice little write-up, even if I do say so myself. But I want to give you more than two and a half column-inches, Ellis. I want to know why you're the best candidate for the appointment as Judge of Orphans."

I'm in the witness box. Aliana is watching me with her dark, intense eyes. Every trace of every drug, even the drug of pride, has worn off. They are all waiting for me. The judge, the cops who picked me up, the two lawyers. They want me to tell them why I attacked Harpur Blane and tried to choke her to death. Depending on my answer, I will go to jail or I will go free. I look around the room. Suddenly I can no longer recognize anyone, not even the intense young woman whose long black hair brushes her page as she writes.

"Aliana, I have nothing to say to the *Daily World*—or to any paper for that matter. I'm trying to resume practice as a lawyer. I haven't the least intention of ever being a judge again."

It was a lie and we both knew it, but she did a little huffy thing with her jacket and her briefcase and sashayed out. I was relieved to see the back of her. And then I was sorry she had left so soon.

"We're going to the parade, and Chief Justice Stoughton-Melville is going to the slammer."

"Angelo, be quiet and watch for the clown. He might throw you some candy."

The raw November wind didn't seem to bother my grandson, but it was killing me. I couldn't concentrate on the floats as they lumbered by our choice viewing spot on the front steps of the Royal Conservatory of Music on Bloor Street by Philosophers' Walk. I did notice that no float, banner, sign or flag bore the "C" word. In a metropolis in which possibly half the four million inhabitants had been born elsewhere and in which every conceivable "religion," including atheism, was represented, political correctness frowned on a public holiday being called by a religious name. "Christmas," some feared, was becoming a relic of the past. "We're only allowed to call it the Festive Holiday," Angelo explained. "So we are watching the Festive Holiday parade."

A cheery buffoon in a big blue wig waved at Angelo, winked in an exaggerated fashion and tossed the boy a candy cane, which my grandson caught without missing a beat of the chatter he'd carried on the whole time we'd stood there freezing. "Mommy says justice has to be done no matter how important a person is, because everybody is under the same law. That's true, isn't it, Grandpa?"

"Here comes Santa Claus. Do you want me to pick you up so you can see him better?"

"Don't be ridiculous. I'm not a baby. And it's not a him. It's a her. It's the Festive Lady."

I studied the figure on the white sparkling sleigh. It was indeed a middle-aged woman. An Asian woman dressed in red trimmed in white fur.

"Mommy says next year Sal will come with us to the Festive Parade. She says by that time Chief Justice You-Know-Who will be in a real jail instead of Club Fed."

"Angelo, what are you rattling on about? Forget about jail and watch this damn parade. Look at Santa Claus's helpers. Aren't they funny? They're Christmas elves."

"They're Festive Season assistants, and don't say 'damn,' Grandpa," Angelo answered.

The next day, Monday, I got a call from Queenie. "What are you doing over there?" she asked. "Have you got any clients yet?"

"I went up to see Stow . . ."

"And?"

"And not much. He made me his lawyer. And a lot of good it's going to do him. I can't find anything out about him that other people couldn't find out."

"You've got to get out on the street. You're not going to find anything sitting in an office."

"Did you call me just to give me a hard time?"

"Yeah. And I'm not done yet. I need you down here to do what you promised. To give my clients some survival advice."

"Down here" meant Tent City. When I arrived later that afternoon, I found twelve men and seven women huddled around a fire they'd built in a rusty old barbecue. They were about as interested in hearing me lecture as I was in lecturing them, and I suspected the whole exercise was a ploy on Queenie's part to get matching funding for her

clinic by hauling me in as someone who was making a con-
tribution.

"I realize I'm a little late in telling you about preparing
for winter," I began.

"Whatever," I heard someone mutter under her
breath.

I glanced around the shabby circle and started again.
"It's usually best to have your winter site chosen and your
shelter pretty much built by the first week in October because by November, all the good spots are usually taken."

"Tell us something we don't know," muttered the same
woman.

"The valley is much warmer than the city streets," I soldiered on, "so you'll want to sleep down here instead of in
a doorway."

"Especially if you don't have Queenie to keep you warm
like you used to."

This malicious statement from Johnny Dirt. His com-
panions seemed to find the remark hilarious. I shot a
glance at Queenie, expecting her to reprimand her mot-
ley assortment of misfits. I was surprised to see that she
was smiling along with the rest of the vagrants.

"Go on, Your Honor," she said gently when she saw how
angry I was at being mocked.

"The best place to make a home in this valley is a cave,"
I said. "But they're few and far between, and you'd have to
leave the downtown area and go upriver where the banks
are much steeper than they are here."

"I ain't climbin' down no high banks," an old crone
protested. "It's bad enough I gotta sleep down here in the
damp."

"Shut up," a man shouted at her.

"She's right," I said. "You people shouldn't be this close
to the river. You should . . ."

"Stick to your helpful house-building hints, Judge," Johnny Dirt taunted, "and leave the location of Tent City to us. It's none of your damn business where we set up." He shifted from foot to foot at the edge of the fire, moving between light and shadow, like someone waiting to rob the unwary. I tried to ignore him.

"A good way to keep warm even in a damp location like this," I told them, "is to build what the old-timers used to call a 'fagot shack.'"

The name elicited a commotion. When the hoots died down, I demonstrated how to take long straight branches from the trees, stand them upright by implanting them in the ground about a foot apart in two rows, then make bundles of smaller twigs and stout grasses and jam those bundles between the standing sticks to make a wall a foot thick. They tried it. It took them awhile to catch on, and the ground was hard, nearly frozen, but as soon as the wall was only a couple of feet high, they could feel it block the cold wind off the water.

This minor success resulted in a seemingly sincere invitation for me to return, which I did a couple of days later, to hold what I planned as the first of a series of wilderness cooking classes. To the credit of my little group of students, as many men as women attended. Unfortunately, the first part of the lesson, about the necessity of marinating wild meat, broke out into an argument over whether the drunks in the group would ever part with enough wine for the procedure. When I suggested using juice instead, we were able to get down to business.

"Today I'm going to show you how to cook small animals that you catch in the valley. Always be sure to catch and kill what you eat yourself. Don't ever—I repeat—ever—take an animal that's dead, even from your best friend. And also, don't eat rats. Don't ask me why. Just don't."

"This is going to make me sick," one of the younger women said. "Can't we just, like, pick the garbage at a fast-food place?"

"That ain't healthy," somebody remarked. And they all burst into laughter.

"The point here isn't what you should eat," I told them. "It's what you can eat if you absolutely have to."

"Like what?" someone asked.

From my backpack, I took out a book that I'd ordered on the Internet. It had a lot of recipes for game and the names of places in Canada that shipped frozen caribou and venison, moose and bear to gourmet cooks around the world. The recipes called for vintage wines available only by special order from the Liquor Control Board of Ontario. Also required were balsamic vinegar, pure olive oil, capers, pine nuts . . . . The irony of the publication was not lost on the more literate of my students. "Do they tell rich people not to eat rats, too?" one person asked.

I ignored the question and explained, "There are some pictures here that I want you all to look at. They show you that the edible valley animals—raccoons, squirrels, groundhogs, porcupines, muskrats—all have a few things in common. If you know how to cook one of them, you can pretty much cook all of them."

I showed my rapt audience how to locate the scent glands under the legs and on the back of a raccoon, how to remove those hard little nodes so that the meat stayed sweet and delicious. I showed them how to skin the animals in such a way that the fur never touched the meat. "That's so that no germs get on it," Queenie explained. "Fur is dirty—like your coats. Or else covered with animal saliva. Not anything you want to touch your food."

Spoken like a true public-health nurse, I thought with pride.

"Groundhogs are not too hard to find in the valley," I told them. "And if you ever feel that you can't bring yourself to eat something like that, just remember that groundhogs are vegetarians. They only eat healthy food themselves."

I explained that porcupines were edible but maybe not worth the risk, and I didn't even bother mentioning skunk. "As for squirrel, you can eat one if you can catch one, but I wouldn't bet on that . . ."

Though I had once been adept at snatching apples and onions from sidewalk markets and stealing bottles of juice out of stores, I refrained from imparting suggestions in regard to the acquisition of ingredients, though I did tell them that muskrat cooked with onions and celery could be called "Marsh Rabbit" and served to guests. That got another laugh.

"Next time," I told them, "I'll talk about wild geese, ducks, pigeons and doves. And the time after that, about frog legs and fish."

"Count me out. I'm going to the food bank," a man in ragged jeans and a beautiful leather jacket said.

"He's the type who can take care of himself without wringing the necks of squirrels," Queenie said of him later.

"Maybe they all are," I replied, convinced my homeless survival lessons had bombed.

"I think maybe you need to teach them something simpler," Queenie suggested as we walked toward the doughnut shop on King near Church Street that we had frequented for years. I remembered times when we'd only had enough money to order one coffee and one doughnut between us. Sometimes we still ordered like that because coffee now gave Queenie heart palpitations and doughnuts were bad for my cholesterol.

"Simpler? How?"

"What they really want to know is how to sleep in shelters without getting their stuff stolen or exposing themselves to T.B. And they'd like to ride transit without having to stand in line at some charity and beg for tickets one at a time. They'd like to have telephones so they could call family members—or even each other. Most of all, they'd like what everybody else would like: an easier, calmer, freer life."

"Queenie," I said, reaching across the table and touching her hand, "you're working too hard. You're going to burn yourself out."

She turned her hand under mine in a gesture of intimacy that surprised us both. She pulled away, but then her fingers returned to mine, and she lightly stroked my gold ring, running the tip of her forefinger over the embossed symbols that adorned it. "You still wear this," she declared. I slipped the ring from my finger. This gesture seemed to shock Queenie.

"It's okay," I said. "It's not a wedding ring."

She glanced away in discomfort, as if I'd embarrassed her. "What did you promise Stow's wife before she died?" she asked after a while.

"She asked me to do the one thing I just couldn't do."

"Hurt her again—on purpose, I mean?"

"Yes."

"It's easy to make promises," Queenie said, taking the mug of coffee from me. "When you owe promises, that's a different story."

"To whom do you owe promises?" I asked in alarm.

"Not Stow, if that's what you mean. You two ought to leave the past buried," she added. Her eyes strayed to the window. It had started to snow, and I knew part of her mind was, as always, out in the streets and down in the valley with her clients.

"Easier said than done, Queenie. Without Stow's intervention, I would have a criminal record for assaulting Harpur. And that would have cost me not only any future hope of earning money, it would have cost me five years' back sick pay."

"He forgave you. You ought to forgive him, too."

"For what?"

"I got to get back to work." She looked out at the snow again. It was beginning to thicken, to gather in long streamers that skittered across the sidewalk. "He stopped phoning me. So you must have agreed to be his lawyer."

"What does he know about you? How did he get your number?" The sharpness of my voice surprised me. It seemed to surprise Queenie, too.

"Your Honor," she said, smiling only a little, "if I didn't know you better, I'd think you were jealous."

Maybe she didn't know me as well as she thought. I *was* jealous.

"Look," she said, "anybody can get my number. The clinic number, anyway. And as for how he knew about me, I thought maybe you told him."

It touched me to think that Queenie would consider herself a topic of conversation between me and the Supreme Court Justice. "Queenie," I admitted, "I haven't spoken about you, or anyone else, with Stow since . . ."

"Since he said you killed his wife?"

"How do you know about that?"

"He told me you had it in for her because she always rejected you. He told me you tried to strangle her once, but that didn't surprise me because I knew that's why you ended up on the skids. But he told me something I didn't know. He said you were the last person she was with before she died. He said he lost it at her funeral and told everybody it was your fault she was dead. He said all that was five or six years ago. Now's he sorry and he wants things to be better between the two of you. He said you're the only person who can prove what happened the night Harpur died. He said you have to save him the way he saved you."

"Queenie, I can't defend a man accused of murder. And one who blames me for upsetting his wife to the point where she gives up the ghost. Even Stow must know how ironic and just plain stupid that is."

"He's a famous judge. He has to know what he's doing."

"The murder charge is absurd. Harpur Blane died in a hospital. She was failing. There would be records. Every minute of her final hours would be accounted for."

Queenie leaned closer. "It's a cold case, right? Isn't that what you call it?"

"I guess so."

"It seems like a long time ago, but obviously the police have a reason for opening the case back up. They think Stow killed his wife. You have to prove them wrong. That's how it works, isn't it?"

"Sort of."

"All you've got to do," Queenie said, "is figure out what happened every minute of the night she died. Then you can show that Stow didn't do anything wrong."

"What if he *did* do something wrong?"

Queenie looked stunned. "Is that what you think?"

Outside the hospital window, the tobogganers in their bright pink and yellow jackets zip down the hill in Riverdale Park, haul their sleds back up, zip down again. Harpur lies still. I can feel her eyes on my back. I can hear her even breath, not labored, thank God, but not strong, either. Everything is finished between us, and everything is forgiven, too. We're even. She could never love me, and I could never save her from herself. I can only imagine the joyful shouts of the tobogganers, but I can clearly hear the bustle in the hospital hall. Busy place. I ran into a staff member coming out of Harpur's room as I headed in. We collided and something flew out of his hand and landed at my feet. Just then Harpur called my name.

"Your Honor?"

Queenie's voice startled me out of reverie.

"If Stow calls again, Queenie, don't talk to him."

"I just told you," she said, "he doesn't call me anymore."

"You have to come, Daddy. I've got something really important to tell you, and I want to tell you in person."

"Ellen, sweetheart, I can only take so many of these family gatherings."

I stretched out on my office couch and cradled the phone between my shoulder and my chin. So far, stretching out was the only thing I was accomplishing in my new office.

"Daddy, there was a time when we didn't even know whether you were alive or dead. You can't blame us for wanting to spend time with you."

"Ellen, there was a time when you wished I *were* dead!"

"Oh, don't be so melodramatic. It's Jeffrey's birthday and Mom really wants you there."

The thought made me uncomfortable.

"And I want you there, too. When you find out what I have to say, you'll understand why I need to tell you to your face."

"You're not serving me with a writ or anything, are you?"

"Oh, Daddy, such soap opera! I'll see you at Mom's."

Before my fall from grace and goodness, my wife Anne and I had substantial investments, which, due to good advice provided by her own family, had not diminished during my lapse. When I was sufficiently recovered from my brush with the law and my retreat into mental illness to be divorced, we divided those assets. I used my share to leverage purchase of the apartment building Jeffrey and I now ran. Anne had used hers to buy a triangular suite on the thirtieth floor of a building overlooking Lake Ontario on one side and most of downtown Toronto on the other. On a November day, I found myself in the condo and realized that at that time of year, Anne could see the sun rise over the harbor islands from her bedroom window and watch it set over the low blue ridge of hills northwest of the city from her living room.

"I'm glad you came before everyone else, Ellis," she said awkwardly. "It gives us a few minutes alone." She stood outlined against the backdrop of the city. Dressed in a pale blue silk slack suit, her ice-blond hair sleek in the early winter light, Anne looked like a lovely fixture, an art object.

I cleared my throat. "I guess I mixed up the time."

"Ellen and Jeffrey and their families will be here in a few minutes," she said pleasantly, "but before they come, I need to ask you something." She moved closer and lifted her hand. I was afraid she was going to touch my face. Would my skin recognize the once-familiar sensation of her smooth fingertips against my cheek?

Instead, she ran her fingers along the sleeve of my jacket. "Ellis," she said, "I want to know how the case in Stow's defense is going."

I noticed faint shadows beneath her eyes. Age or tiredness was making its mark after all. But she was still beautiful, still the only woman I had wanted to be my wife. Disappointed that her question was not about me, I moved away from her touch.

"I'm not at liberty to discuss that, Anne. I'm surprised you'd think otherwise."

"Thank you, Ellis, thank you." Now she *clutched* my arm. "If you're not at liberty to say anything about the case, that means you're on it. It means that Stow has been successful in convincing you to be his lawyer in this mess."

"Anne," I said, catching a whiff of Chanel, "is that why you invited me here today, to ask me about my practice? Are you afraid I'll slip back into vagrancy?"

"No, of course not! I'm simply concerned about your well-being." She hesitated, her eyes averted. "I'm not an unsophisticated person, Ellis. I know I have to share some of the blame for what happened to you."

"No, Anne," I protested, startled at this idea. "The responsibility is all mine. Forget . . ."

"Ellis," she said, her voice now urgent. "The prosecutor on this case is brand new, but powerful and promising. Whatever the outcome for poor Stow, his murder trial can make or break both counsel, the Crown and the defense. Both of you can be sure of the kind of attention that will elevate you to . . ."

"Anne, Anne," I said, taking both her hands in my own. "Why do you care about this case so much, anyway?"

Before she could answer, the door to the condo burst open. Little Angelo came running in and behind him was his mother.

"Daddy," Ellen said, without prelude, "you need to know that I've been promoted."

"Ellen, how wonderful!"

"As of November 15, I was made Senior Crown. In fact," she glanced at her mother, then at me. "In fact," she said, "I'm going to be the lead Crown on the first-degree murder trial *Regina vs. John Stoughton-Melville.* It's you against me, Daddy, and before you say anything, I want you to know that I'm happy about this, and I hope you will be, too."

Chapter 5

It was totally false—the notion that our possible confronta-
tion was good news to Ellen, that she relished telling me in
person because of her joy in robust competition. Ellen was
the child of my blood, the person most like me in the
world. I sensed that she was not happy to have me as an adversary, that she was distraught.

I, on the other hand, felt a sense of exhilaration that I
dared not show. A prosecutor of power and promise? My
own daughter! I have to admit I felt a sudden relish; it
would be easy to win against so green an opponent. Yet
the juxtaposition of counsel seemed not only unusual but
impossible. Would the law permit this situation? It occurred to me that there was no statute I knew of forbidding such familial confrontations in the courtroom.
Weird as our opposition might seem, it was not illegal. Or
did I suppose I would lose the case, thereby enhancing my
girl's growing reputation?

"Ellen," I said, inviting her to take a seat beside me
while Anne placed goblets of sparkling water on a glass

coffee table in front of us, "I think you're not as keen on this idea as you seem . . ."

"You're mistaken," she answered, refusing to meet my eyes. "I would have asked to be taken off if I'd thought it inappropriate to have you as defense counsel. Besides, I have a very strong case against Stoughton-Melville. He ruthlessly and heartlessly murdered a helpless woman, a woman he had pledged to love, honor and protect. He was an officer of the court and a servant of his country the night he performed this egregious act. Not only did he breach the trust of his wife, he breached the trust of us all. I'm going to nail him. His defense counsel will be a worthy adversary and no more."

"That's the spirit, Ellen!" I said with pride. "I guess you've learned a thing or two from your old man after all."

She smiled but still didn't look at me.

"Do you remember the first time you were ever in court?" I asked.

"You let me sit on the judge's bench so I could get a good look at the place."

"You loved it."

"You loved it, too, Daddy." She didn't add, *Yet look what you did with it.*

"And now we get to play the game together."

"Daddy, it's not a game. We might end up enemies. Did that thought ever occur to you? It may not matter to you, but I don't particularly want an enemy for a father."

"Ellen," I said, raising my hand to smooth her dark curly hair as I had when she was a child, "the day I saw you again and realized that you'd been looking for me when I was down and out was the day I knew that nothing could ever come between us. It's not going to be you versus me. It's going to be the state versus the accused. It's not personal. It's merely an opportunity for us both to showcase our talents."

"I hope you're right," she said as she reached over to give my old cheek a peck.

I looked up then and saw Jeffrey watching us. Too engrossed with Ellen, I hadn't noticed his presence despite the giggling sounds of his wife and babe as they dispensed with their coats and hats, boots and gloves.

"Son," I greeted him. "I'm glad you're here. We need to talk about that land deal when you get a chance."

He nodded, glanced at Ellen and took a step toward us, but Tootie interrupted him to help her with the massive amount of equipment needed for little Sal.

I turned back to Ellen. "This is your first murder case as Senior Crown," I said, "and my first case of any sort in years. We're going to be a sensation."

"Especially if that viper Aliana Caterina gets on the story."

"What?"

"That Euro-trash witch is after you, Daddy." Ellen seemed to be joking, but I wasn't sure. "When the press latches on to the father-against-daughter angle," she added, "we'll both be hot news."

"That's what your mother thinks," I remarked lightly.

A pained look crossed her face. "Speaking of Mom, I'm she sure she needs me in the kitchen."

"Ellen—" I grabbed her wrist. "Don't be afraid. A jury will not be unsympathetic to a young woman trying to bring to justice a man accused of killing his innocent wife."

"I'm not afraid," she said stoutly. "Not of a scoundrel like Stow. And not of you, either."

When my daughter left the room, I approached my son. Surrounded as he was by the demands of his professional

75

life, his young children and his wife, Jeffrey was rather hard to pin down for even a short conversation, so I relished this brief opportunity.

"Have you heard anything?" I began.

"I meant to call you," he answered. "Looks like the land adjacent to Wigmore Ravine is becoming available." Small talk was no more palatable to Jeffrey than it was to me. He continued, "It's the parcel you and I have had our eyes on since we acquired the apartment building. I think it's about a hundred acres . . ."

"And the price?"

Jeffrey reached into the pocket of his black shirt and pulled out a carefully folded piece of lined paper. Though I was sitting opposite him and couldn't make out what appeared upside down to me, I could see the precise columns of figures, the tidy lines of notes. I remembered how proud I'd once been of the neat, meticulous handwriting of both my children.

"The City's trying to unload it as surplus," he said. He shook his fair head. "As if land could ever be extra or something you unload for fast cash. Anyway, we can probably negotiate the price. I'm sure we can make a down payment without having to remortgage the apartment building." He kept his eyes glued to his calculations as he asked, "Want to go back down there with me and have another look, Dad?"

Two days later, we descended the steep path. A light dusting of snow sparkled in the morning sun, which lent freshness to the dark green fir trees and caused the denuded maple and oak to cast long, gray shadows.

We walked in silence directly to the river, easily found stepping-stones above a riffle of rapids and crossed the shallow stream to the parcel of real estate we hoped to buy.

"Litterers," Jeffrey muttered in disgust as we came upon a heap of crushed beer cans. A rusted fork and a bent can opener beside the heap showed that it had been some time since the trespassers had been here. I glanced up. Far above us, new condominiums crowned the rim of the valley. Where they gave onto the ravine, the buildings were protected by tall fences capped with razor wire. No doubt the owners of those condos thought they were protecting themselves from thieves and thugs lurking in the valley. In reality, the fences served to keep people from the street out of the ravine. I was beginning to see that this land would be a safe and secure investment.

Whether Jeffrey was coming to the same conclusion, I couldn't say. He had never been much of a talker, and from the time he'd been a little boy, nature outings had rendered him even quieter than he usually was. He studied the riverbank, the trees with their coating of fine snow, the pale blue sky. After what seemed a very long time, he said, "If we buy this land, people will think we're building ourselves some sort of private domain out here." He gestured toward the river running fast over a ridge of rock worn smooth by the years.

"Does that bother you, son?"

Jeffrey smiled without looking at me. "No," he said, "on the contrary. I love this place. I always have. I remember how I used to look forward to our walks down here. I could hardly wait for the day when you'd bring me down."

"But Jeffrey," I said, stopping and turning toward him so abruptly that he bumped into me, "in those days, you always seemed to come along on sufferance, as though you were accommodating me. If I had known how much you enjoyed our outings, they would have been more frequent."

"No, they wouldn't have, Dad," he answered. "You were always too busy." He shivered. "It's cold. What do you think? About the land, I mean."

"Jeffrey, do you feel confident about handling the negotiations?"

"Yes."

"Then let's do it. I'll draw up a proxy, a limited power of attorney, in case you have to sign anything when I'm busy. Do what you have to do, son. I think this land should belong to us. Jointly." Jeffrey almost always tried to hide his feelings, but I could tell he was pleased.

I met Nicky McPhail for coffee later that same day. "Why is Stoughton-Melville in a maximum-security federal penitentiary when he has never even been convicted, let alone sentenced?" Nicky asked.

"Presumably for his own protection," I answered.

"Against what?"

"Against not being the center of attention!"

Nicky laughed, but clearly Stow's situation was serious. "How did this happen, Ellis? How did he ever end up in so much trouble?"

"Nicky, I've never met an accused who didn't ask himself that question—even when he knew the answer. Whatever happened in Riverside Hospital that night made Stow vulnerable to investigation. Whatever that investigation turned up has led to his arrest."

"It's your job to study the disclosure, to put together the Crown's evidence in direct opposition to the way Ellen will put it together."

I agreed. "Same so-called facts. Different conclusion."

"In what ways is Justice Stoughton-Melville vulnerable here?"

"I suppose, Nicky, that's for me to find out," I answered carefully. But I already knew some of the answers. Stow had been vulnerable to his love for a difficult and ultimately inaccessible woman. He had been vulnerable to the arrogance of judging other men. And now he was vulnerable to time, time that was robbing him of his freedom while he quickly aged.

"But Stow doesn't cease to be a judge because of these charges, does he?"

"Far from it," I replied. "All this has no bearing whatsoever on his judicial status."

"Which makes him powerful and dangerous still," Nicky mused.

Stow didn't need a judgeship to make him powerful and dangerous, but I didn't bother mentioning that to my young friend.

The presumption of innocence and the burden of proof. The merest schoolchild, perhaps even one as young as my precocious grandson, knew that these two principles were the foundation of our system of justice. But few laypeople realized fully that these twin concepts meant that the accused need never open his mouth in his own defense.

Stow knew. Of course he did. And when I visited him a second time at Fernhope, he was still unwilling to tell me what evidence he had that could counter Ellen's case.

"She's going to run with this, Stow. It's the biggest case she's ever had." He eyed me evenly. Of course he had known all along that the Crown was my own daughter. As a judge of the Supreme Court, Stow would know every detail about the justice system. But what about the medical system?

"First, I need you to tell me everything you did that night. What time did you arrive at the hospital? Who saw you there? What were you driving? What were you wearing? Who had you been with earlier that day? I know it's been several years, but nobody's memory of that night is likely to be sharper than yours."

All I had been allowed to bring into the interview room were a pad of yellow lined paper and a cheap ballpoint pen. Stow sneered at these items contemptuously, as if they were unworthy of taking notes about him. Perhaps that was the reason for his reticence. I waited. The room was so quiet that I could hear the two guards breathing. One of them realized I was listening and held his breath for a moment. My patience began to thin. "Look, Stow, you're in a precarious position here. Ellen may seem new at this, but she's good. She's going to be on us like a junkyard dog. I need to know every single thing that happened the night Harpur died, and I need to know it from you. I can dig things up, but I can't invent facts. You've got to give me something to start with."

"Ellis," he said dreamily, as if he hadn't heard my questions at all, "you were such a skilled cross-examiner in the old days. Do you remember how you used to wear them down? You'd get some poor sod to swear he was completely certain about something. Then you'd ask him one more time while you searched your files as if you had some piece of paper that would prove him wrong. It drove witnesses crazy the way you searched through those papers."

"I'm not here for chitchat, Justice. Nor for old times' sake, either."

"Oh, really?"

The two words were spoken in a chilling tone that brought Queenie immediately to mind. I didn't know what hold Stow had over her, but she thought "old times" a sufficient reason for me to help him. "There are dozens of ways to intimidate by stalling on a criminal trial, Stow. I'm sure my learned adversary knows all the tricks, considering that I taught her quite a few when she was only a child. Which brings me to my next question . . ."

I wanted him to tell me what his stake was in all this. Why was he insisting on me as his lawyer? Was he guilty or innocent? Was he trying to save himself or to harm me? If the former, how? If the latter, why?

But his attention drifted away from our conversation, his eyes seeming to seek those of the guards. His hair had lost the sharpness of its previous cut. His skin was sallow, his posture stooped. It was now two months since the day of the Red Mass, and already he was exhibiting behavior typical of a prisoner. He didn't need words to tell me that he wanted to go back to his "house"—his cell.

"Please, Stow, at least tell me why you are here," I persisted. "Why are you not out on bail, or at the very least in a remand facility?"

"I have friends," he said, as if I had asked him about some exclusive club. "They look after me."

He signaled. The guards approached, and without a word, he was escorted away. I noticed that he was wearing the same clothes he'd worn during our first interview at Fernhope. The lean, well-cut trousers, the pale finely woven cotton shirt and the cashmere sweater looked clean and fresh. There was no laundry in the prison capable of washing a four-hundred-dollar cotton shirt without ruining it. Stow's clothes were fresh because between visits he was probably wearing jail clothes—either a bright orange pumpkin suit or, worse, prison-issue sweats that were passed from prisoner to prisoner after having been laundered, and sometimes before.

"I'm going to build a case whether you help me or not," I called after him. He stopped abruptly, throwing the shorter guard off balance. The man swore under his breath as he missed a step and reached out his free hand to right himself.

Stow glanced at me for a split second. There was a tiny movement at the corner of his mouth, a low light suffusing his eyes. He stood taller, inclined his head toward me just a fraction, then turned away. His smile, his glance, his posture formed one smooth, consistent gesture. Was it a gesture of gratitude? Or was it contempt?

"How do you go about reconstructing one day in somebody's life?"

Nicky McPhail and I walked along Queen Street West, passing cafés, funky little clothing shops, a bookstore with a black metal bin of tattered titles on the sidewalk. We hung a sharp left and headed up McCaul Street. Ahead of us loomed a two-story rectangle about the size of a football field. It was raised above the other buildings on the block by gigantic multicolored metal poles rising from the ground.

"That is so cool," Nicky said. "What the heck is it, anyway?"

"It's the new building for the art college."

"I know that, you silly geez. What I mean is, what does it symbolize?"

"It's a profound statement of art's ability to soar above the mundane at the same time as it is deeply grounded in the everyday experiences of the man on the street."

"Wow," Nicky said, "did you just make that up?"

"Sure." I laughed. "Seriously, Nicky, I've got a client who won't help me at all, so where do I start?"

"Start looking for another client." We turned again, this time onto busy Dundas Street.

"Not an option. I owe Justice Stoughton-Melville big-time—for reasons I can't explain, by the way."

"Explain to me or to yourself?"

"You'll make a good lawyer, Nicky. Did anybody ever tell you that?"

Over doughnuts and coffee at the Tim Hortons on the corner of Dundas and Simcoe, Nicky's conversation grew more serious.

"Until you get full disclosure from the Crown," he began, "you're going to have to wing it. Best way is to start from what you can get right now, then work your way back."

"Meaning?"

"Let's talk hospital. That's where Harpur died. The scene of the crime. We still haven't heard what the police learned that caused them to bring charges. So you need to know what they found at that hospital." He thought for a moment. "Wasn't there a preliminary inquiry, a hearing to set out all the evidence?"

"The Attorney General waived the prelim."

"On *murder one?* How can that be?"

"I don't know. Nothing's been done according to procedure here. I do know that there's some sort of bizarre medical evidence. It seems the police were called in by the hospital when researchers got some inexplicable results from one of those studies that require follow-up every five years."

"Where did you get that information?"

I smiled at Nicky. He was such a pleasant young man. Everything about him was easy to take: his casual good looks, his unassuming air, his understated manner, his intelligence. I liked to please him. "I found it on the Internet."

"Good, Judge Portal," he said grinning, "good start. But now you have to get on the ground. That hospital, does it still exist?"

"It's a government facility. It's still in operation, but it's sort of been commandeered."

"You're going to have to get in there, which is tough. Since SARS and 9/11, hospital visiting is not so easy. You're going to have to do some sneaking around. Are you up for that?"

"Yeah," I said. I bit into a strawberry vanilla doughnut and munched for a few minutes before I conceded, "But whether I'm up *to* it remains to be seen."

We went back to my office. Nicky patted the distressed leather of the chair in front of my desk. "Nice," he said. He threw himself into it and swung his leg over the chair's stout arm. "I could get used to this."

It never occurred to me to be bothered by his frequent show of what I once would have considered disrespect. All I felt at Nicky's nonchalance was amusement. "So get used to it," I joked.

He glanced up at me a little surprised. I let it pass. "We need a plan," I told him.

Nicky turned his lithe body around so that he was sitting properly. He reached inside the pocket of his jacket and pulled out his electronic organizer. "I thought you'd never ask," he said.

We talked for the next two hours, beginning with an honest assessment of the amount of work it would take us to get through the mountain of disclosure material that would soon arrive. "Major work. And Stow's reluctance to help us with his own defense? Major problem."

"Yes. Sooner or later," I told Nicky, "Stow is going to have to relinquish his silence and tell us how he wants this case conducted. I've known the man for years, but I can't claim to be able to figure him out. His uncooperativeness may be shame, or fatigue, or despair. Or consciousness of guilt."

"Never say guilt," Nicky recited. It was an old law school adage.

"I accepted a retainer, so like it or not, I'm committed to Stow as my client," I said, "and I'm committed to his acquittal, too. So, in the absence of any instructions to the contrary, I intend to mount a straightforward defense."

Nicky nodded. "We'll check out all their potential witnesses . . ."

"Right."

"The people at Riverside . . ." He began to count off on his fingers, but I lost track of the names he mentioned. All I could think about was how hard it would be to get inside the hospital. What had been a low-security private care facility when Harpur had died was now a high-security contagious disease isolation unit.

" . . . the police . . ."

"For sure. I can contact my old friend Matt West. I think it would be wiser to deal with him than to try to get anything out of Ellen's police contacts."

Nicky nodded again and made a note. "We'll need to check out that rental car that Stow is supposed to have driven to Riverside that final night," he said, "and the bank for anything we can get on Stow and Harpur's finances."

I was beginning to feel dizzy at the thought of all this work, but I could see that Nicky was growing more enthusiastic with each addition to our task list.

"And Pipperpharmat," he said. "That's the far-out name of the pharmaceutical company that was conducting the drug trials, isn't it?"

"Yes. And we should also try to get a look at the drug vault that Stow is accused of raiding." Once again, the problem of getting into Riverside arose. And even if we could find a way to get in, there was no guarantee that the present layout of the hospital would even resemble what it had been at the time of Harpur's demise.

Nicky furiously jabbed his stylus at his handheld device. He didn't look up for several seconds. "How do we do this?" he finally said.

"Have any ideas?"

I expected him to remind me that I was the boss, which is exactly what he *did* do. "Whatever you have in mind will be fine with me," he said.

I went over the onerous list of tasks in my mind. *Nicky should do the running, and I should do the digging.* "How about you check out those witnesses, and I handle the pharmaceutical company?"

"Sounds good, but . . ." He hesitated, checked the screen of his handheld. I waited for him to ask for clarification on some particular matter. I was surprised when he said, "All these lines of inquiry sound fine, but where is it all leading? What are we trying to prove here?"

"Nicky, you know as well as I that we don't have to prove anything. All we need to do is to make the jury doubt Ellen's proof."

"Yeah, yeah, sure," he said impatiently, "but what I mean is, what's our theory?" He reached for the folder on my desk that held my summary of Ellen's proposed case. "What are we holding forth as the explanation for Harpur Stoughton-Melville's death? For Stow being seen at the hospital the night of his wife's death? For his using a rental car to get there instead of his own vehicle? For leaving fingerprints on surfaces in the hospital's drug vault? For his wife having died with elevated levels of an experimental drug in her blood, a drug stored in that same vault?"

"Nicky," I said, getting up from my new, beautifully aged leather armchair and putting my hand on his shoulder in a paternal way, "Nicky, my boy, Stow's defense is the most time-honored one of all. '*I didn't do it!*'"

We both laughed, even though it was an old joke. "What about natural causes?" Nicky asked when I had resumed my seat. "Can't we use that as a defense?"

"If there were some way we could eliminate the blood-level evidence," I answered, "there might be a natural-cause defense. After all, Harpur was ill and had been for a long time—years, in fact. But I saw her myself the same night . . ."

Nicky looked shocked. "What?"

"It shouldn't come as a surprise to you, Nicky, that I knew Harpur. I went to law school with Stow. So did she. We were friends. True, we had become estranged, but in her last months, Harpur asked me to visit her, and I did."

"Ellis," Nicky said, "I'm a little concerned . . ."

"That I visited Harpur? Common knowledge."

Nicky didn't look convinced by my nonchalance. "Everyone at Riverside," I went on, "including the volunteers who visited her, knew that the greatest conundrum of Harpur's condition was how close or far from death she might be. Physically, she had rallied more than once. Her strength seemed to come and go. Mentally, however, she was gone all the time. She could have died that night—or she could have lived on for years."

"Doesn't that uncertainty itself present a motive for murder?" Nicky asked. "I mean anyone around her might consider mercy killing."

"Yes. But nobody is accused of killing Harpur except Stow."

"But what if one of the nurses administered the fatal dose?"

"Don't you think Ellen would have checked that out, Nicky? Don't you think every suspect, every witness would have already come to her attention?"

"I don't know, Ellis. I don't make assumptions. I make it my job to discover anything that serves the interest of my client."

He sounded determined, almost belligerent. Perhaps he had some new idea for our large to-do list. I made a mental note to check the police fingerprint files and the surveillance videos from the hospital lobby.

"Ellis," Nicky said, "I'm not blowing you off. When I spoke of people near Harpur having a motive to kill her, I didn't mean . . ." He hesitated.

"Me?" I inquired, hurt innocence strong in my tone.

Chapter 6

"*Disgusting!*' is the general consensus on your cooking lessons," Queenie told me. "My clients like the idea that you come down and talk to them, but they don't want to hear one more thing about squirrels and frogs and . . ."

"All right. All right. Maybe I can think of something else. If they don't want to eat squirrels, maybe I can show them how to make a hat out of squirrel fur."

"Oh, puh-lease!"

"I'm kidding."

"There was a woman down here the other day handing out baked potatoes," Queenie said. "And it was great. Everybody put them in their pockets to keep themselves warm. The potatoes stayed hot for hours. When they were still a little warm, we all sat down and ate them."

"I don't think I can beat that, Queenie," I said, holding back laughter.

"You don't have to. Come down and see us anyway."

The next night, I parked on a small side street just east of the Queen-King Bridge. As I made my way down the embankment, mulling over the relative heat-retention properties of Styrofoam versus bubble wrap, I overheard a loud voice raised in a rant.

A bonfire roared in the middle of the riverbank Tent City site, throwing light on boxes, shacks and tarp-covered lean-tos laid out in neat rows with paths between them. A few figures huddled in the shadows between these makeshift dwellings, caught fleetingly in the headlights of a car passing overhead.

But for the most part, the twenty-five or thirty squatters gathered near the blaze had their eyes glued to the figure who stood beside them, waving his arms and stamping his feet.

"This is public property. This whole city was once public property. Now rich people are everywhere, and they got everything, including all the land that really belongs to us. We should get all this land back instead of being kicked off it whenever rich people want us out of here."

Johnny Dirt's notions of private and public property were a little confused, but his command over his audience was total. "City Hall and them counselors say we got two weeks left and then we gotta go? Well, I say they gotta go!"

A cheer rose from the little crowd. Quite a hearty cheer for people whose meals, when they didn't come from the garbage, came from the leftovers of the food bank.

Queenie, I noticed, was not cheering. I made my way to her. As I did so, Johnny Dirt caught sight of me among his listeners.

"Some people," he said, "act poor even when they're really rich. Them people we got to watch out for special because them people got friends at City Hall." A low murmur rumbled around the camp, echoing the rumbling of the cars above.

"Lay off His Honor, Dirtbag!"

Grateful for this vote of confidence from an invisible supporter, I moved through the crowd, acknowledging a wave here, a nod there, until I reached Queenie's side. I hunkered down near her and she reached out and gave my arm a squeeze.

"Thanks for coming," she said softly. The red firelight made her hair look like the fine copper wire I used to steal scraps of as a boy on my father's building sites. It seemed to erase the years from her dusky face and smooth the planes of her high-boned cheeks.

"The firelight makes you look beautiful," I said.

I could see surprise flash in her dark eyes before she lowered her gaze.

"I came to take you home. You shouldn't be down here so late," I whispered. "You've put in a full day at the clinic, I'm sure."

She nodded, sending the copper lights dancing. "Yes. And I suppose you've put in a full day lawyering. Tired?"

I shook my head. "I'm up to my ears in papers. Ellen has finally finished shipping boxes of photocopies to my office. Under the law, she has to disclose all information that she intends to use against Stow."

"I don't get it," Queenie said, speaking close to my ear in order to be heard over the great orator. "How come she has to show you what she's got?"

"In order that my client—Stow, of course—in order that my client can make full answer and defense."

"Meaning?"

"Meaning that should he so choose, Stow can answer the case the Crown is making against him and raise a reasonable doubt in the minds of the jury."

Queenie looked up at me. "Is that all you've got to do, Your Honor—make them doubt that Stow could have killed his wife?"

"Yes. That's all. Seems simple, doesn't it? Especially considering his position in this world."

Queenie gave the matter some thought. "You know," she finally said, "it works both ways."

"What do you mean?"

A biting wind seemed to rise from the river as night deepened over the waters. Queenie pushed a lock of hair away from her eyes. "It's a two-way street, his being a famous judge. Some people feel sorry for him. They think he's getting picked on because he's rich and successful. After all, why does the court want to open up a murder case against him now? It's been five years since his wife died, hasn't it?"

I thought of the rows of banker's boxes growing like mold up the wall of my little store-top office. "That's what I've got to figure out," I answered.

"You're not going to figure it out sitting down here," she said. She glanced across the river. Near the bank, the water was dark and still. But a current roiled in the center of the stream, breaking up the reflections of lights from the bridge and the street and the buildings into a scattering of jewel-like sparkles. "There was a time," Queenie said, "when you and I could go without seeing each other for a month, then catch up in about five minutes flat. But it's not like that now, is it?"

"No," I said, reaching for her hand in the dark shadows between us, seeking the warmth of her skin. "We were bums then—and for quite a while, we were drunks, too. We didn't have a lot to report to each other."

She laughed quietly. "Yeah. That's one way of putting it," she said. "But now I'm running the clinic, helping out here at Tent City, going to meetings, sitting on committees . . ."

"Yes."

"And you, you're working on a murder case again." She slipped her fingers away from mine. "So if we don't pay attention to each other, we're going to lose track. I wouldn't want to do that, Your Honor."

A loud burst of applause drowned her words. Johnny Dirt had apparently reached the rousing climax of his speech.

"Tent City stays!" the crowd began to chant. "Tent City stays!"

"Queenie," I suddenly thought to ask, "what's gotten Johnny going, anyway?"

"There was a newspaper reporter down here," Queenie answered. "That one you know, Aliana Caterina." She made a face. "She and her photographer were looking to take a picture of you teaching one of your so-called cooking classes. When she realized you weren't here, she got the photographer to take pictures of the shacks and lean-tos. Next thing we know, five city counselors are down here making loud noises about poor homeless people camping out in the middle of the city. Whatever they said about improving the situation set Johnny Dirt off. Now he's a crusader. And you know as well as I do that when a crusader gets a crowd worked up, the crusade itself is sure to follow."

Queenie refused my ride home, claiming she still had work to do at the site. Leaving her, I crossed the river and walked north through the valley for half a mile or so until I crossed again and came near Riverside Hospital, the imposing semicircular building from which I'd once watched tobogganers on the hill from Harpur's room.

It was pitch-dark and cold, and the white tents of the isolation units set up in the parking lot behind the hospital stood out like tombstones. Riverside had gone from a private care facility to what my mother used to call a "pest house," a public facility for contagious disease. Anyone admitted to the hospital was forced to stay for a minimum of ninety days. No visitors were allowed, even to attend the dying.

I crept closer to the barbed wire that separated the park from the hospital. Two armed officers stood beside the door to the building, but no one seemed to be guarding the tents themselves. A ventilation system, connecting all the tents and composed of twisted pipes and stream-releasing valves, hissed its white breath into the frigid night. Suddenly the guards snapped to attention. A heavily gowned figure, masked and with a white plastic helmet, moved from one tent to another, genderless in thick protective garments, taking slow laborious steps hampered by heavy white rubber boots.

I moved farther into the shadows. The last time I'd been in Riverside was the night Harpur had died there. Unless I contracted something like a flesh-eating disease or antibiotic-resistant T.B., I'd never get in there again.

I trekked back to my car and drove straight to my office. I spent quite a long while washing my hands, as if the contagion of Riverside had somehow crawled onto me.

Then I searched the pile of boxes for one I knew must be there—the medical records that had made the police change Harpur's death from a closed case to a cold case.

My daughter had been tidy and thorough. Each box was labeled with a printed sticker. I had to move a few around before I found the one I needed, but it was there, just as I thought.

I undid the tape around the box. Red tape. That wasn't Ellen's joke, it was Nicky's. After we'd made a preliminary assessment of a box's contents, we taped it shut as a reminder that we'd cursorily examined it. Masking tape would have done just fine, but Nicky said red tape was "more Dickensian."

I lifted the relevant files out and began to read, making a list of things to check. I was concentrating so hard that I didn't hear footfalls on the stairs. Suddenly, someone was standing right behind my chair. Startled, I jumped up, dropping papers in a shower at my feet.

A teasing liquid laugh changed my fear to anger.

"Aliana! How did you get in?"

"Through the door. You should be more careful about locking it. There are a lot of crazies on Queen Street."

"Why didn't you call first?"

She held up a waxy white bag. "I've been looking for you. I drove by and saw the lights on. So I got us a couple of subs. I thought you could use something to eat."

I *was* hungry. I took one of the sandwiches, sat down behind my desk and allowed her to make herself comfortable.

"Wow, Ellis, this is a great chair. Where did you get it?"

I wouldn't tell her I'd spent enough on the chair to keep Tent City in shacks and tarps for a year.

"Forget the furniture, Aliana," I said, gesturing toward the banker's boxes that filled the place. "I'm busy. Whatever you want, keep it short. And," I thought to add, "lay off Queenie and Tent City."

"Don't be so unfriendly," she said, pursing her remarkably red lips into an attractive pout. "How do you justify living so well when your friends are sleeping under a tarp, by the way?"

"Why is it, Aliana," I said, only half teasing, "that when *I* slept under a tarp myself, *you* were interested in my story? You made it into quite a good one."

"A lot of thanks I've gotten for it," she said. Her dark, long-lashed eyes never left my face. She had the reporter's trick of always appearing totally engrossed in her subject.

"What do you want now?"

"To hear the rest of the story . . ."

Her voice was sweet, cajoling. But what story? I couldn't tell her about Stow. And I didn't want her bothering Queenie. So I told her what it felt like to be a lawyer again after being a nutcase and a bum. Somehow, it got to be midnight before she left. I walked her downstairs and stood with her as she posed on the curb, arm gracefully outstretched to snag a cab. I watched the taxi speed east on Queen until it disappeared.

When I got back upstairs, I realized that I had just wasted my whole evening. But the sight of the photo-copies urged me to continue my search.

The oldest-looking medical records were routine re-ports on Harpur's deteriorating condition. It pained me to read them. "Advanced Alzheimer's disease." "Rapidly progressing dementia . . ." Nothing new there. I reached into the open box again.

The records with the most recent date were on the let-terhead of Pipperpharmat, a pharmaceutical firm with worldwide interests. I forced myself to analyze what these reports were saying.

There were two sets, one referring to tests done on Harpur before her death, a second dated about five years later, just about the time the police had decided to bring charges against Stow.

The language was scientific and difficult. Columns of figures blurred and danced. After about half an hour, my eyes grew too heavy for reading.

A thin layer of snow covers the low bushes beside the river. Our breath is a silver cloud against the whiteness. Is she singing? Is that the sound I hear? Behind me the footfalls of the doctor, the hospital volunteer. But I am first to round the curved path. She wears the loose hospital gown. Her long red hair against it is like the wing of the cardinal against a branch. Come back. Oh,

Harpur, please come back. Her feet are bare. She is standing on ice. Tears freeze on my cheeks.

Startled, I looked down to see a document I had not expected, although I should have known it would form part of the record of any hospital patient: a list of Harpur's visitors on her last night. I took the single sheet with its list of names to the desk so that I could see it better. I read it, then I read it again. I felt an overwhelming sense of relief. The record was incomplete. My name was nowhere on it.

I gave up and fell dead asleep in my chair without dreaming.

The next morning, I awoke to find that Nicky had been in while I slept and had rearranged the files. I spent twenty exasperating minutes until I could pick up where I'd left off the night before. Nicky was going to get it when he returned.

Morning light filtered through the windows as I read some old medical journals detailing a few studies on Somatofloran, a drug that had been tested on Harpur. Beneath me, Queen Street was springing into life, but not the desperate life of the blocks near Queenie's clinic. There, the late-night drinkers were relinquishing the least desirable sleeping places, those on the open sidewalk. Here, young people on their way to work carried lattés in one hand and the morning paper in the other. I opened the window and breathed deeply to wake myself up and went back to the boring journals.

Only about a thousand elderly people had ever taken Somatofloran. The drug had proven benign. From what I could understand of the cumbersome medical jargon, when the drug worked, it made breathing significantly easier for those with previous and mild respiratory impairment. When it didn't work, the subjects, for the most

97

part, just seemed to fall harmlessly asleep. Perhaps I was missing something. Somatofloran didn't seem like a murder weapon to me.

Or did Ellen intend to use this evidence in a way that I didn't yet understand? She was obligated by law to reveal to me any evidence she had found that could incriminate Stow, but she was under no obligation to let me know how she proposed to use her material. In fact, the strength of her case might well lie in tricking me into thinking that a piece of evidence was harmless to Stow's defense when, in fact, it was fatal.

When Nicky arrived, I intended to give him hell for messing up my papers, but the sight of him cheered me after my long night in the office. I wondered how he could look so fresh when he, too, had been so late. "Thanks for not waking me," I told him, "and no thanks for getting my files out of order."

"What?"

"I appreciate your coming by after hours, but the next time you decide to sneak up on me like that, let me know you're here so I can show you what I'm doing and save you from redoing work I've done already."

Like all the other youngsters on Queen that morning, Nicky sported the requisite gigantic cup of expensive coffee. He took a dramatic gulp. "I guess I need this more than I thought I did," he said. "I must still be asleep. Nothing you're saying is making any sense."

"Forget it," I answered. "Take a look at this."

"Somatofloran?" he asked. "What's that?"

I found it a puzzling question coming from someone who'd just read a file on the topic. "It's the drug Stow is accused of using on Harpur," I answered. "When patients overdose, they just conk out."

"Conk out? What does that mean, exactly?"

I laughed. "They fall asleep."

"No," Nicky said, cocking his head, partially leaning over my shoulder to see what I'd been reading. "How can that be?" He studied the page in front of me. I didn't know how he could read at such an odd angle.

"That's old stuff you've got there," he concluded. "Let me go over to the Med Sci Library and see what I can dig up."

"Never mind," I said, "I'll go over myself."

"Whatever," he answered.

At the Medical Sciences Library on the campus of the University of Toronto, I did find more information about Somatofloran, but I couldn't say it was current. I noticed that Ellen had been there before me. Nearly every journal I signed out had previously been signed out by "Portal."

In an appendix to a report published by Pipperpharmat, I discovered a list of test subjects that included the name "Harpur S.-M." I photocopied all that I found to discuss it with Nicky. But there would be no discussion of the effect on me of seeing Harpur's name in the cold print of a table of statistics, or of reading about the blood that had once coursed through her heart. My youthful love for Harpur had been foolish, but like most foolish love, it had endured long beyond the fleeting moments in which I thought it might be returned.

"Any luck?" was Nicky's greeting when I got back.

"Bad luck," I answered. "Wrong-place-at-the-wrong-time-type bad luck."

I opened my battered briefcase, which I'd bought secondhand so that I could have an old one like the other old lawyers, and pulled out the copies I'd made at Med Sci. "Somatofloran was a loser drug from the start," I told Nicky. "It was abandoned as useless only two years after the Riverside Hospital trials."

"If it hasn't been used in years, then why the follow-up study?" Nicky said. "I don't get it."

"I don't get it, either. Why would anybody care about a drug that didn't work and was never even marketed?"

Nicky rifled through some papers on the desk. "According to disclosure," he said, studying a page of close-typed text, "Stow's involvement in the case was discovered when Pipperpharmat conducted follow-up tests on breakdown products in the subjects' blood."

"Yes. We know that. One set of tests when Harpur was alive. Another set five years later. Ordinary follow-up. So?"

"So—" Nicky screwed up his face as though he were thinking hard. "I'm thinking litigation one-oh-one. I bet somebody sued the hospital. Put them up against it bigtime"

"You mean the second set of tests might have had nothing to do with the first, but rather with litigation resulting from the administration of a debased drug to a patient?" I thought about that for a minute. "It's possible, I suppose. But who sued?"

"I don't know. And I haven't seen anything to suggest that in any of this." Nicky gestured toward the pile of files.

"If somebody sued, and Pipperpharmat went back to check its original study, discovering irregularities, there'd be a hefty class-action vulnerability on the part of Pipperpharmat, wouldn't there?" I speculated.

"Yes. But there'd also be some record of that," Nicky concluded.

I decided to try the law library at Osgoode Hall to investigate cases that might shed light on our speculations.

Ah, the beauty of the afternoon light streaming delicately through the etched-glass windows of the library onto the long oak tables and the tall portraits of famous old judges! Was there any other research venue that could match this one? Beneath the molded plaster garlands of the ceiling, there was no sound except for the occasional whisper of a turning page or, far in the distance, the click of someone's heel on the mosaic tile floor. I loved the smell of Osgoode Library, the feel of books old Magistrate Tuppin had called the "leather-clad soldiers of long-ago battles won and lost."

I found no cases that enlightened me about Pipper-pharmat, but I did find precedent for Stow's predicament. *Regina vs Smith*: A man is accused of clubbing his son to death, calls no defense and is found guilty. The appeals court sets aside the verdict and orders a new trial because the judge on the original trial suggested to the jury that the accused was *unable* to defend himself, which was illegal, rather than that he was *unwilling* to defend himself, which was his most basic right.

If Stow refused to defend himself, there would still be a case against him, and I was in charge of that case. Maybe I could win it by causing a judge to make a mistake.

Or maybe not. Perhaps I was the judge making a mistake by taking on a client like Stow.

I was pondering that angle when I looked up and saw that the past—the distant past of my earliest years at the bar—had returned.

Illuminated in a ray of red-gold sunlight stood my ex-wife. Her hair was not its normal ice-blonde, but the soft golden blonde of the early years of our marriage. Motherhood had added curves to Anne's slim figure, and the years had added lines to the face I had gazed at across the pillow, across the table. But now, by a trick of the sun, those lines were gone. The black cashmere coat with its upturned collar looked identical to one she had worn in the early years of our marriage, and so did the diamonds that sparkled at her ears. A gift from her father, she'd worn those gems nearly all her life.

Just as she would have done forty years earlier, she took a step toward me and raised her hand in a wave that asked, "Are you finished working? Can you get away? Can you spend time with me?"

Once, I would have closed the books immediately and gone off in a New York minute for a romantic dinner in some cheap but charming restaurant.

Now, as she took a step toward me out of the golden light, she became a sixty-year-old grandmother. I realized then I was never truly in love with Anne herself, only with her image. But she had been in love with me, and sometimes that is all it takes to make a successful marriage.

"You look tired, Ellis. Can I tempt you to take a break?"

"How did you find me?" I asked, flustered.

"I took the liberty of inquiring of Queenie Johnson where you are spending your time these days. She was kind enough to give me suggestions."

It bothered me to think about Anne and Queenie communicating. I almost said something to that effect, but Anne spoke first. "Let's do dinner—the way we used to."

She must have been reading my mind. I put away my papers and followed her out of the room.

Chapter 7

Anne asked me to spend Christmas Day with what she called "our family." So, early on Christmas morning, I dutifully had breakfast with them all, but I was distracted because I couldn't get Stow and his case off my mind and neither, I could tell, could Ellen. "Everything I have so far bolsters your case, not mine," I told my daughter with a rueful smile.

"Come on, Dad," she answered, "don't be such a wuss. You'll think of something. And if you don't," she added, "I'm going to cream you!"

That was such a harsh warning that I left before lunch.

The day was bright and cold, which was about how I felt myself, my mind too occupied to notice the pleasures of the season. I remembered how it used to feel to pass the homes of people celebrating the holidays when I was on the skids. All their bright decorations were a rebuke, their kindnesses extended to a stranger, to me, a profound embarrassment. I wandered up from Anne's and stopped by the community center that Queenie and I used to call "the Shelter" in our days on the street. I peeked in long enough to see that she was serving the homeless Christmas dinner. But I didn't have the heart to join her.

At the end of the day when the sun was a golden red behind the black outline of bare trees, I heard the sound of carols flooding out from a tiny church on an obscure block running up from Queen Street.

I nearly turned away from the Yule cliché, but somehow I found myself sliding into a pew just in time to hear the sermon. The gist of it was that it's never too late for a new beginning. I wondered whether picking up the threads of the past counted as starting all over again.

The next day, the Feast of Stephen, found Aliana Caterina once again in my office.

"I'm doing an article on you and your involvement with Tent City," she said without preamble.

"I'm not involved," I protested. "I've just gone down there a couple of times to help out."

"What I'm thinking," she continued as if she hadn't heard me, "is that it would really enhance your chances of obtaining the new judicial appointment if we can tie together what you're doing for the homeless now and what you did for them when you were on the bench."

"Aliana, please don't assume anybody even remembers what I did as a judge. It was all a very long time ago."

"Not so long," she replied. "You make us sound ancient."

"Not you," I teased. "You're by far the youngest woman I'm seeing at the moment."

She did a double take. "You're seeing women?" Her voice lost its light quality and became professionally investigative.

"I have no social life. What I was about to say is that public attention is probably more detrimental than helpful to one who is seeking a judgeship. Keeping a low profile would be more appropriate under the circumstances."

"What other women are you seeing?"

"Aliana, please." Why had I jested to such a bloodhound?

She pushed away her half-finished lunch, many dollars' worth of take-out sushi. "One thing's for sure," she said. "The last article I wrote got City Council to back down on its plan to evict the Tent City denizens by the end of this month."

"City ordinances would have prevented an eviction at this time of year, anyway," I corrected her.

The scent of lemon and jasmine wafted toward me. "You were going to go to bat for them legally!" she said, bringing herself nose to nose with me. "You were going to use the anti-eviction laws to save their tents and shacks. Just as if they lived in rental properties! That's brilliant, Ellis. Are you still considering it?" I saw her slip her hand into her bag.

"Before you start interviewing again, kiddo, let me tell you that it was just an idea. I'm too busy to be building up precedent-threatening cases unless it's a last-resort scenario."

"And you don't see Tent City that way?"

I heard a minute click. "Turn that thing off."

Aliana lifted her hand. A tape recorder the size of a lipstick sat on her palm. "It's off."

"Listen, Aliana," I said, "there's a strong chance public opinion is going to save Queenie and her band of vagabonds. For one thing, Torontonians are capable of quite a bit of humanitarian generosity. Queenie tells me that ordinary people come down quite regularly with donations of food and clothing, especially now that the weather has gotten so cold."

"Is Queenie Johnson the woman you're seeing?"

Now it was my turn to smile mysteriously. "I'll confess if you'll give me something."

"What?"

"How would a person get into Riverside Hospital? Don't pretend you don't know, you wrote about it last month. I saw the article. You got in. How?"

"Well I didn't have SARS or bird flu, if that's what you're thinking."

"It's not," I said. She was stalling.

"Ellis," she said, "anybody who so much as goes near there stands a chance of being incarcerated for at least ninety days. Why would you want to risk that?"

"Didn't you risk it, Aliana? Didn't you risk being quarantined when you wrote that piece? Obviously you were *not* quarantined and not ill, either. So?"

"What's your angle?" Her voice was even and low, the voice, I thought, of a conspirator. No, the voice of a deal-maker.

"I'm not at liberty to say," I answered, trying to keep my tone light, as if the whole query were a joke.

But Aliana wasn't a joker when it came to her work. "Ellis," she said, "you tell me what's going on with Justice Stoughton-Melville's defense, and I'll tell you how I got into Riverside."

I thought about it for a moment.

"I can't," I finally said.

"Ditto."

Queenie *was* the woman I was seeing. At least for New Year's Eve. "It's just business," she'd said cryptically. "I can't explain. I'm paying. Will you come?"

It had been quite a while since I'd worn a tuxedo and quite a while since I'd spoken with my son except for a few words of holiday greeting at Anne's Christmas brunch. I knocked on his door, hoping to borrow cuff links.

"You look real handsome in a tuxedo, Dad," Tootie Beets told me. "Jeffrey's all dressed up, too. You guys look like twins."

I have to say that both Jeffrey and I did look sensational in our black ties, but "twins" was not the appropriate comparison of me and my son. He looked like his mother: blond, slim. Unlike Ellen, whose dark curls, dusky complexion and solid build were just like my own.

"These belonged to Granddad," Jeffrey said, as he handed me a pair of gold cuff links with a delicate scroll incised into them.

"Your mother's father always had beautiful jewelry," I said. "He gave your mother something new every birthday."

Jeffrey kept his eyes on the bits of gold in my palm. "Wrong granddad," he said. "They belonged to *your* father. Gramma gave them to me when I was confirmed."

"My father! I never knew he had anything made of gold. He was a working man. A—"

"Keep them, Dad," Jeffrey said. "Maybe someday you'll have another son. You can give them to him."

"Jeffrey—my boy! Why would you say that? You're my one and only son."

"Don't be so sure. You're a hottie," Tootie declared.

I blushed at the vote of confidence and headed out for Queenie's place. Her house was on a short street in an old restored downtown neighborhood. Once it must have been a worker's cottage, but it had come up in the world. A white fence surrounded the one-story bungalow. There were no curtains on the two windows that graced the front of the place, but brightly painted shutters seemed to glow in the faint illumination of a nearby street lamp. She was very secretive about her living arrangements. "Just call me on your cell when you get here and I'll come out," she'd said.

The little dead-end street was alive with people leaving for parties or arriving. I was watching the action and wondering how long before Queenie would appear to join me and my hired limo when, through the window of the car, my eyes caught a striking figure partially visible in the sidewalk's shadows. A small woman in a low-cut, close-fitting black dress, revealed by the opening in her long black coat, stood there. She patted her upswept hair, which, in the light of a nearby street lamp, looked white. She touched a finger to her necklace of black stones. And then she pulled the coat closed, hiding a smooth and youthful throat.

I looked away. I was filled with such loneliness that I wished, as Aliana had suggested, that I really was seeing a woman.

The limo door opened, and I jerked to attention. Without a word, Queenie slid into the seat beside me.

I stared at her in astonishment. Again, she touched her hair and the necklace at her throat. "What's the matter, Your Honor?" she said. "Do I look okay?"

"I didn't even recognize you," I replied. "You look beautiful, Queenie."

"You don't look half bad yourself," she answered.

Often, in the good/bad old days, I had been a fixture at head tables across the city. Elevated at the front of the room. Gazed at by people either drunk and starving or drunk and stuffed. Trapped into talking to pompous strangers.

Now I was experiencing a new twist on the old arrangement. I was the guest of honor's date! "You should have told me!" I whispered in Queenie's ear as she stood to accept the ovation of the distinguished public health supervisors who had voted her the most valuable health-care provider of the year. "I would have brought you an orchid corsage."

"Thanks," she said. "You're cute—quaint. But this is just a New Year's party given by some people I'm on committees with."

"Some? It looks like a few hundred to me," I told her as we looked down over the room, where crystal and silver glowed softly on white linen.

"I didn't bring you here to honor me," she said. "I brought you here for good luck."

"What do you mean?"

"The person you're with at midnight on New Year's Eve is the person you'll be with most during the year," she said.

The van pulls up. Queenie and I stand shoulder to shoulder so the drunks behind us can't steal our spot in the line. She reaches up to take the cup of soup. Her hand trembles and she spills a few drops. She spills more when I push her out of my way. "Happy New Year to you, too," she spits at me.

"Want to dance, Your Honor?"

Some idiot is playing a trumpet. I take her in my arms. It's like holding a bundle of Goodwill donations. We whirl around and around on the icy pavement until she falls and I fall on top of her. "Did you learn to dance in finishin' school?" she slurs. I'm laughing too hard to answer.

"You don't know how to dance, Queenie," I whispered. "Try me!"

She leaned against me, the top of her head touching my jaw. Her perfume was the scent of musk and rose. Surprised,

I remembered her scent of wood smoke from the distant past. I held her lightly, thinking that I liked wood smoke better than musk, and slowly we began to circle the dance floor. Maybe she was concentrating on her steps, but she said not a word during the tune. When it was over, I led her back to her seat. From our vantage point, I looked down on a room that I suddenly realized was full of medical personnel.

"Queenie," I said, "will you do something for me?"

She glanced up. The room's low light was not reflected in her eyes. They were dark and unreadable, but her whole demeanor seemed charged with expectation. "I'd do anything for you, Your Honor," she said. "For old times' sake. You must know that by now."

I moved my head closer to hers. "You know a lot of doctors and hospital administrators," I whispered. "I need you to help me find a way to get into Riverside. Before you say no, I must tell you that if I don't see for myself the layout of the floor where Harpur died, I won't be able to defend Stow. And don't say the floor plan will be different now. From maps sent to me by Ellen, I know it isn't. But," I added, "they're not enough. I *must* get into the facility. Will you help me?"

Before she could answer, the master of ceremonies approached with the mayor in tow. Queenie took the mayor's hand, and was then swept up in a crowd of people offering their congratulations. Too soon, the band announced it was midnight. Amid the balloons and noisemakers, I searched for Queenie in the crowd, but she was nowhere to be found. Sullenly, I drove home in my rented limo. *Happy New Year, Your Honor, you old fool.*

"Do the homeless people sleep outside even when the ground is frozen? How do they wash? How do they make a fire? Mommy says they can eat at Osgoode Hall and lawyers—even judges—serve them like waiters. Is that true?"

I was reluctantly preparing to visit Tent City and its New Year's Day dinner. My grandson, Angelo, who had stopped by with his mother, was begging to go with me. I hadn't slept all night, realizing I'd asked Queenie a stupid question and she had faded into the congratulatory crowd to avoid answering me.

"Please let me go with you, Grandpa," Angelo begged.

"Take him," Ellen said. "There'll be lots of volunteers down there today. Besides, I want him to see how other people live," she added. "It will be a good lesson."

Yes, I thought, a good lesson not to grow up like your grandpa. "Okay, then, kid. It's me and you," I told Angelo. "Get ready."

He talked the whole way there. "Why didn't we take the streetcar, Grandpa? Homeless people don't ride in cars, do they? I think it would be better to go like they go. Should I say Happy New Year to them? Do you think their New Year could really be happy if they have to live outside?"

I was nearly worn out with question-answering by the time I parked the car and crossed Queen Street to climb down. Before descending, we stood for a moment on the bridge. "Wow!" Angelo said. "I didn't know there would be so many people."

I didn't either. The population of Tent City seemed to have doubled. The narrow bank of the river was jammed with hundreds, about a third of whom were children. Frigid wind off the river pierced the fur-lined hood of my parka. I reached down and pulled Angelo's wool cap over his ears, adjusted his scarf. Cold as it was, some of the children there had no hats, scarves or gloves.

"They're freezing, Grandpa," Angelo said. He pulled off his mittens and handed them to a child who backed away as if frightened by my grandson's offering.

"Put them back on, son," I said to Angelo.

Reluctantly, he did as he was told and followed me wordlessly through the underdressed and shivering crowd. We made our way toward a large white tent where a portable stove billowing a cloud of steam gave off peculiar cooking smells. Stirring the pots was the hazy silhouette of Queenie.

I approached gingerly, feeling all sorts of emotions. So I had miscalculated the appropriate time for asking her a favor? She should have understood how important that favor was to me. After all, she was the one who'd wanted me to defend Stow. She was the one who preached that friends should help each other out. And she was the one who had disappeared rather than answer me.

"This must be Angelo," I heard her say. "Haven't seen you since you were a little baby."

"Yes, ma'am," Angelo said, taking off his gloves once more and accepting Queenie's outstretched hand. "Grandpa and I are here to help. What would you like us to do?"

I smiled at this exchange, but Queenie paid no attention to me. "You can both help serve," she said to Angelo, gesturing toward a huge pot of chili or stew. "You can hand up the bowls and your grandpa can ladle out. How about it?"

My grandson stared doubtfully at the parade of shabby figures lined up for the contents of those pots. There were other smells in the tent besides the food. Sterno. Coffee. Baked goods. Just a hint of the smell of the street. I thanked God it was winter.

"Cool, Grandpa," he finally said. "Let's get going."

We worked in silence, Angelo and I juggling bowls, at the same time handing out cheese cubes and bread and fruit. I kept waiting for Queenie to take a minute from her own tasks to come see how we were doing, but even when the homeless were finished and the volunteers were having their meal, she didn't stop by.

But Nicky McPhail did.

"Yo, Ellis," the young lawyer said, "starting the year off with a good deed, I see. And enlisting the help of relatives, yet." He sat down with Angelo and me for hot drinks at a table littered with paper plates, plastic cups and discarded cutlery. "What a sterling example!"

Angelo seemed properly subdued at the number of people in Toronto who needed food and clothing. His legs dangling over the edge of the bench on which we sat, he tried to balance hot chocolate and a butter tart in one hand, as he observed the others doing. "They sure make good tarts at the food bank," he said, but he sounded like he was only being polite.

"I don't think I get this," Nicky said. He was watching the action, listening to the slurps and gulps of hundreds of people filling their bellies. I thought he was referring to the couple in front of us. The girl's hair was bright green and the guy's blue. Both of them were dressed in long yellow plastic bags with "Toronto Parks and Recreation" printed on them in black letters. I hoped they had sweaters or sweatshirts underneath.

"Young people today," I said, grinning.

"No. I mean Stow," he said. "Maybe he doesn't talk because he's innocent. And if he's innocent, then he's being framed. But why? By whom? The police, to save face now because they failed to thoroughly investigate Harpur's death five years ago? I'm beginning to know those disclosure files by heart, and I can't see where the Crown claims anything about Somatofloran except that it alone couldn't have killed Harpur. I can't see any evidence that Stow augmented the effect of the drug in any way."

"No," I answered, a little concerned that Nicky didn't seem able to take a break from the case long enough to concentrate on the humble New Year's feast.

"So you agree it could be a trumped-up case?"

This was neither the time nor the place. "Look, Nicky, today's a holiday, and Angelo and I . . ."

"Malicious prosecution. Maybe it's malicious prosecution."

"Are you accusing Ellen of something like that?"

"Why not? She's a sharp one—and it looks like she's done her homework. Her name is on just about every document we've checked."

I couldn't let him get away with criticizing my daughter. "She's the Crown. Of course she's going to sign off on potential exhibits. But she's also . . ." I tipped my head toward Angelo. Nicky took the hint and shut up.

Now, I caught a glimpse of Queenie. She was hoisting a giant pot so that one of the volunteers could scour it. Angelo saw her too and walked over to lend a hand.

It's freezing. I'm lying in a doorway, Queenie curled up beside me. My arm strays to her waist, encircles it. We fall asleep like that for hours. But when we wake up in the morning, she slaps me. Hard. And tells me I'm a dirty drunk who should keep his filthy hands to himself.

"Ellis?"

"Sorry, Nicky. I should just keep an eye on Angelo." I trained my eyes on my grandson, who had helped move the pot and was now deep in conversation with Queenie.

"I wouldn't worry about anything as imaginative as framing people or prosecuting them for punishment or to prove some point other than their guilt. That's not what Ellen's about. I've spent as many hours going through those boxes as you have. There's little in them except photocopies of useless stuff: endless police memo books, Pipperpharmat annual reports, junk. I'm not only mystified about Stow's case. I'm mystified about Ellen's. What makes her think she's got a case strong enough to nail my client? It looks weak to me."

"Stow must be thinking the same way, Ellis."

"Oh, great. So he thinks this is an easy case—so easy he doesn't even have to talk to his attorney? I solve it and my big comeback is a done deal?"

"Yeah. You succeed. You get him off. Your comeback is a triumph and . . ."

"And I ruin my daughter."

"What?"

I looked at Angelo. Maybe he was too far away to hear us.

"I'm working on those witnesses," Nicky said. "And—"

Whatever Nicky was about to say was drowned out by the sudden sound of applause. Johnny Dirt was standing on a table, and his posture and the motions of the crowd around him told me that he was about to launch into another tirade about wresting ownership of the downtown core from the rich.

"This guy sucks," Nicky said. "I'm out of here—and so is he in about ten minutes. My father donated the tent and the tables and chairs. The truck's coming to pick all this stuff up." He waved goodbye to Angelo, who seemed mesmerized by Johnny's fiery oration.

"That guy talks really loud," Angelo said as we headed away. "Why is he so mad?"

"Angelo, sometimes people sound angry just because they care so much about what they are saying."

"If Mommy puts Mr. Justice Stow in prison, will he be mad at you, Grandpa?"

I unlocked the car door and waited for the boy to climb in. "I don't think you really need to worry about that," I answered.

"But will he?"

Angelo had only just become big enough to sit on the regular car seat. I had to admit a certain pride in having him riding with me and asking questions about the profession I had passed down to my daughter and perhaps carried on by my grandson. When I was Angelo's age, I had ridden beside my father in his truck, avoiding at all cost any tales of the old man's livelihood. And Jeffrey had never shown the least interest in the law.

"If I did something that resulted in Stow going to prison, I suspect he'd be very disappointed indeed, Angelo," I said.

Then why does he choose to remain in Fernhope?

"Grandpa?" Angelo wrinkled his smooth little nose. "You mean you can't feel sorry for a guy if the jury says he has to go to the slammer?"

I laughed. "Not exactly, son, but that's close enough for now."

We rode through the empty city streets for a few minutes longer before Angelo asked another question.

"Grandpa, is everybody who talks in court called a witness? Mommy says if she thinks a person knows something, then they have to talk in court and be a witness."

"Witnesses are people who promise to tell the court the truth when the lawyer or the judge asks them questions about facts," I told him. "The answers they give are called evidence or testimony. Everybody who testifies is a witness. But not everybody who talks in court is testifying. Lawyers like your mother and me are not witnesses."

"So a person can't be a lawyer and a witness at the same time?" the boy inquired.

I shook my head no, but I didn't have time to explain further because we had reached the house, and Angelo flew to his mother to tell her about our afternoon together.

But something about this last innocent query stuck in the back of my mind, and it was still there several hours later when I was in the library in my apartment, mulling over the case.

I pulled a pad of paper toward me and began to list all that I knew about Harpur's last day on earth. She had awakened in a state of agitation. It was the Feast of Stephen, the day after a Christmas she had been too ill to spend at home. Our long history of failed flirtation, of jealousy, of the near violence I had perpetrated on her so long ago, was almost over.

But Harpur still seemed to want something from me. Whatever it was could not make its way through the mists of her Alzheimer's-fogged mind. Did she want me to forgive her for never loving me or did she want to forgive me for loving her? I remembered her desperate last embrace. I remembered disengaging her from my arms and laying her back down onto her deathbed.

I thumbed through some files I'd brought home from the office. I took a look at a log kept by the volunteer coordinator of visitors to Harpur's floor. It was vague. It listed "private visitor" for anyone who was not part of an organization. From this slight information, I couldn't figure out the exact hour of my own visit that last day. But I must have left before the end of visiting hours at 8:30 p.m.

I'm holding her in my arms. I have spent a good part of my life dreaming of holding Harpur, but now all I want is to get out of here. I want the stupid Christmas carols to be silent. There is no other sound except—

Suddenly I remembered something I'd forgotten. I remembered that the phone had rung. That I had picked it up and said "Hello." There had been no one on the other end. Or had there?

If whoever had answered that phone had recognized my voice, he or she would know that I had been in Harpur's room shortly before she died.

The thought gave me pause, but why? I had seen and heard nothing that night. None of this had anything to do with Stow. No matter how many lists I made and how many times I went over them, I found nothing that would inculpate my client—but nothing that would exonerate him, either. I couldn't prove to myself that he was guilty and a scoundrel. I couldn't prove to the court that he was innocent and a victim.

Back at the office on Queen Street, I quailed at the sight of all those boxes. Sealed with that absurd red tape, they had an air of leftover Christmas presents. Apparently Nicky had cleaned up his act. Everything was piled in the order in which the boxes were numbered. There were so many still to go through that I just picked one on top of a pile. "Financial Records." Why not?

I slit open the tape, removed a number of files and dug in. Soon there wouldn't be any more paper files, not even in the law trade. Soon everything would be electronic. But not yet. The papers gave off the scent of the old ways. My ways.

As had been a requirement when he'd been elevated to the Supreme Court, Stow had transferred all his personal financial assets to a trust. An affidavit to that effect taught me nothing I didn't already know. I was also not surprised to see that Harpur's assets had been put into a separate trust at the time of her demise. The couple had no children. Perhaps, however, another relative or a charity had inherited her money. I made a note of the trust company named in the documents pertaining to her fortune. I would check out that company next.

Among the papers in the box, I also found copies of deeds: the deed to Stow's amazing pied-à-terre, a twenty-thousand-square-foot condo occupying an entire floor of a building balanced at the point of a spit of land that stretched out into Lake Ontario. There was no deed to the family mansion on Highland Avenue in Rosedale. Perhaps Stow himself had never owned that sprawling Victorian hulk. No doubt his immensely wealthy father and grandfather had had trusts of their own.

At the bottom of the box, I found a sheaf of papers clipped together. There were twenty or thirty of these, and each appeared to be the deed to a single-family dwelling situated in the older sections of the downtown core. There had been a time—though not within recent memory—when ordinary houses like those could have been had for less than a hundred thousand dollars each. Now that handful of deeds represented property worth about fifteen million dollars.

Later that afternoon, I made a few phone calls, aided by my own banker. "I spoke to your son," he told me.

"About the Don valley property. We . . ."

We were cut off for some reason, and I wasn't able to get back to him, but it didn't matter because I had enough information to wrangle a half-hour appointment with the trust company that handled the real estate portion of Stow's estate.

"Under ordinary circumstances, sir," the trust officer told me, "we would require several days' notice and a notarized written request before we could allow access to the personal records of a client."

"I understand, of course," I answered, "but I am entitled to see anything that the court would consider a matter of public record."

I am drunk out of my mind. The room is reeling, and the employees of the bank are standing still and circling wildly. "It's my damn money, and I want it now." I am shouting. No one is paying any attention to me except the two big police officers headed my way.

"Sir?"

"Yes, as I was saying, I'd like to see any record of a significant change in any trust held by my client or his family, that is, anything registered in the public record of transfers and trades."

The officer led me to a small room, touched a computer mouse and discreetly withdrew, while the screen sprang to life.

It took a couple of hours of searching databases before I found what I was looking for. Stow regularly transferred the ownership of downtown houses to other parties. I wondered whether he was using them as lesser men might use currency: for gifts, for payments, for bribes.

When I finished checking Stow's name, I checked Harpur's. It took less than one second because all her assets were sheltered in one numbered account. Naturally the number itself was not available to unauthorized parties.

On the way out, I was required to sign the obligatory visitors' log. The officer thrust the book at me and stood right behind me as I signed. As I wrote my name, I managed to glance at a few names on the opposite page, those,

I assumed, who had been in the building the previous day. Apparently Ellen had been among them. I saw "Portal." Was there nowhere I could go that the Crown had not been? I craned my neck to see the exact time and date of her visit, but behind me, I heard a disgruntled sigh. I crossed the "t" in my name, turned and walked out.

Chapter 8

When I first fled to the Don River valley to live alone with my madness and my regrets, I had done nothing but sleep, forage for food and think. Time, however, taught me many skills, one of which was how to make ice skates. I tried wood first. Being a pretty good whittler, I was not wholly unsuccessful. But metal was best, and I soon learned how to make blades out of scraps I found in back alleys, strengthening them by a process of folding and refolding the metal, heating it, hammering it and eventually sharpening it with stones I found in the river. By the time of Stow's murder trial, I'd graduated to store-bought. Nothing cleared my mind like a few sweeps around the rink in front of City Hall, even on a bitter January afternoon. Everyone who lives in Toronto owns skates, or so it is rumored, so I wasn't surprised when Nicky pulled up beside me. By now, he knew me and my habits.

"Can you take a meeting?" he asked.

"Sure. Shoot."

"The Crown's got the usual police witnesses," he began. "Set the scene, establish the time . . . I went over the file on them, but I didn't think it necessary to make any calls."

"Okay." I executed a rather skillful little turn right around Nicky, who seemed suitably impressed.

"Where'd you learn to skate?" he asked.

"Private instruction," I lied. "What else have you got?"

"I think the Crown is basing its case on three main witnesses," he answered. "The first will probably be a Dr. Swan. He's the chief research specialist at Pipperpharmat—now and at the time Harpur died. He's the man who ran the drug study. Iceman. You're going to have trouble with him."

"Point taken," I replied, glancing across Nathan Philips Square where people were beginning to gather on their way home from the offices, hotels, stores and legal buildings that surrounded this plaza at the heart of the city. I could see the courthouse on 361 University Avenue at the northwest edge of the square. I felt a sudden surge of eagerness to get into the court arena, to do battle for my client, however evasive and elusive he might be. "Who else?"

"Well, number two witness for the prosecution has got to be some hospital administrator, most likely the volunteer coordinator. Five years ago, she was the person whose job it was to keep track of the comings and goings of any nonstaff."

"I took a look at those volunteer records," I told Nicky. "They're uninformative. That's to our advantage because they're not going to help Ellen, either."

"Yeah, right. Anyway, everything's different now. Those amateurs have been replaced with professional security personnel since 9/11 and SARS." Nicky shook his head. "Fort Hospital."

"Who else?"

Nicky skated with effortless ease all the time he talked. I remembered how I had tried and failed to teach Jeffrey to skate when I had been Nicky's age. Then my son had been as old as little Angelo, who, I recalled now, wanted to grow up to be Wayne Gretsky.

"Who else? Our nemesis—the fingerprint man, that's who else," Nicky answered. "He's a world expert, and he's really got the goods on Stow."

We were both silent for quite a while. "So Ellen will bank on those three. What about witnesses on our side?" Nicky asked.

"Let's have a separate meeting on that," I replied. "On dry land."

We did meet later, but it was a short encounter. It was clear that I had never worked on a case with so few compelling—or compellable—witnesses. The classic Crown case that Ellen seemed to be preparing was always designed to lead the jury toward one spectacular witness whose testimony would pin the accused like a butterfly to a board. Where was the eyewitness testimony that Ellen had to put Stow on the scene?

Ellen had disclosed nothing about such a witness. And Nicky and I had found no one, either.

As for our own potential witnesses, without Stow's co-operation, there would be none. And Stow's cooperation was still not forthcoming, even when he called and commanded that I come up to see him.

It had been snowing for four months at Fernhope. The startling whiteness against the bright blue sky hurt my eyes. They kept wandering away from the road, toward the deep green forests of fir and the black waters of small streams.

I tried to be hopeful, but mainly I felt frustrated by my lack of progress on Stow's case and angry that Stow had summoned me in his familiar imperious way. *Come immediately; I need you.* As if I were his servant. But I had to watch myself. To lose control with Stow would be to endanger both of us. As his reluctant but de facto attorney, I couldn't take that risk.

I managed to sit calm and still in the little waiting room. I heard him coming long before I saw him. Far in the distance, a buzzer sounded. A door slid open with what seemed like infinite slowness. Then it slid closed. Then a nearer door opened. Another buzzer. Another set of sliding sounds. And then the click of three sets of heels on concrete. Just before the door to the room in which I sat was thrown open, I heard a sound that truly shocked me.

A key turned with a rasping sound, followed by the soft clink of metal on metal. Then I heard the same sound nearer the floor.

These rasps and clinks need to be heard only once to be engraved on one's memory. I had heard them a thousand times before.

The first was the sound of handcuffs being unlocked. The second was the sound of shackles.

I felt a jolt of panic. Why was Stow suddenly being treated like a dangerous criminal? Had he become violent during his incarceration? I waited forever while the guards removed the restraints and escorted my client to the small wooden table that would be the only barrier between us.

As on my two previous visits, Stow was wearing the Turnbull and Asser shirt, the cashmere sweater, the bespoke slacks. He even had his ring and his watch. All of these items were as pristine as the first time I'd seen him inside.

126

But Stow himself was dramatically different. His hair had turned from blond to white. And it was untouched by a barber—even a jailhouse barber. It brushed his shoulders. The costly clothes, once carefully tailored to his measurements, hung on his shockingly thin frame. His skin was gray, and so was the stubble that covered his jaw. With embarrassment I noticed that his nails were broken and dirty.

I almost took pity on him.

Almost.

For Stow was glaring at me from gray-blue eyes that were perfectly steady and clear. His touching decrepitude was nothing more than an elaborate act. Beneath the damaged exterior of the "prisoner" lay the same undiminished sense of power. It was as if he wanted his appearance, his refusal to cooperate, to ruin me. It was as if he wanted Ellen to handily win her case. If I lost my temper with Stow and, subsequently, the case for my high-profile "comeback" client, even Aliana's skills wouldn't make me look good. Not to mention the judgeship that would fly out the window.

For a few seconds we stared at each other like two adolescents in a contest of endurance. I dropped my eyes. "As you know," I began stiffly, "it is my obligation to put before you the particulars of the case the Crown has against you—"

I expected Stow at least to nod in response to this simple information, but he just kept staring straight ahead. I felt the urge to tell him to stuff it, but the guards were like hawks on a couple of chickens.

"Stow, as you are well aware, you have the right to make full answer and defense to these accusations."

His eyes shifted, met mine, but still he said nothing.

"My assistant, Nickel McPhail, and I are in the process of interviewing witnesses and examining records. You can assist us greatly if you'll just clarify the facts as we present them. For instance, it appears you drove a rental car to the hospital the night of Harpur's death. Naturally the question arises as to why."

"Did anyone get the license number of the car?"

Finally he had deigned to speak, surprise almost silencing me. "N-no," I managed to stutter out. "No one had reason to at the time. However, car rental records show that a late-model Buick had been rented earlier the same day by a young assistant prosecutor who worked at the courthouse on University Avenue. In the space on the rental application allotted for the business phone number of the applicant, the private number of your Ottawa office appears. This same young person refused to speak to us."

Stow shrugged, his sudden verbosity apparently quelled.

"When we couldn't locate her through the Crown's office, we learned that shortly after Harpur's death, she set up practice on her own in an office downtown."

A small smile crossed Stow's thin lips, but he continued his silence.

I pressed on, hoping to startle him once more into speech. "Ellen's disclosure states that several employees at Riverside intend to testify that they saw a man that might have been you in the hospital lobby, in the first-floor corridor and in the elevator at some time on that date." I hesitated. "I've not been able to get into Riverside myself," I admitted, "but Nicky has checked out each of these witnesses. We're confident that none of these people can say with any certainty that you were on Harpur's floor or in her room until the next day."

I didn't add, *By which time, she was already dead.*

128

Stow looked at the ceiling. I had an impulse to vault the desk and get my fingers around his throat. But I only looked down at the two sheets of paper I had been allowed to carry into the visiting room. One was the indictment.

"I know you've seen this," I said to Stow, holding the document up. I felt the guards move almost imperceptibly closer to us as Stow moved closer to me.

He examined the indictment carefully but silently.

"And you know the police would not have been able to lay this charge of first-degree murder without much more than the circumstantial evidence I've just described."

"So—"

"So now we have to talk about Pipperpharmat."

"I don't own stock in it, if that's what you're worried about," he broke in, as if only the topic of money could make him talk. I thought of other high rollers who had fallen and landed in jail because of stock deals. Did he identify with them?

"Okay, Stow, be as wiseass as you like. It doesn't bother me. It's not my future that's on the line here."

Nothing was further from the truth, and we both knew it.

I searched the second piece of paper I held for the exact name of the drug that was the reason Stow was in so much trouble.

"Ellen's case relies heavily on the Somatofloran evidence," I said. "I'm not going into the technical details here. Suffice it to say, Ellen will attempt to convince a jury that you poisoned your horribly ill wife, and that even though it took scientists almost six years to discover that, the proof is incontrovertible."

Stow turned inward again, demonstrating not the slightest interest, not even boredom, in what I considered a damning piece of information.

"It may work in your favor that a jury will almost certainly find the pharmaceutical information hard to understand. It will take a lot of explanation on Ellen's part to suggest to them that you injected a fatal dose of a harmful substance. That's *her* problem. The fingerprints are *our* problem." I was almost babbling, so anxious was I to get Stow to respond.

I heard a loud yawn. But when I looked around the little room, it was impossible to tell who was the culprit. A rush of embarrassment heated my face.

I'm on my hands and knees like a dog. A man is yelling at me and swinging a newspaper. He finds his mark. My face stings with his blow. Twenty other people are laughing. "Get out!" the man yells. "Get out, you filthy beggar, and don't come back."

"Portal," I heard one of the officers say, "get on with it, man."

"I've not yet confirmed this to my own satisfaction," I said, conscious I was rushing my assertions, "but I believe Ellen is going to maintain that you broke into the drug vault on the floor beneath Harpur's and stole a quantity of hypodermic syringes. Five years ago, at the time of that theft, there was no reason to connect it to Harpur's death, which was considered natural. Years later, Pipperpharmat had reason to revisit the results of the study it had conducted at Riverside. It was then that excessive blood levels of Somatofloran in Harpur's blood at the time of her death were discovered."

As I gazed hopelessly at the silent man before me, a thought came to me, based on the conversation Nicky and I had had about civil litigation. "Unless you were the one who reopened the issue by suing Pipperpharmat!"

This statement apparently hit its mark. "What would I have to gain?" he inquired, as calmly as a normal person.

"You tell me, Stow."

He rubbed his hands together in a gesture that had the effect of directing the overhead fluorescent light onto the golden surface of his ring and into the intricate shadows of the embossed design. It looked as though he were trying to wipe prints off his own fingertips.

"Stow," I said, "the fingerprints on the drug vault at Riverside are yours, and you know they are. You knew that long before the day of the Red Mass. You knew it because Ellen subpoenaed those prints. There is no record of your having refused to be printed—or even of calling a lawyer at that time. Why? Why won't you defend yourself? Who are you trying to hurt, besides me?"

"How much longer have I got here?"

This was addressed not to me, but to a guard, who did not look at his watch before he answered. "Three minutes."

"Three minutes," I repeated. Plenty of time to remind him of one other little fact that will be easy for the jury to understand. "On Harpur's death," I said, "her entire estate would have passed into your possession. You and she were childless. She had no siblings. Her parents had long since predeceased. No will has been probated. No money has been transferred into the trust that you set up to handle your own assets since you became a judge. Harpur's fortune at the time of her death was approximately seventy-eight million dollars. That money is still intact. Why has it remained untouched—not even aggressively invested? What nefarious plan do you have for that money?"

Stow made a show of beginning to rise. "What's the difference, Portal?" he asked. "Motive is *not* one of the elements of a criminal offense."

"Yes, but the sudden acquisition of nearly eighty million dollars would strike any juror as a good reason to kill one's wife. Eighty million dollars is beyond ordinary people's comprehension."

Stow was now standing, studying me as if to assess some previously undiscovered quality after forty years. "The jury will not be ordinary, Ellis," he said. "You are going to see to that."

His parting words rang in my head on the way back to Toronto, until a blinding blizzard drove out all thoughts except safety. The squall abated when I got to the northern outskirts of town, and I thought of Queenie down in Tent City with her ragged regulars. I'd not seen her for twelve days—not since I'd taken Angelo down on New Year's. I had no idea how she would receive me, for she had certainly ignored me on that day, so I prepared myself for at least more coolness, if not outright anger. I wasn't prepared for the calm with which I was received. She appeared to have forgiven me for spoiling New Year's Eve by my inappropriate request that she help me breach the security of Riverside Hospital.

"Your Honor, it's good of you to come down. We always can use help."

The frosty cloud of Queenie's breath wreathed her face. The wind was so bitter that my breath froze on my eyelashes after a few moments' exposure. How did she work out here day after day? I buried my face in the warm folds of my cashmere scarf and made my way single-file behind her along the ice-encrusted path of the Tent City site.

"Your friend Aliana has been writing about us again, I think," she tossed over her shoulder. "Some people from the city were here earlier. They said we've got to get out right now, but they promised the move would just be temporary. They said we have to evacuate for our own good."

It was 5 p.m. and getting dark. The river, which was almost always too warm to freeze, danced with a soft light that I knew was telling Queenie and her little band of vagrants to hang on, that despite today's lung-numbing cold, the sun was inching north toward the vernal equinox and the first day of spring.

"Most of my clients have been evacuated to shelters, anyway," Queenie explained. "I promised those who couldn't carry their belongings that I would lock up their valuables." She shrugged. I knew what she was thinking. The valuables of a street person are not like the valuables of anyone else.

We worked side by side for an hour, our hands protected by several layers of latex gloves. I kept hoping she'd start a conversation, but she was totally silent. As for myself, I didn't even try to talk. I knew that unless Queenie spoke first, there would be no dialogue.

By six, we'd filled two shopping carts with tattered plastic bags, frozen cardboard boxes, rusty coffee cans and all sorts of shabby fabric bundles.

"That nice Nicky guy gave us this," Queenie finally told me, leading me to a sheltered bend in the river where a new metal shed with a good strong lock on it graced the riverbank. "We can lock this stuff up until everybody can come back."

I helped her heave the pathetic bundles into the shed and lock it up again. I felt filthy, and there was nowhere to wash my hands, so I walked to the riverbank and hunkered down over the water. "Don't put your hands in there, it's not very clean," Queenie said over my shoulder. "We can go back to the clinic to clean up."

I stood and faced her. The sun had set, but in the glow of the city, in the light that never dies, I could clearly see her face. She was tired and no longer young, but I thought she looked more beautiful there in the semidarkness than she had in all her finery on New Year's Eve.

"Use this," she said, pulling a small plastic bottle of alcohol from her pocket. "I said *use it*," she joked, "not *drink it*."

I cleaned my hands, handed her back the bottle. She smiled at me for the first time. "Come with me for supper," I invited.

"After we shower," she answered.

"Shower?"

"Separately, of course," she answered mischievously.

I took her to a cozy place I knew in Little Italy. It was getting harder and harder to find anything Italian in the neighborhood where I'd grown up hearing my parents' language more often than my country's own.

"What do you call this?" Queenie asked, spearing a piece of chicken with her fork.

"Chicken cacciatore," I answered. "It means 'chicken hunter style.'"

"Like you'd really need to hunt a chicken," she laughed. "I'm surprised you came over here to eat. If you want Italian food, why don't you just cook it?"

"Except for tomato sauce, I don't know how, Queenie. It was my wife who always cooked when we were . . ."

"Together?"

"Yeah."

It made me uneasy to talk about Anne with Queenie, so silence came between us again, and the evening ended no more warmly than it had begun.

In Toronto, there is always a day in February when the temperature soars a degree or two above freezing, the sun melts the snow and spring pretends it's just around the corner. Such days are most often followed by the swift return of merciless cold and virulent wind, but on such a day it was nice to walk down Yonge Street toward College. I turned off the bustling main drag onto the wide side street crowned by the massive pink-granite police headquarters.

In the not-too-distant past, I would have dropped in to see my best friend in the police service, Matt West. But Matt had been booted upstairs big-time. He was now a superintendent heading up a large division in the east end of the city.

Fortunately, however, a mere phone call from Matt to headquarters had resulted in my being given my own private office for an entire day, with a secretary and a police detective on call to answer any questions.

I had to admit that sitting somewhere in the center of a huge law enforcement complex, in the middle of a city of millions of citizens, with the latest technical equipment and expert personnel at my command, almost prevented me from getting any work done.

I started by scanning six-year-old surveillance videos taken from Riverside Hospital. The angle of the camera was such that only the backs of heads were visible. The day in question was December 26. Most people wore winter hats. I marveled at how much things had changed since people had become serious about security post–9/11. Great gaps in the video record, times when the camera had been off or out of videotape, were the norm. On one occasion, a cleaner had left a dust cloth draped over the camera for two days before it was discovered and removed. Stow appeared nowhere on the tapes, though I myself was on them a number of times. Had Stow been on the tapes, I would have used them to show his devotion in caring for his wife. I decided against using them. They really could not prove that he hadn't been at Riverside. Plus, the thought that he could never be proved to have been there could turn some jurors off, making him look like he didn't care enough about Harpur to visit her.

Even Matt's clout did not permit me to see on-the-scene police memos or any originals of supplementary reports on the case that officers might have submitted. For these, I learned, I would have to find the photocopies Ellen had included in those red-taped boxes. Ellen only had access to photocopies of the police records, too, but originals might have showed me something she hadn't seen. No such luck.

But I did gain an advantage about fingerprint evidence. Ellen had reports only, but I had a password that allowed me direct access to the police file of all fingerprints found at Riverside five years earlier during the investigation of the drug vault break-in.

Technological advances over the past ten years were astonishing. In the old days, the police could get fingerprints in only three ways: by finding a visible print; by securing materials, such as mud or soap, in which an impression had been made; or by "raising latents," a process of applying fine black dust to an area suspected of having prints, which produced images as the powder adhered to the oils secreted by fingertips.

But now, I concluded, police were using a handheld digital laser beam. By pointing the beam at any area of interest, fingerprints stood out like diamonds in coal. When I entered the password on the computer, page after page of prints sprang into view, each accompanied by a time, date, location and, sometimes, the name of the owner of the print. I was startled to see my own name twice, until I realized the location was the elevator button on Harpur's floor of the hospital. Much more damaging were three crystal-clear prints on the shelves and inside door of the drug vault itself. They were labeled with Stow's name.

Several hours later I left headquarters. On the way home, I phoned Matt West to thank him for his help. I also took a chance and asked him whether he could get me past the heavy security at Riverside. He just laughed at such a naive question.

When I got to my apartment building, I stopped off to help Jeffrey prepare the February rent payments for deposit.

"Son," I said as we worked on our financial records, "I don't know what I would do without you here, but shouldn't you and Tootie be thinking about your future?"

"What do you mean?" Jeffrey looked up from the piles of paper. Despite his avowed love for the outdoors, his daily walks in the ravine abutting our building, his cross-country skiing in the valley, he was pale and seemed so much less robust than his sister—or his wife.

"Well, you're spending a lot of time supervising this building. And now that we're looking into that extra acreage down by the river—well, I just hope you're able to spend time with your child . . ."

"I'll be able to take Sal down in the valley with me soon, Dad," he said, showing no irritation at my implications. "And Tootie'll come too. We'll show little Sal where her mother stayed in a cave by the river when she ran away."

It was a pretty odd sort of legacy, showing a daughter how her mother survived as a street kid. But Jeffrey was so clearly in love with both of his girls that I wasn't worried about Sal's roots.

I left him to his accounting.

Sometimes I worried about Nicky, too. I often found him burning the midnight oil. He was being extremely careful with the files and boxes, I noticed. Whenever he opened a box, he took great pains to seal it up again, as if he were trying to replace the red tape exactly. I appreciated his care. However, I did not appreciate it when I got a call from a senior security official at Riverside, complaining that someone from my office had tried to gain entrance into the hospital.

"I understand from the head of security at Riverside that you inquired about access. I found that a little surprising, Nicky, considering that you and I had not discussed the matter."

Nicky had been so diligent, so skillful, in all the work we'd done thus far on the case that I hated to question or criticize him, but I did feel some explanation was called for.

"Ellis, please," Nicky said, his voice trembling, whether from fear or anger, I wasn't sure. "We're not on the same page. I have never deviated from any agreement we've had on handling this case. And I would never jeopardize our eventual access into Riverside. Accusing me of that is totally uncool."

"Nicky," I answered, trying my best to sound fatherly, "I'm sorry. I certainly didn't mean to offend you. But I was informed that a young man mentioned my name at the hospital a few days ago and—"

"It wasn't me," Nicky said, more confident now, "so forget about it."

With that, he stormed out the door.

After half an hour, the phone rang. Naturally, I thought it might be Nicky regretting his impetuousness. It wasn't.

"I need you to help me," a melodious voice breathed.

"Aliana—what's up?"

"I need a story for page one of the Life section this Saturday. Can I interview you again?"

"Forget it," I replied. "There's nothing to say. The judgeship won't be decided for months."

"How about interviewing Queenie and you together?"

"Double forget it. There's no story there."

"If that's true, then how about dinner tonight?"

Of course I'd been tricked, but still, we met at a café on Queen Street a couple of hours later.

"How's your big case coming?" Aliana asked me even before she tucked into a smoked salmon, caper and sliced potato pizza the size of Lake Ontario.

I was wary of telling her too much. But Aliana had a lot of contacts, an impressive fund of general knowledge and a ferretlike ability to dig out anything that could suit her purposes. "The case is going fine," I said carefully, "but I could use a little more financial information."

"Financial? Like what? I know some guys on the money page. What do you have in mind?"

"Well," I said, eschewing my own plain tomato and cheese pizza and reaching over to cadge a piece of hers, "I wouldn't mind knowing a bit more about Justice Stoughton-Melville's personal fortune."

"Such as?"

"Little-known-fact types of things . . . You know, whether he has any blind trusts—any secret bank accounts or hidden assets he might not want to come to the public's attention."

Aliana delicately cut a sliver of pizza and dipped it into a pool of spiced oil. "I could help you out if you were a little nicer to me." I felt her eyes on my face, but I didn't glance up from my plate. After a moment she said, "Why don't you put that faithful little Nickel what's-his-name on the case?"

"Because this might be a dead end." I paused and gave her a conspiratorial look. "But maybe *you* could dig something up."

"Oh, so it's okay for me to waste my time chasing down tidbits of info, but not Nicky?"

"No, Aliana, that's not what I mean. The thing is, you can do this without anybody realizing that I'm checking on Stow's finances as part of his defense."

She cut herself another piece of oil-drenched pizza. How did she stay so slim?

She must have read my mind. Attacking the pizza again, she said, "I run it off chasing after useless tidbits of info . . ."

Chapter 9

"Your client would make this a lot easier on himself if he would just plead guilty." Ellen leaned forward across the expanse of her desk, her countenance severe. "And a lot easier on you and me, too."

My little girl. Not literally, of course. Ellen was in her thirties. But my girl all the same. She wore her dark curls pulled back from her face, a severe style intended to give her a look of maturity and professionalism. I was absurdly proud of her, proud not only that she had followed my profession, but proud that she would be a worthy adversary—whether she liked it or not.

"Ellen," I said, "today I'm an unknown legal quantity, but I wasn't born yesterday. You might hope for a guilty plea first off, but you know as well as I do that Stow's actual guilt or innocence is not the point here . . ."

She stood up quickly, sending a little perfumed breeze in my direction. I found it odd that she wore Chanel No. 19, the same as her mother, when the two were such different personalities. For one wild moment, I actually wondered whether she had chosen that scent to disarm me, to remind me in some unconscious way that to oppose her was to be disloyal to my family.

While I quickly dismissed this idea, the notion of such a tactic remained with me. People seldom realize how much they depend on their sense of smell. Unless, like me, they have lived rough and learned to avoid odors that threaten survival: sickness, animals, fire, storm, police.

"Daddy," Ellen said, "come on! Are you implying that you would defend Stow knowing beyond a reasonable doubt that he killed his wife?"

"Ellen, you won't get us to plead guilty by accusing me of doubts, reasonable or otherwise, about Stow. That won't affect my defense. The jury will make the decision about his guilt or innocence, not me. My opinion is completely irrelevant."

"Daddy, Daddy," Ellen declared, shaking her head and releasing some of her curls. "Who could possibly really believe that Stow isn't guilty! First of all, there's no other suspect . . ."

"Oh, come on yourself, Ellen," I objected. "That's absolutely the weakest argument possible. There doesn't need to be another suspect. Harpur was a sick woman. On some days, she was at death's door."

"Are you going to try to prove she died of natural causes?" Ellen asked with dramatic disbelief.

"I don't have to answer that."

"Okay, but just in case you *are* considering natural causes, Daddy, let me remind you that I have two doctors fully familiar not only with the details of any conditions that Harpur may have had, but also with her own particular case. If you've read all the material I sent you," she went on, "you'll also recall that I have several scientists from the pharmaceutical company that manufactures Somatofloran, as well as independent scientific evaluators— all of whom will testify concerning the chemical properties of that drug in Harpur's system. They will convince the jury that there was nothing natural about the way Harpur died.

"On the other hand," Ellen persisted, "if you decide to take the position that someone other than her husband was with her that night, I trust that you realize just how many witnesses I have to the contrary." She sat back stiffly. She was bluffing.

"Give it up, Ellen," I teased. "I may have been out of the loop for a while, but I'm still capable of proving to the jury that my client is nothing but the victim of overzealous police officers."

"I beg your pardon?" Ellen asked. More of her curly locks were coming undone, framing an exasperated visage. I almost smiled, remembering the awesome temper tantrums she had thrown as a child. "You're the one playing a game here. We have fingerprints, Daddy. We have witnesses. We have motive. And we have the accused in custody."

"Custody! In Club Fed where he's allowed to wear a fifteen-thousand-dollar watch? What kind of custody do you call that?" Why was I arguing with her out of court, continuing a replay of our encounters from her childhood?

"Daddy," Ellen said, "in case you've forgotten, your client is an officer of the court. He's a man with many enemies among Canadian criminals. Would you rather have him detained in some provincial jail where he'd be at the mercy of thugs?" She shook her head in disgust. "Whose side are you on, anyway?"

"Is it because I'm past it and shouldn't have fooled myself into thinking I could be a lawyer again? Everybody, even the Crown, otherwise known as Ellen Portal, is yelling at me these days."

Nicky and I, our differences temporarily quelled, sat in the Barristers' Dining Room at Osgoode Hall eating a let's-be-friends-again lunch. It was Friday, casual day, which meant that the trio playing for the fifty or so gathered attorneys was a jazz group rather than chamber music, that the featured dish was sole instead of beef, and that the dress was blazers and slacks instead of suits.

Nicky took a deep swallow of his Chardonnay before he deigned to speak. "Ellis, you know, I trust, that the Crown's case is flawed."

"Flawed?" Nicky was irritating me again, even before dessert.

He nodded. "All those eyewitnesses putting Stow in the hospital but never in Harpur's room—they're worse than useless. No jury is going to fall for that tactic."

"You may be right, Nicky, but what about the scientific testimony?"

He shrugged. "Those pharmaceutical weirdos? They're useless, too. Jargon junkies. People tend to ignore what they can't understand. Which leaves us with our only real problem."

"The fingerprints." Was I more than a little annoyed at his slick analysis? Yes, I was, because he happened to be slick *and* right.

"Yeah. We've got to get those prints thrown out. And I know just the man to do it."

"Who?"

"Why *you*, naturally," Nicky answered, picking up the wine again and tipping his goblet toward me.

"Especially since the police have *my* fingerprints, too," I muttered into my sandwich. Now wasn't the exact time to be candid about that point.

"They're lovely, Ellis. I'm charmed that you remembered." I followed Anne through the white expanse of her living room and watched in silence as she found a Waterford vase for the tall blue irises I'd brought her. She stood contemplating the flowers for a moment, and her slender figure in cream-colored silk reminded me again of the advantages of a wife with every asset. Anne was an artist at decorating in the clean, uncluttered style I had come to love. This room and her adjoining solarium, for example, held little except a white sofa, a white grand piano, a few glass tables and two low-slung chairs in white leather and brushed aluminum. The irises added a splash of color to the one-tone room, and I supposed that her artistic side was charmed by the contrast.

"I spoke to Ellen today," Anne said, moving away reluctantly from the flowers. "It sounds as though you two are managing to work together well after all."

I didn't know how she'd come to that conclusion, but I didn't argue. I merely sat and waited for her to reveal the reason she had summoned me.

"Ellis," she said, casually studying her long fingers with their perfect nails, as if to avoid my gaze, "do you ever think about the way things used to be?"

"What things, Anne?"

"Us. Our children."

"Of course. Sometimes."

Now she glanced past me out the window toward the blue expanse of the lake. "Do you ever wish you could have back what you've lost?"

The awkward question embarrassed me. "My dear, how could I not miss the life we shared? You were a perfect wife."

I realized how crass this sounded the minute the words left my mouth. If I had thought her so fantastic, why had I chosen to sleep in a cardboard box in a ravine rather than in her bed?

"Not so perfect that you cared to stay," she said, embarrassing me further.

Now it was I who glanced away. "Anne, I can't explain my breakdown or ask your forgiveness. It was not something I chose to happen." I spoke to the vista outside the window. "I'm sorry I turned out to be such a loser."

Anne captured my gaze and replied vehemently, "You have always been the man I wanted you to be. What a person does and what a person is aren't the same thing."

"Oh, Anne," I exclaimed, "you're so wrong! We are what we do. That's prima facie evidence."

"Does that mean there can be no going back?"

"Going back?" I asked, my eyes on the exit. "Going back to what?"

She rose, moved to the piano where she had set the vase of irises and began to rearrange them.

I stood, too, and approached her. I needed to head off this personal discussion. I caught a whiff of that scent again. She used to wear it even in bed. "Anne," I said, "why does Ellen wear your perfume?"

She shrugged. "I don't know. It *is* unusual for a mother and daughter to both choose No. 19, I suppose. But it's a scent we both like. And wearing it makes us feel connected. Is there something wrong with that?"

I recalled something I hadn't thought about in thirty years. "Do you remember the time Jeffrey gave the dog a bath with the bottle of Lisle Douce aftershave that your father had given me?"

"A four-hundred-dollar bath," Anne said. "It's interesting, isn't it, that of all of us, Jeffrey cares the least about such things: expensive clothes, fine cologne."

"I guess he just doesn't take after his father," I said jokingly.

"No," Anne said with surprising seriousness. "He does not."

"I always felt that was another reason I was a disappointment to you," I said.

She looked at me with an expression of deep puzzlement. "Whatever do you mean?" she asked. "Surely you can't think I'd be disappointed because our son isn't a carbon copy of his father?"

I smiled. "Sometimes I don't think he's related to me at all!"

"I would give anything if I could make things right between us, Ellis," she said. And she leaned close and kissed me on the cheek. So this was her reason for inviting me. A regal woman with a pathetic plea is the saddest of humans.

"We can't go back, Anne. We can't repeat the past."

"I wasn't talking about the past," she said.

I was really worried. She had been in court every day of the pretrial motions. Since these covered mundane matters of procedure and the admissibility of evidence, I felt both annoyed and flattered at her presence, though I felt it was Ellen's work she was interested in. It seemed now that I was equally the source of Anne's pride, and she wanted me to know that. The thought of the potential consequences made me want to head for the ravine again.

147

Quickly I made my farewells and escaped. Once out on the street, I felt less like a cornered rat. I didn't want to renew anything with Anne. That was yesterday. Today held new promises. Why didn't she feel the same?

I was equally puzzled by the persistent and intense scrutiny of Aliana Caterina in the courtroom. Every day, she sat scribbling away from the first "All rise" to the last "Court adjourned." I felt as though she were stalking me. Two or three times a week, I'd pick up the *World* and find myself quoted in one of her hard-nosed pieces. Daily I felt more indebted to her—and less inclined to pay. The day the final three candidates for the Judge of Orphans position were leaked to the press, Aliana was on me like a bird on a bug at the court's morning break.

"Ellis, it's super! I knew you'd make the short list!"

The weather was cold, but Aliana was wearing a remarkably skimpy dress. She was a woman who would not see forty again, but she had spectacular legs.

"Look, Aliana," I said, "you can't talk or—good grief—*write* about a judicial appointment as though it were a popularity contest. There is no 'short list' as you call it. There's just . . ."

"Come out with me after court is finished today. I'll treat you to a special Shirley Temple. Maybe even a double Shirley Temple." The woman had no shame.

"I can't. Nicky and I have to spend all evening going over jury selection to present to Stow."

"Are you driving up to Fernhope tomorrow, then?" she asked.

"I suppose so. Yes."

She hooked her arm through mine. I couldn't draw attention to us by shaking her off. We were in the main corridor of the courthouse, surrounded by robed lawyers, students, members of the public and the press. "Let me drive you up," she cajoled. "I can interview you as we go. You can tell me what sort of jury you're hoping for."

"Aliana, please!" I responded. "Don't you ever give up? I can't discuss jury selection with you—or the judicial appointment either. And I'll be driving up with Nicky."

"Nicky," Aliana repeated with a snort of contempt. "Why do you let that spoiled brat work with you?" She looked around as if to make sure Nicky wasn't within earshot. She didn't see him, but I was taller. Nicky was nearby, deep in conversation with someone who was shielded from my view by his body. Some witness he hadn't told me about?

"What part of the case is he handling, anyway?"

"What?"

"Nicky. What exactly is he doing for you? Maybe I should talk to *him.*"

"Forget it, Aliana. You're not going to pump me about the angles he's working on, and you're not going to pump him, either. So quit wasting your time." At that, she turned and left me standing on the sidewalk like a leper. But the next day she wrote a glowing account of my loyalty to my "underlings" and my willingness to trust them with important elements of Stow's case. She said my efforts to shield my "staff" from anyone who tried to interrupt them in their work were "stalwart."

The only woman of my acquaintance who never came to court was Queenie. I regretted that. When the day arrived and I stood before a judge to open a case for the first time in almost two decades, I would have liked Queenie to be there. Obviously, her interest in my new career was minimal. I put her absence out of my mind.

Late winter snow slowed our progress the next day, and it was noon before we reached Fernhope. Both Nicky and I were allowed inside. On this occasion, the prisoner looked unchanged from my last meeting. His clothes were neatly pressed. His expensive watch and leather belt were in place. His Gucci loafers were pristine. His hair was combed, but still uncut. I saw Nicky study him the way he had studied the tenants of Queenie's domain. If Stow noticed this scrutiny, it did nothing to affect his haughty hello when he was introduced to my assistant.

"Housekeeping matters first," I chirped, hoping to put both Nicky and Stow at ease, but only managing to increase the palpable tension in the little room. "I've managed to speak to the preliminary motions without your being present in court, Stow, but that's over. Now, you must be there every day. Do you want me to arrange some sort of secured accommodation for the duration of the trial?"

Stow made a dismissive gesture, as though he couldn't care less about where he stayed or how many security officers watched over him.

"All right, then," I responded, "I'll see what I can do."

Nicky handed me a file. Now that the trial was about to begin, I was allowed more latitude about bringing documents to my client. In fact, the guards had got so used to our meetings that they practically ignored us.

"Let's get down to the reason for this meeting," I said. "Time is short. First, we need to talk about the challenge for cause. We intend to question each juror . . ."

"On what grounds?"

The three-word question demonstrated Stow's first sign of interest that day. But I kept my surprise to myself and pretended his query was no big deal—the way a parent will pretend a baby's first word is not worth making a fuss over, so that the word will be said again and again. With a glance toward the guards, I handed Stow a sheet of paper with a few lines of type on it.

"This is the question Nicky worked up."

Stow's eyes flashed across the lines of type. I waited, but he said nothing, showed nothing. He handed back the paper, his hands steadier than mine, which trembled slightly as I took it.

"In a high-profile murder case like this one," I told him, "they'll have a large panel. I believe the jury office has arranged for two hundred people to gather in courtroom 6-1 tomorrow."

Courtroom 6-1 was easily the most notorious in the city, perhaps in the country, if you judged it by the famous cases that had been tried there: the husband-and-wife team who had tortured and videotaped teenaged girls before killing them, the shooters who'd rounded up middle-class customers eating dessert in a small café and then gunned them down.

But unlike some places haunted by the ghosts of the wicked, 6-1 had the uncanny quality of seeming to wash itself clean after each hideous case, as though somehow it were born anew, ready again for whatever the cells might vomit up.

"Six-one," Stow said with a smile. "The court of the damned!" He gave a sneering laugh that was both contemptuous and, I suspected, ashamed. "That's rich!"

I ignored his comment. "I need to make sure you understand the challenge fully, Stow. As each prospective juror's name is pulled from the drum, the registrar will swear him or her in and ask the following question. Indicate to me any changes you feel ought to be made."

I cleared my throat. "Justice John Stoughton-Melville is a public figure. He has been written about extensively in the media. Would the fact that he is an officer of the court, or would any other thing you might already know about him, affect your ability to render a true verdict in this case?"

Stow was silent for several minutes. I made the mistake of thinking he was actually considering the question. When he finally spoke, Nicky and I exchanged puzzled glances.

"I won't be able to turn around when I'm in the dock. I won't be able to see who's behind me."

"Of course not, Stow." Two sentences! He was becoming positively loquacious. I hastened to explain. "The guards are trained to keep you from having any contact with spectators. Even eye contact. Especially eye contact."

"Who's there? Who's behind me? Sometimes I can see someone out of the corner of my eye. A woman. She sits to my left. She's never there when I'm led in or out. I've tried to catch sight of her face, but I can't. Who is that, Ellis?"

Nicky's mouth hung open. I kicked him under the table. "Stow, I think we're through for tonight. I take it you approve the challenge question. That's enough for now. We can proceed with the jury selection based on your lack of objection to—"

"Is there a woman who comes? Maybe I dreamed her. Was a woman present during the prelims?"

I kept my eyes glued to my notes. "I don't know, Stow," I told him. "The court is open to the public."

Was his confusion an act? If so, it was a good one. But I could act, too. I could, for instance, pretend that no woman had come every day to follow the progress of Stow's case. I could pretend that Anne, like Stow himself, had never been in the courtroom.

"What's his problem?" Nicky asked the moment we got to the car. "He totally flipped!"

"Stow will be okay once he's in court."

"You hope," my young companion commented, doubt clear in his voice.

I didn't bother to respond. I didn't want him to hear doubt in *my* voice.

The next day, when Nicky and I met at Old City Hall courthouse, its Victorian hulk almost ladylike with the rising sun casting a pink glow on every cornice, crenellation and curlicue, I remembered myself in a pink glow, too.

I have just turned forty, one of the youngest men ever appointed to the bench. But am I afraid? No. I bound up the steps, I wink at the figures carved above the main door, I sweep past the McCausland stained-glass window with its depiction of the founding of the city, I race across the two-toned polished wood floor. I tear open the double etched-glass doors to the courtroom, I run to the empty bench, sit behind it, throw open my arms and embrace the whole damn room. I am home at last. The elderly guard finally catches up with me. When he sees who it is, he says, "Welcome, Your Honor." Your Honor. Your Honor. Your Honor.

"Earth to Ellis. What's wrong?"

"Nothing, Nicky. Old City Hall looks pretty good, doesn't it?"

"If you say so." Nicky took a swig of coffee. "You okay?"

"Yeah, sure." I changed the subject. "We should have told Stow more about the judge who'll try his case." I took one more peek at Old City Hall. "But Justice McKenzie is so young. He looks your age."

"No way! Bobby McKenzie's forty-five," Nicky laughed. "But old as he is, he's still too young to remember who you are—er—were."

"Very funny, boy. Too bad F. Robert McKenzie isn't such a comedian. Are you forgetting he allowed every bit of Ellen's evidence?"

"Which we agree contains a lot of stinking garbage . . ."

I conceded that with a nod. "But," I said, "he's a stickler for efficiency. And what about his legendary hair-trigger temper? He's already torn a strip off me three times for 'woolgathering.'"

Nicky looked up. "What's that about, anyway?" he asked. "The daydreaming?"

"If I knew, Nicky, I'd tell you. I guess I just have a lot to think about these days."

"Well, don't forget about Bobby's temper. And don't forget about your own, either."

"You're getting me mad at you right now, Nicky!"

He just laughed again. Then he became dead serious. "We never did get around to talking to our client about the jurors we need."

"If we were in the States," I said, "we could hire experts to question potential jurors, but here we must do it ourselves, and all we can know about them is that they are Canadian citizens, that they speak English, their addresses and what they do for a living. And of course, we can inquire whether they're prejudiced for or against Stow by anything they already know about him. We have to deduce all we can from their dress, their demeanor and our instincts."

"Sucks," Nicky said. Then he added, "So what kind of juror are we looking for?"

"When I used to defend men accused of sexual assault," I replied, "I tried to stay away from jurors who were in any way similar to my client. I reasoned that if both the client and the juror were male, white, thirty-six, blue-eyed, for example, the juror would be more inclined to convict because he would want to separate himself from the accused as strongly as possible. "But here," I emphasized, "I think the opposite would apply. I think the more a juror identifies with Stow, the more sympathetic he will be to our cause."

"Yeah, right. We'll get ourselves a dozen more Supreme Court Justices."

"Not quite, Eddie Murphy! I meant older men."

"I disagree. I think we need women. Young and old. Women are always more sympathetic to domestic ordeals."

"They might identify with Harpur. Or worse, with Ellen. They might take a feminist stance."

"Rats." Nicky admitted, "I hate this. It's going to make me lose lunch."

"You won't lose lunch. Jury picks on big cases are always in the morning," I replied, trying to be as funny as he was—or thought he was.

"I'll call twenty names at a time," Judge McKenzie told the two hundred gathered in the cavernous courtroom, paneled in red maple that seemed to swallow his voice, even though he used a microphone. "When I call your name, form a line to my left."

As the court clerk spun the wooden drum that held a card for each of the two hundred names, I looked over to the oak table on the other side of the room, where Ellen sat with her Officer-in-Charge and her Assistant Crown. I couldn't get my girl to look at me. I longed to tell her we were simply adversaries, not enemies, but I hadn't spoken a personal word to her in days. It was an odd feeling knowing that if I won, she lost.

It sounded easy enough to pick twelve suitable jurors out of two hundred prospects, but it wasn't, because half the crowd had excuses for being unable to serve. Prepaid vacations, appointments with medical specialists, elder-care obligations, work assignments that could be done by the prospective juror and nobody else. I whispered to Nicky, "Bunch of lousy slackers!"

"Are you ready to ask your question, Mr. Portal?" the judge interrupted.

"Yes, sir," I answered, sputtering and jumping to my feet as the first prospect, an Allan Martin, entered the witness box. A female court officer in gray slacks and a dark blue blazer stepped up to him and asked if he wished to swear on a holy book—she gestured toward several piled on the railing before the witness—or to affirm the truth of his answers on his own word.

The man chose the Bible. The officer, a woman who would become the jury's matron as soon as the twelve were chosen, asked him to place his right hand on it. Instead, he yanked the book out of her hand, grabbed it tightly and brandished it aloft.

Nicky cringed and so, I saw, did Ellen. The sour little man swore his oath. His voice was too loud, too determined. I studied him for some clue as to his attitude toward the duty he faced, his fairness, his intelligence. If he indicated that he could, in fact, remain impartial despite his previous knowledge of Stow, I could still reject him as a juror. Ellen and I each had twenty peremptory challenges. We could each reject twenty jurors just because we didn't like the look of them. But we could ask them no questions except the one Nicky had worded and Stow, by his silence, had approved.

I stood. "Mr. Martin," I began, "Justice John Stoughton-Melville is a public figure. He . . ."

"I know damn well who he is," the prospect shouted. "And I know who you are, too, Ellis Portal. You're a drunk, a womanizer, a drug addict and a convict. You and that criminal over there," he pointed at Stow who, for once, seemed to be taking some notice, "you two are a disgrace to this country. You both belong in jail, and I for one would be happy to help send you there."

I had to laugh. One tiny snicker.

But Justice McKenzie heard me. He launched into a tirade.

"You find something funny about this juror, do you, Mr. Portal?"

"No, Your Honor."

"You think it humorous that a citizen of this country would use the sacred trust of the duty set upon him to demean the court?"

"No, Your Honor."

"You find it a laughing matter that a man who is innocent until proven guilty is condemned by the very people who have been charged to fairly judge him?"

McKenzie's face was growing red. The veins were standing out on his neck. His fists were balled so tight that his knuckles were blue.

I glanced at Ellen who, like me, was trying not to enrage the judge further by bursting into laughter.

As for my sidekick, Nicky was looking from the outraged juror to the outraged judge as if it had occurred to him that McKenzie was going to hold me in contempt of court. That would mean that he would have to defend Stow himself.

Justice McKenzie, however, had enough of humiliating me, and waved to three uniforms to assist the jury matron in clearing the two hundred potentials from the courtroom. In about one minute, they all disappeared as if swallowed.

Then McKenzie turned his attention to Allan Martin. Throughout, the potential juror stood rigid and self-righteous. A fearless smugness suffused his face. Unfortunately, the courtroom is a place above all others where a person can make himself the center of attention and wreak havoc by doing so. The prospective juror did not flinch when Justice McKenzie turned on him. He was waiting for it.

"You, sir," the judge began in a voice that was calm, cold and authoritarian, "you, sir, have jeopardized these entire proceedings. Do you realize that?"

"I do," the juror answered defiantly.

"And you appear to be entirely unrepentant?"

"I am."

"Mr. Martin," Justice McKenzie said, his voice beginning to rumble ominously, "you have no right to judge anyone in the court until such time as you become a sworn juror and have heard all the evidence presented relevant to the case at bar."

Justice McKenzie steadied himself with his two fists on the bench, gave me a meaningful look and declared to the juror, "It is *you*, sir, who are a disgrace to this court! It is *you*, sir, who are a reprobate and a scoundrel. It is *you* who have engaged in criminal behavior. It is *you*, sir, who belong in jail, and I am sending you there right now!" Mr. Martin's belligerence disappeared like air from a popped balloon, and he trembled as he found himself being escorted to the cells. Stow was staring at the offending citizen with a bemused expression. He, like me, understood that the judge's fine display had been meant to warn me and my daughter that we must be on our guard for the duration of the trial.

"Your Honor." I rose. "I move that we call another panel. Today's prospective jurors have been tainted."

Ellen rose. "Not so, Your Honor. There's no need to delay these proceedings. The accused . . ."

"Sit down, both of you. I'm not calling for another panel. Get together and figure out how to go with the panel we've got. This court is recessed until 2 p.m."

Ellen and I managed to agree that we'd talk over lunch. But then we argued as to whether we should have Oriental or Italian. Then we argued over whether we should go to Queen Street or Chinatown. Finally, unable to concur, we took Nicky's suggestion. Over pastrami sandwiches, we discussed everything but the jurors. Nicky listened in fascinated silence as Ellen and I bickered. First, she brought up her mother.

"Why do you think she comes to court every day, Dad?"

"I don't know. I guess she comes to see how you're doing on your big case."

"Oh, get real, Daddy," Ellen answered. "I've been a prosecutor for eight years. Mom's never been in court before. She's not there because of me."

Ellen balanced a delicate sliver of dill pickle between two fingers. She looked at it and not at me when she said, "Mom is in love . . ."

"Just one minute," I answered, deciding that Nicky might as well know all my secrets. "She divorced me. And to marry somebody else, as I recall. What happened to that plan, anyway?"

Ellen popped the pickle into her mouth and waved her fingers dismissively. "It didn't work out. She broke the engagement. Not that you can blame her for wanting to do something. You were considering moving to a larger cardboard box prior to the divorce. What happened to *that* plan?"

"How can you be so disrespectful?"

159

Nicky looked a little surprised at the growing heat of the conversation.

"I'm not disrespectful, I'm realistic," Ellen declared. "And you should be, too."

"About what? I thought we came here to discuss the jury panel. You'd better get realistic about that. We need a new panel. This one is spoiled."

I turned to Nicky, sure he'd agree with me, but he seemed to be hanging on Ellen's every word.

"McKenzie said no and he means it," Ellen declared.

Again I turned to Nicky. He was nodding yes vigorously. "Whose side are you on?" I asked him.

"The side of justice," he said, tucking into his sandwich.

"You call it justice when you're ganging up on me?" I challenged. "And as for your mother, I don't know what she wants from me. Maybe you'd better tell her to lay off."

"Take it easy," Ellen snapped. "I didn't say Mom is in love with *you*." Frostily, she changed the subject. "Look, we're here to discuss the jury panel, and I suggest we get to that topic right now."

"All right." When we fought, I was always the one who felt guilty. When Ellen was small and now that she was a major player. I was willing to do anything she wanted. Except jeopardize my case.

We all came up with a compromise. McKenzie agreed that the same panel be recalled and that they be questioned not only as to any prejudice they might harbor due to Stow's reputation, but also any bias they might now hold due to what they had seen and heard in court that morning. Sixty names were pulled from the drum, and by noon the next day, the first few jurors had been chosen.

"Number one's a fan already," Nicky whispered. "Watch how she looks at you. She's flirting. In a grandmotherly sort of way."

160

"Shut up. McKenzie's on us."

It took until 5:30 that day to get twelve suitable jurors. As I participated in the selection, I stood close to the prisoner's box in the middle of the courtroom, close enough for Stow to whisper instructions to me. This was standard procedure, and I decided to do it more out of respect for the traditions of the court than from any conviction that Stow would actually express interest in the men and women who would sit in judgment upon him.

As it turned out, I was wrong. "Too young," he whispered to me when a university student was called. I agreed, but I didn't need to spend a challenge. I felt I could force Ellen to use her challenge to dismiss the kid.

I was right. Ellen challenged the student. I still had all twenty challenges left.

"Too timid. Won't stand up to pressure," Stow whispered. I agreed with him and spent a challenge to get rid of a slight woman who looked about to burst into tears.

"Stay away from the women," Stow whispered. "They'll sympathize with the so-called victim."

Did he mean Harpur? The instruction chilled me.

Ellen was taking her time. She painstakingly scrutinized posture, eye movement and voice as each prospect stood in the witness box for evaluation.

"Watch her," I told Nicky, sitting back down at the defense table, where I could get a better look at Ellen's reactions to the prospects. "She's trying to load the jury with people who hate Stow on sight."

"It's her right!" Nicky hissed. "She's one smart lady. Why aren't we doing the same thing?"

Yes, my daughter was going for the jugular. Cutthroat. That's what everybody and everything seems to be these days, too cutthroat for an old man. "Help me, then."

Nicky nodded. The next prospect entered the box. Nicky never let his eyes leave the man's face as he stood and began, "Justice John Stoughton-Melville is a public figure. He has been written about extensively in the media . . ."

I watched the juror's face. Because he was looking at Nicky, I could concentrate on his eyes, his jaw. As Nicky said Stow's name, the juror's expression tightened. It was almost imperceptible, but it reminded me of when I'd hunted for my food in the valley. Wild animals have facial expressions that tell the hunter whether to pursue or give up.

I got rid of that juror, then turned back to Stow to see whether he approved of my decision. His face had closed again. No clue for the hunter there.

Chapter 10

Waiting for me outside the courtroom was Aliana, who had continued to scratch on her little pad throughout the last two days. She had witnessed juror rage, judge rage and Crown rage. "Got time for a coffee?" she asked, disarmingly. I expected her to wink at me.

I began to fit my face into a frown.

"I've got what you asked for," she said. Her voice was sharp, and something told me that what she had I shouldn't ignore.

"Can you walk with me?" I said, heading toward the escalator. She went first, and I stared at the top of her head all the way down to the main floor. No gray hairs.

The minute we got outside, I stopped. "Please, Aliana," I said, "could we skip the coffee? Could you just tell me what . . ."

"You asked me to check on Stow's finances," she said, looking around rather dramatically. Nobody near us, neither my daughter, who had left in a huff, nor my assistant, who had a date. "He's clean as far as I can tell. No unreported accounts. No lawsuits outstanding, either against him or initiated by him. All his assets appear to be in his own trust. And Harpur's are in her own account, which is held in trust for a family member."

"A family member of Harpur's?"

"No," Aliana said, "a family member of Stow's."

"Who?"

"I don't know."

"But how could you find out that it was a family member of his without knowing the name?"

She gave me one of her looks, as if I should know better than to ask her anything about her sources. "That's all I got, Ellis," she said, "and you're lucky I've even got that, considering how unfriendly you are."

"We'll have coffee next time, Aliana. Thanks for the info."

I left her standing there looking as annoyed as Ellen. But her irritation didn't stop her from being in court bright and early next day, scribbling away as usual.

That was the day Ellen opened her case. "Ladies and gentlemen of the jury," she began, glancing down at her neatly typed notes, "it is my duty and my privilege to address you today."

As she began to carefully lay out the evidence against my client, it sounded hopelessly damning. Despite the weeks Nicky and I had spent combing her disclosure material, Ellen's alleged facts stood out with surprising brutality. I imagined I saw disgust on the faces of the jury, those so-called peers of John Stoughton-Melville. Stow, however, surveyed the court with the expressionless calm of a man who considers himself peerless even in the dock.

In spite of our differences, I listened to Ellen with pride—until I homed in on what she was actually saying.

"There is no more sacred trust than the trust between a husband and a wife. No matter what life might throw into the path of either, loyal spouses know that each has a champion, sometimes even a savior."

"What's with the sermon?" Nicky silently slid a scrap of paper across the polished oak table.

I shrugged, hoping McKenzie was looking at Ellen and not at us.

"In times of trouble, to whom do we turn first? On whom do we lean most?" Ellen's eyes scanned the twelve, whose intense faces bore the expression of people about to chop the legs off an idol.

"And who do we least expect to be our betrayer, indeed, our executioner?"

At the use of that word, two of the jurors flinched.

"No," Ellen said, "no matter what our creed, we believe that a husband and wife are there for each other. That is what Harpur Blane Stoughton-Melville believed. She believed it all her married life—the better part of three decades." Ellen paused, moved a little to make sure she was not preventing any juror from looking at the accused as she spoke, not that anyone did so overtly. It was rare to catch a juror looking directly at the accused, rare for any-one in the courtroom to do so. But everyone could be ex-pected to sneak peeks at Stow incarcerated in his glassed-in box.

"Men and women, you will hear that poor Harpur Blane Stoughton-Melville was wrong to place her trust in her husband. Dead wrong."

She let the pun sink in. No one sniggered. She was lucky.

"Motive," she went on, "is not one of the elements of this case that must be proven beyond a reasonable doubt. You may discover that you need to know *how* Harpur was killed,

165

but you need not know *why* in order to render a verdict in the matter before you."

This was elementary stuff, made interesting only by Ellen's grandstanding, which was beginning to annoy me. I wished I could turn around to check out Anne and Aliana. Was Anne staring at Ellen? Nicky sure was. I didn't like the look on his face. Was he falling for all this nice-nice junk about husbands and wives?

"Over the course of this trial," Ellen said, "I believe you *will* ask yourself why a man like John Stoughton-Melville might kill his wife." She paused, looked up. Now every eye was on her, including McKenzie's. She slowly turned a page of her notes without looking at the paper. *Good touch.*

"To begin," she said, "let us be kind in our theories. You will hear from medical professionals that Mrs. Stoughton-Melville was not a well woman. That she was suffering. In fact, that she was declining daily. You will learn that on some days, she had no idea who she, herself, was, let alone knowing clearly who anyone else might be. She had once been a brilliant and beautiful woman. Now, all she had to look forward to was a mindless and embarrassingly pre-mature old age. I think you might want to ask yourself whether someone who loved her might have wanted to spare her the shame of such decline. Might he kill her in order to save her from the humiliation of becoming noth-ing more than the empty shell of her former bold and lovely self?

"Or," Ellen said, pausing again and rising onto the toes of her small feet, "should we be less kind? You will hear, ladies and gentlemen, from several bookkeepers, ac-countants and bankers that Mrs. Stoughton-Melville was a very wealthy woman, a woman whose illness, even her con-finement in a private institution—Riverside Hospital—

made barely a dent in her fortune. These witnesses will tell you as well that she was a childless woman with no living parents. That she died without siblings, nieces or nephews."

The jurors pondered this information, and Ellen not only paused to let them consider the implications of what she was saying, but also let them see her search each of their faces for her cue to continue. So solicitous! I glanced up at McKenzie, wondering how he took this rather intimate communication with the jury. He looked pleased. I was beginning to feel defeated before I even began.

"You will hear," Ellen repeated, shaking her head almost imperceptibly at the odious notion, "that the accused is a man of very expensive tastes. You can see for yourself the fineness of his clothes, his jewelry. You will be given the opportunity to consider whether such a man might be led by greed to double—even triple—his own holdings by adding the inherited holdings of his wife."

Nicky was scribbling furiously throughout all this, preparing notes for our cross-examination of the witnesses Ellen was planning to call. I listened, waiting for her strategy to become clear to me. She needed more than motive.

"I don't wish to mislead you, ladies and gentlemen," she said. "A person can have every reason to do a thing, yet still never think of carrying out the act. So I will not ask you to weigh reasons as to why the accused would kill his wife—at least, I would not ask you to do that without showing you how such an act was carried out."

I leaned closer, eager to see how Ellen would put her knowledge of Stow's movements before the jury.

"On the night of December 26, approximately five years ago," she recited, "Chief Justice John Stoughton-Melville entered Riverside Hospital with the intent to deceive. He arrived in a rented car, rather than his own. You will hear witnesses testify to seeing him in the neighborhood, in the hospital lobby and on the stairs leading up to the floor on which his wife's room was located."

But not in her room. No witness could place Stow anywhere near Harpur's room that night. Ellen had disclosed the existence of no such witness. Nicky had found no such person.

Like everyone else, my daughter didn't seem to know that I had been in Harpur's room, and I was under no obligation to inform her. Not that it mattered. I had seen no one that night. I had been alone with Harpur. And she had been safely asleep when I left.

I had gone over my final moments with her again and again. Now I retraced them in my mind. The ride to the hospital. The cold wind blowing up from the valley that lay beneath the northern wall of the great building, a building shaped like half a circle with its round side looking down onto Riverdale Park and the Don River. Then the walk through the lobby of the hospital, where the same carols that had played cheerily all month had begun to sound tinny and stale, just as the green bows and red and white poinsettias had lost luster.

Then the long trek up to Harpur's room.

I remembered that the elevator bank was being repaired and that three of the four elevators were out of service. A man waiting for the fourth elevator commented that he'd been there forever.

So I take the stairs. I begin to climb. I seem to be the only person in the stairwell, but when I get to the first landing, I stop, startled, hearing noises behind me. The sounds stop, too, and I soon understand they are my own echo. As I resume my ascent, I

think about how the crowds of people who visited the sick before
Christmas have disappeared.

The staircase leads to a glass door on each landing. I climb
past a few more floors. When I get to Harpur's floor, I open the
door, slip through and peer down the long hall. At the farthest
reaches, a hunched old woman labors at her walker, coming to-
ward me a centimeter at a time. She makes so little progress that
she seems to have moved not at all by the time I turn a corner into
the hallway where I figure Harpur's room must be. I'm uncertain
because I've never walked up before.

". . . walked up before."

Ellen's voice cut into my reverie. I looked up in alarm.
In my daydreaming, I had missed a significant portion of
what she'd been saying.

What was wrong with me? I had never let my mind wan-
der when I had been a young man before the bench or an
older man on it, but now, as an even older man, I found myself too often out of it, lost in my own interior world. I con-
centrated vigorously to analyze Ellen's every word, necessary
if I were to catch her or her witnesses in some inconsistency.

"The evidence will show that the accused deliberately
broke into a secure vault, first distracting the nurse who
guarded it and then manipulating the lock. He shame-
lessly stole several items from that vault, including about
two dozen prepackaged doses of Somatofloran, any three
of which would have been sufficient to place a woman of
Harpur's size into a coma. A larger number of doses
might possibly have been capable of killing her, which
was, you will be shown, exactly what John Stoughton-
Melville intended."

I longed to rise and object to this shocking display of
bravado: the sappy references to husband and wife, the
standing on tiptoes when an especially important point

was to be made, the use of silence to frame the Crown's most important pronouncements. Pause. "He left behind . . ." Pause. "As every thief does . . ." Pause. "A silent witness . . ." Pause. "To his nefarious act." Pause. "In fact . . ." Pause. "He left three fingerprints . . ." Pause. "Three silent witnesses." Pause. Cough. Longer pause.

"And he left behind something else," Ellen said, surprising me. There had been no disclosure about Stow leaving anything on the scene.

"He left behind a shocked country. A country that had put its trust in him. A country that was counting on Chief Justice John Stoughton-Melville not only to uphold its laws, but even, when necessary, to correct them.

"How can any trust be greater than that? I'll tell you, ladies and gentlemen. I'll tell you of a greater breach of trust than that of a judge who is a disgrace to the nation he serves. I'll tell you of a greater breach of trust than that of a husband who fatally betrays his beloved and long-suffering wife. I'll tell you of the greatest breach of trust here. When John Stoughton-Melville turned from being an esteemed judge to become a petty thief and a common murderer, he breached the trust he should have had in himself. He fouled his integrity. He blotted his own spotless record."

The jurors stirred in their padded but uncomfortable seats. Someone among them coughed. The matron hastened to pour a plastic tumbler of water from a jug she kept nearby. I could see that the chosen twelve were moved by the eloquence of this young woman. I was moved myself. "Now," she said, "I am bound by my duty as an officer of this court to remind you that what I have told you today is not fact. It's not even my personal opinion—which counts for nothing in this case, or any case. What I have told you, as Judge McKenzie will explain, is nothing but the theory of the Crown. Something which remains to be proven. You will hear a great deal of testimony in the days to come. I trust you will listen carefully. And if you exercise the common sense that is the mark of a jury of twelve citizens, I believe you will be convinced beyond a reasonable doubt that the accused who sits before you—"

She turned and glared at Stow. I had never seen a Crown make a face of loathing at an accused. I expected McKenzie to intervene, but he, like everyone else in the courtroom, waited in silence. I slid around in my seat to check on Stow. He was glaring right back at my daughter. Powerful negative energy leapt between Ellen and my client. I felt afraid for both of them. *Of* both of them.

Was it my imagination, or did Stow make a fist? I saw the guard beside him edge closer to the prisoner's box. I heard Nicky sigh. And I saw Ellen glance for an instant past Stow and toward the body of the court where, though I couldn't see her, I was sure Anne was sitting. Ellen seemed almost to falter, but only for a moment. She found the power of her full voice, and she let it rip. "That the accused who sits before you, despite his rank, his influence and his wealth, mercilessly slaughtered his defenseless wife."

Chapter 11

"Can you slaughter someone with a plastic vial?"

I wasn't amused by Nicky's question about Ellen's choice of the word "slaughter."

"I think she may damage her case with excessive dramatics," I said, worried about my girl using techniques I myself would never stoop to.

Nicky shrugged as we walked quickly away from the courthouse. "You'll change your mind," he said. "She's a smart lady. She's got everybody in that courtroom in the palm of her hand already."

At 5 p.m., University Avenue was busy. Across the street from the court, a steady stream of rush-hour cars sped by the U.S. Consulate. No traffic had been allowed to stop in front of it since 9/11. My car was a couple of blocks west near the art college on Dundas. Nicky seemed determined to follow me all the way there.

"She's going for the husband-wife betrayal angle," he said. "She's playing on the sympathy of those old ladies we picked." He nodded as if in approval. I was going to have to talk to him.

"They're not that old."

"Not as old as *you*, anyway." Nicky smacked my back in a gesture of camaraderie that made me stumble. "To-morrow she'll call her first witness," he went on, oblivious that he had practically knocked me off my feet. "It'll be the police officer who handled the crime scene."

We dodged a convoy of white cube vans, court vehicles full of prisoners headed back to jail after the day's trials. Stow was in one of them. All by himself.

"We're ready for that cop, of course," Nicky said. "You've got the copies of his memo books and . . ."

"Nicky," I interrupted, "let's give it a rest. I don't want to carry too many preconceived ideas into court. I want to concentrate on his actual testimony. It's the only way to cross-examine. Word by word. I need to clear my head." As Nicky got the idea I wanted to be alone, he looked crestfallen. "Anyway," I added, postponing the moment of his departure, "I don't know how long Ellen will be in her chief examination of that police witness. I may not even get to the officer tomorrow."

"Yeah, well, if you do . . ."

"If I do, I'll be ready. Why don't you just leave it to me?"

We said goodnight at Dundas and University, the side-walk thick with people leaving the office towers, court-houses, government buildings and banks that lined Uni-versity Avenue. The fickle late-winter sun was remarkably warm, and a soft breeze carried a hint of spring freshness, incongruous against the exhaust of the cars jamming the intersection.

"All right, I'll leave it to you," Nicky said. "Ciao, then." He waved, but when he had gone a few yards, he turned back and glanced at me doubtfully, as if he wondered if my confidence was not misplaced. True, except for practice in the classes and moot courts of my retraining, I had not cross-examined a witness in almost twenty years. Either it was like riding a bicycle and would come back to me the minute I got on, or else I was about to make a total fool of myself.

Predictably, I found myself heading east toward the clinic and Queenie because I had a problem I wanted to talk about.

"Have you got time for a quick supper?" I asked as I found her sorting through a huge pile of file folders.

"No, thanks."

"Because you're still angry with me?"

"How's the big case?" she asked, not responding to my question, but not unfriendly, either. "I went there one day, but I didn't see much."

"You were there? In court?"

She shrugged. "No big deal. I guess you were too busy to notice me. You never turned around. But I did talk to that friendly young man."

"Nicky?"

"I guess so. Anyway, you didn't answer my question. How's it going?"

"Okay."

"But it would be better if you could get into Riverside?"

I moved away, toward the window, and studied the huge flakes of snow that were suddenly falling between the clinic and the store next door. They never made it to the pavement, disappearing into the wet air. "Queenie," I said, "I'm truly sorry that I gave offense by asking you to do something wrong."

I felt her hand on my shoulder. "Don't be sorry, Your Honor. I'm working on it, I'm working on it." She shook her head, but whether in exasperation or frustration I couldn't tell.

"Come to supper with me," I asked again.

"I've got to finish this report tonight." She flipped through the pile on her desk. "But then, if I leave it alone for an hour, it won't disappear, will it? Looks like you talked me into it."

I took her to a little Chinese place at Broadview and Gerrard in the heart of Chinatown East. It pleased me to watch Queenie eat. She was so delicate in her movements that to watch her eat spareribs with her fingers was like watching someone else play the clarinet.

"Are you afraid, Your Honor? About tomorrow, I mean," she said when she noticed that my usually too healthy appetite was nowhere in evidence.

"Afraid? Why would I be afraid?"

She took a sip of tea, then refilled both our cups. "It's been a long time since you've done this."

"Eaten with you in a Chinese restaurant?"

She frowned at my feeble joke. "Your Honor," she said, "do you remember the time you and I ate at that restaurant around the corner from the courthouse and really got sick? When we thought somebody was trying to poison us?"

"That was pretty bad. Not something you'd forget."

Queenie nodded. "You know, Your Honor, we've been through trials and tribulations that an ordinary person couldn't survive. I think you and I are tough enough to handle anything now, because there's not much worse than being a street drunk that begs food when he isn't too hungover to eat." She hesitated, smiled. "We sure know how to suck it up."

"As long as a man can say, 'This is the worst,' the worst is yet to come."

"Who said that?" Queenie asked.

"I can't remember. A Roman or a Greek. Maybe Virgil."

"Virgil from down at the shelter?" she asked. I saw that Queenie had a sense of humor after all. "Listen, Your Honor, you may not have been lawyering for a long time, but you know about murder cases . . ."

"Queenie, a long time ago, I promised Stow I'd help him one time in his life, no questions asked."

She touched the gold ring on my finger. "I remember all of that, Your Honor," she said. "I remember that the day you became a lawyer, you and the Justice and his wife and a couple of other lawyers made that promise. When he asked me to talk to you, he reminded me."

I felt a stab of anger. I'd almost forgotten that Stow had sought Queenie out. "What else did he say, Queenie? Did he tell you why he needed an intermediary?"

"What are you getting so hot about?" she challenged. "It's a free country. He came to me late last summer. He said he'd run into a little trouble, and he needed someone to help him out. He said you were our mutual friend. He said he needed you to defend him in court, but that you were a proud man."

A master of timing, Queenie sipped her tea before going on. "He said he was a proud man, too, and that it's easy to ask a favor through an intermediary. But now I'm not so sure I did the right thing."

I wasn't sure myself. "Why?"

She cleared her throat and blurted out, "Because the day I came to court, I saw how you were with him. You didn't talk to him, didn't look at him."

"Queenie, I can't show how I feel about my client. It would be unprofessional."

"I didn't say you didn't show how you felt," she answered. "Everybody could see how you felt. Like you weren't absolutely sure that your client was innocent. That scared me. How can you defend somebody if you think he's guilty? Isn't that, like, lying?"

"Queenie," I answered, "it's not my job to convince a jury that Stow is innocent. It's my job to raise a reasonable doubt."

She glanced around the small restaurant as if some stranger were more capable of clarifying matters than I was. "All I know," she said, "is that if you really believe Stow killed his wife, if you yourself don't have that doubt you talk about, how're you going to convince a jury?"

How many times had I encountered laypeople with the same question? They believed we lawyers were morally reprehensible. And how to explain this aspect of the law to my old friend? I took a deep breath. "Queenie, you have to understand that my personal doubts about my client have nothing to do with the case."

"That's what you think," she declared, as if she had known more about the law than I did all along—or more about Stow.

After dinner, Queenie said she wanted to take a look at her charges at Tent City before returning to the mass of work in her office. Our trek along Queen Street East was mostly silent. By the time we reached the bridge over the Don River, the final red rays of light had faded from the western sky behind us, turning it first to leaden gray, then to deep blue. From the north side of the bridge, we could see the Don wind up toward expensive residential neighborhoods. Ellen was up there somewhere. Maybe little Angelo was getting ready for bed. I could picture my daughter reading her son a bedtime story, or regaling him with tales about her day in court.

From the south side, we could see the campfires and lanterns of Tent City.

I told Queenie, "I feel guilty that I haven't been able to go down since the trial started. But everything looks under control."

"There's where you're wrong." She gazed at the homes of her misfits and sighed.

"Things are worse out here than they've ever been."

Along the narrow east bank of the river the tents and shacks stretched like beads on a black ribbon. The night was quiet. No raised voices, no music. "What's so terrible?"

She shook her head. "As soon as the worst of the cold weather passed," she said, "the drug dealers moved in. If it seems quiet down there right now, that's because it's too early in the evening for the coke market to open."

I turned away from the peaceful scene below and wished I had it in my power to right the world's wrongs. A piercing scream rose from the depths of the valley, and a slim figure—I judged it to be a young woman—ran from a tent that burst into flame seconds later. Soon the tranquil scene below me became a riot of dark figures running in every direction.

"They're at it again!"

I followed Queenie without question as she darted down the embankment. Pushing through people climbing up to the bridge, she quickly made her way to the burning tent. Beside it the young girl watched her home become ashes with a mixture of horror and disbelief. "It came right out of the sky. Like lightning! I was standing by the tent and I saw it come, and I just run."

The girl clung tightly to Queenie, sobbing that her stuff was gone and she could never get any more, that somebody had tried to kill her, that she didn't know what to do . . . Queenie gently pulled the distraught young woman away from the fire and patted her head as though comforting a child.

179

"Queenie, what is it?"

"Firebombs," the girl said before Queenie could answer. "It's been happening every night for a couple weeks. Some yahoos are throwing burning rags down on the tents from the bridge or from cars on the road. Mostly they just go out in the air, but not tonight. Tonight they landed on me. I'm a lucky bitch!" She smiled weakly, and Queenie patted her again.

I was appalled. Drug dealers. Firebombs. "The tenters have to be removed at once. How about back to the shelters?"

"No," the girl answered immediately. "It's better to burn than sleep one night in a shelter." As if in confirmation of what she'd said, most of those who'd run at the sight of the fire from above were making their way back down.

One of the shack dwellers whose home was still intact agreed to take the young girl in for the night, and with many backward looks at the embers of her home, she went along. As for me, I was anxious to get Queenie and myself away before the next firebombing episode commenced or the drug market opened for business. But we didn't go back to the office. Instead, we walked up the embankment, over the bridge and along King Street to her house. I'd not been there since New Year's Eve when I'd been forced to remain outside. This time, she invited me in.

"Why are you so secretive about this?" I asked her as we entered a small hallway that opened onto a comfortable living room.

She rearranged a few books on a table, as if I'd criticized her housekeeping.

"It's so nice, Queenie, with all your Indian art and your plants. Why wouldn't you want to show me?"

"No reason, Your Honor. Why are you so questionable all of a sudden?"

"Inquisitive," I corrected. "I'm not questionable. I'm inquisitive. Did someone give you the money to buy this house?" I persisted.

A stronger notion hit me. "Did someone *donate* it to you?"

Queenie balled her hands into tight little fists at her sides, as if she were about to attack. "Are you a nut case? I'm not a charity!"

"How about bribes? Do you accept those?"

I'd gone too far. Why couldn't I stop harassing my best friend? Queenie unballed her fists and said, "If you weren't just about my only pal, I'd throw you right out of here. Why don't you ask the real question, the one that's bugging you?"

Okay, I thought, *I will.* "Queenie, did Stow give you this house in exchange for talking me into taking his case?"

She appeared embarrassed, but only a bit.

"Oh, Queenie!"

Now she fired up again. "He didn't donate it or give it to me. He sold it to me and made the mortgage one I could afford. It was legit. Fair and square deal."

"And in exchange, you convinced me to become his lawyer?"

"Nobody convinces you of anything." She looked around the cozy room. "Anyhow," she said, "so what if I *did* do Stow a favor? One hand washes the other. No big deal!"

Uncomfortable with her rationalizing, I left a few minutes later, went home and tried to get some sleep. When I was still tossing and turning at 5 a.m., I gave up, showered and headed downtown to the office.

It took me a minute to realize that the lights were on, as though someone had been working from dark until after sunrise and had forgotten to turn them off. Nicky? He'd said he had a date.

I glanced around. Nothing seemed out of order. The boxes were still neatly stacked, generally in numerical order. We had cut most of the red tape away. I could see nothing different about the boxes or the tape. As before, the tape had been resealed carefully but without the appearance of tampering.

Perhaps I'd left the lights on myself. Prepared to dismiss the puzzle, I moved toward my desk. There in the middle of it was a courier's envelope that had definitely not been there the day before. A smudged black time stamp indicated 1:06 a.m. as the time the envelope had left the courier truck. I turned it over to see whether Nicky had signed for it. All I saw on the signature slip were the words "Signature not required."

I tore open the envelope. A sharp edge caught my knuckle, so that a smear of blood sullied the front of another envelope inside. On this second envelope, I saw the bold black globe that was the logo of the *Toronto Daily World*. I tore that open too.

A note was scribbled in blue ballpoint on a single piece of letter-size paper. "Ellis," I read, "I found something more on Harpur's trust. Here's a one-page record concerning the transfer of the trust to that family member I mentioned. What does it mean? Let me know when you figure it out. Aliana."

I turned the note over. On the other side was a photocopy of a few lines of legal jargon. I interpreted it to mean that the person who had signed the document agreed that some preexisting claim to inheritance had not been relinquished. My eye raced to the bottom of the page. The signature I saw there was more than a shock; it was mind-boggling: a neat, precise, familiar "Portal."

Chapter 12

It was the same signature I'd seen on the financial records that I'd checked, on the Pipperpharmat drug trial records, on so much of the Crown's disclosure material. I mulled it over for more than an hour. I pulled a few random pages from my files, from the stacked boxes. I was so sure that Ellen had signed all the Crown's disclosures that I hadn't stopped to ask myself why she'd have to sign them. And indeed, most of the material I now looked at was not signed. There were initials here and there, including at the bottom of typed memos from Ellen, but only a few full signatures. They looked very similar to the document Aliana had couriered, but now I realized that I couldn't be 100 percent sure. But I had to ask myself: Was I only now questioning the signature because the document I held in my hand was questionable? Why would my daughter have signed a paper stating that she refused to relinquish a claim on Harpur's money?

I had no more time to figure it out. I shoved the paper back into the courier envelope and stuck it in a drawer.

Nicky was waiting for me at court, and I had to get there before he got nervous and Judge McKenzie got furious. I ran down Queen Street, but any time I gained by rushing was lost as I went through an exceptionally thorough search of my person and belongings. Security at the courthouse seemed to be getting tighter by the day.

I shouldn't have worried about Nicky. He was engaged in friendly banter with Ellen when I arrived in the courtroom, and as she called her first witness, he stared at my daughter with the smarmy gaze of a hero worshipper. I had seen junior defense lawyers in awe of senior Crown lawyers many times. This time it really ticked me off.

"Constable Simms," Ellen began, "you were the first officer on the scene the night Riverside Hospital was broken into and Harpur Stoughton-Melville died?"

"Correct."

"Can you tell the jury what your duty that night entailed?"

The officer, a woman dressed in a suit a bit too tight in the jacket and in ankle-length trousers answered, "It would have been my job to secure the scene, to make sure no evidence was misplaced or disturbed . . ."

Even though Nicky and I knew the answers to such basic questions, we wrote furiously on our pads to intimate that the officer was saying something controversial. It was a technique we intended to employ with all Crown witnesses, to keep the jury on edge, to give them the impression that what each witness said was disputable.

Nicky and I had agreed to share the cross-examination of the routine police witnesses. We asked each of them about eyewitnesses to the actual events in Harpur's room. There were none.

When he concluded his questions with the last police constable, Nicky indulged himself by speculating in front of the jury. McKenzie didn't stop him, which we imagined would be a tiny coup for us.

"So, Officer," Nicky said, practically puffing out his chest, "looks like the only witness to the death of Harpur Blane Stoughton-Melville was the unfortunate deceased herself."

"I wouldn't say that," the officer answered calmly and with what I suspected was a twinkle in his eye. "I never worked on a murder case yet where the only witness was the corpse."

Every day of the trial, Aliana sat and scribbled as much as we did. I realized I needed to get her take on the "Portal" paper. Anne was in the body of the court, too. I caught her watching Ellen with an intensity I couldn't remember her displaying before. I flattered myself that she was watching me too, imagined I could feel her admiration, even approval, when I rose to cross-examine the first of the more specialized police witnesses. Why did I care what Anne thought?

For whatever reason, I was conscious of the attention of both women as I rose to address the witness. "Detective Wellesley, your notes taken the night of the break-in at the drug vault in Riverside show that you found three full vials of Somatofloran on the floor near the vault."

Wellesley thumbed through his small black memo book. "Yes."

"But you have not indicated that you fingerprinted those vials. Am I right?"

Wellesley stared at me for a moment, aware of my tactics.

"Are you asking whether I indicated fingerprinting the vials in my notes or if I actually did fingerprint the vials?"

"Both, sir," I said with a slight air of exasperation that was designed to make the witness look less intelligent than he clearly was.

"I did not indicate that the vials had been fingerprinted by me immediately upon their discovery," he answered calmly.

"Why?"

"Because I was the officer in charge of the case," he explained with exaggerated patience, as if trying to communicate with a backward child. *Tit for tat.* "I don't conduct fingerprint examinations. That would have been done by forensics at the scene sometime later."

"I see." The faces of the jury had come alive with interest. Fingerprints. Crime scene. This was more like *Law and Order.* Good for keeping them awake. "So you would have received a report sometime after the break-in alerting you to the results of the fingerprint examination of the vials?"

"Yes, but—"

"But?"

"But the results were negative."

"Officer, does that mean there were no fingerprints?"

"Fingerprints were found on the three vials," he answered, "but they were partials. We couldn't get enough to make a conclusive match."

I appeared to give this information careful consideration. This was precisely the opening I'd been going for. "So, Officer," I declared ponderously, "you are telling me that the fingerprints of my client were *not* found on any vial of Somatofloran retrieved at Riverside Hospital during the time in which his wife was a patient there."

The officer was no rookie. He weighed his options and chose the one most damaging to me. He turned to Justice McKenzie and spoke directly to His Honor.

"Sir," he said, "I believe the defense is putting words into my mouth. I . . ."

"Withdraw that question, Mr. Portal," the judge commanded without hesitation. Turning his gaze on the twelve, he instructed, "You are to disregard Mr. Portal's last query. Move on with your cross, Counselor."

"Thank you, Your Honor," I said. *Always thank 'em.* I glanced at Nicky, who smiled faintly. It is impossible for the jury to ignore a dramatic and apparently logical statement. They would remember that no fingerprints of Stow's were found on any vial related to the so-called murder long after they had forgotten the judge's instruction.

On the third day of the trial, my son Jeffrey was there. I was pleased that he was interested enough in a display of family rivalry to take time off from his duties at the apartment building and as a new father. He sat beside his mother and whispered in her ear from time to time. I had limited opportunities to observe them, but I resented that Jeffrey distracted Anne's attention from Ellen and me. I mean, who were the stars here?

Immediately after lunch, two security officers escorted Stow back from the cells and into the prisoner's box. He was still shackled, a humiliation generally reserved for the violent or the mentally disturbed. Angry, curious, I stepped toward the prisoner's box to ask why he was being treated in such a manner. Before I even reached Stow, however, I caught sight of Jeffrey and Anne now sitting only a few yards away from the prisoner.

Anne was distraught and weeping. Jeffrey was comforting her. Stow was completely uninterested or unaware of the disruption behind him.

A second later, Ellen breezed in, followed by her coterie of police witnesses. Anne appeared to compose herself. Jeffrey removed his arm from his mother's shoulder. Stow gazed off into space. The fascinating little drama ended as quickly and as mysteriously as it had begun.

Ellen examined more police witnesses, and Nicky conducted routine cross-examinations. The case was slow in getting off the ground, but then I have always felt that way at the beginning of a trial. Many lawyers believe it is necessary to carefully and firmly establish the crime scene and its effects in the minds of the jury before proceeding. I don't disagree. I just find the prelims excruciatingly boring. The jury, however, was alive and alert.

"How was it today? Did you speak? Were you afraid? Surely not . . ."

She has a cocktail waiting for me, but hasn't made one for herself. There's a startling new idea going around: that a baby in its mother's womb can feel the effects of alcohol. I don't make the connection. Not at first.

"I've an announcement," she murmurs with uncharacteristic coyness. I'm in my armchair, and she sits on the corner of our couch, facing the room. I see her alabaster face in profile, her skin translucent, her radiance arresting.

"What?"

Before she makes her revelation, I hear a squeal of delight. The most beloved voice I know cries out my name—"Daddy!"

Ellen, a toddler with untameable energy, bounds through the door, crosses the living room in a leap and lands in my lap. She throws her pudgy arms around me and squeezes my neck so hard that I can't breathe, until she releases me with a peanut-butter-scented kiss on my cheek.

"We're going to have a new baby, Daddy!" Ellen declares. My eyes fly to Anne's face. Is this coming event a good thing?

"Ellis," she says softly, "it's true. And I hope you'll be as happy as I am."

A small smile curves her perfect lips. I'm tempted to say, quite truthfully, that such a perfect woman should have many chil-

dren, but I can't quite buy her supposed bliss. Nor can I contain my surprise that our infrequent and perfunctory sex has resulted in a miracle. I reach out and stroke her face, grateful and touched. Anne gives me all her love, while I play with the fire outside. Does she know that cocaine is more important to me than family?

"What do you say, Counsel?"

Shocked, I realized Justice McKenzie had addressed me. As if emerging from a deep sleep, I struggled to focus my attention. What had he asked me?

I looked around. My eye fell on the clock. It was nearly four. "I note the time, Your Honor," I said. "I realize it's early, but perhaps with the court's indulgence, we could break until tomorrow and I can address the matter then."

Nicky looked startled. And Ellen was frowning at me.

"Not funny, Mr. Portal," the judge said after a long pause. "I'll call a ten-minute recess, so Mr. Portal can *think* about the matter."

"Order!" the deputy called out, and McKenzie rather majestically sailed down from the dais and out of the courtroom.

"Why did you tell him you need to adjourn until tomorrow to decide whether the heat needs to be turned down?"

"Nicky," I answered, "I was out of it again."

He looked at me with a pained grimace. "Get a life," he suggested.

When we came back, Ellen had yet another police detective on the stand, this one a photographer who had taken a series of shots of the hallway and staircase of Harpur's floor.

"Is this the door leading to the corridor?" she asked.

The Crown's resources for the production of court exhibits were practically unlimited. The picture was not a snapshot-size photo, but a huge blowup, at least three feet by four feet. As I approached the exhibit, I had the uncanny feeling of approaching not a photo of a door mounted on foam-core board, but the door itself.

I leave the old lady and her walker. I turn the corner.

I shook my head, focused my eyes on Ellen. She had a laser pointer device attached to the easel to draw the witness's attention to the exhibit without marking it. Very high-tech. Very Ellen. By the way Nicky was smirking, you could see how impressed *he* was by this gadgetry.

I approach Harpur's door. I have something to tell her. Perhaps I need to remind her of something. Over the tinny intercom come those incessant Christmas carols.

I leaned toward the photo of the door and gave it just the right amount of scrutiny. Too little and the jury might think me contemptuous of the Crown's thoroughness. Too much and they might think I needed to learn from Ellen's exhibit.

I push open the door and as I do, I brace myself. I have to tell Harpur one more time that the answer is no. I will not help her to kill herself.

Startled at this unbidden recollection, I staggered, bumped into the exhibit and knocked the little laser pen out of its handy holster.

"Mr. Portal," McKenzie intoned from on high, "if there is no problem with this exhibit, would you please step back and wait until your cross to examine the Crown's submission?"

I obeyed. "Forgive me, Your Honor," I responded with as much dignity as I could muster. "I'm merely identifying the location of the photo for reference."

"Very well, Mr. Portal, but do stand back. Proceed, Ms. Portal."

I slunk back toward my seat and waited for the last half hour of the day to pass with merciless slowness.

Nicky and I were packing our files into our briefcases when Anne, paler than ever, leaned over the bar and addressed me. Since viewing Stow in shackles, she had sat silent and white-faced during the afternoon's proceedings. I left Nicky and escorted her out of the courtroom and down three stories into the lobby, where we sat on a bench and gazed at the rapidly diminishing crowd off for happy hour.

"It has to do with Sal," she began. I almost sighed, reflecting that I didn't need more problems right now. Jeffrey's little girl had seemed bursting with health the last time I had seen her. But when had that been?

I glanced around the nearly empty lobby. Nicky appeared, lugging the files and two briefcases. "I'll be over at the office as soon as I can," I told him. "I promise I won't leave you alone to work on all this tonight." He was the picture of concern as he looked at Anne and me, obviously distracted. But "Cool" was his only reply. And away he went with the rest of the crowd.

I brought my mind back to Sal. Her mother, Tootie, had been a street kid before she went straight. Could she have passed on some condition that now, more than five years later, had manifested itself in her child? Or was Jeffrey about to flee, aware finally that he and Tootie were a fraying conjunction of misfits?

"Ellis," Anne said, holding out her hands to me in the sort of motion she used to welcome guests at her frequent dinner parties. But now there was desperation in the gesture.

I took her hands in mine and kissed her cheek. "Let's take a walk while you explain."

She agreed and we slipped down to Queen Street.

As we strolled, I found myself inadvertently noting each doorway I'd slept in with Queenie during my street days. On an exceptionally mild March day like this one, we'd have been happy to sleep in the fresh outdoor air. I felt Anne relax at my side, as if she, too, had gained some composure from the warmth.

"The trouble's really with Tootie," she said, "but there are implications—uh—things that we need to know for little Sally's sake. Tootie has been very cooperative, very frank and forthcoming. There was a time when she was quite heavily involved in drugs, you know."

"I admire Tootie," I replied. "You can be sure I know quite a bit about her. She's forsaken her past." I felt defensive about my erstwhile landlady.

Anne nodded.

"Are you saying that Tootie's drug use has affected Sal?" I prompted. "How can that be? Tootie stopped using drugs a long time ago." A new fear suddenly hit me. "Didn't she?"

"Oh, Ellis," Anne said, reaching for my hand to illustrate that we were two grandparents with a common concern. "Tootie is a devoted mother, straight as an arrow. But the fact is that drugs can damage a woman's body long after she has ceased using them. The pediatrician wants to test Sal for genetic damage."

"That doesn't sound like a big deal to me."

But apparently it seemed like a big deal to Anne. She gave me a tentative glance. "Part of the procedure is to have the parents' DNA tested."

"That's nothing to worry about, Anne," I said, exhaling abruptly in relief. "DNA testing is done on a regular basis by the police these days. It only involves a small sample of blood, or even just saliva, from Tootie and Jeffrey."

"It's not just Tootie and Jeffrey," Anne said, impatience at my seeming lack of concern in her rising voice. We had had a lot of disagreements in our long and bumpy marriage, but all the voice-raising had been on my side.

"They don't just want DNA from the parents. They also want DNA from the grandparents. That means me and you."

Like the rest of the world, I valued my privacy. I wasn't keen to submit myself to a permanent record. But on the other hand, I no longer had anything to hide. If a mere pinprick, a mere mouth swab, could prevent future difficulties for my son's child, I was not unwilling to undergo a bit of physical discomfort, even a large invasion of my privacy.

"Why do we have to do it?" Anne interrupted, her voice strident. "It's not fair. Tootie has no parents. Why do *we* have to provide samples when they can't test *her* parents? How can they force us to give our DNA samples?"

"No one can force you, Anne." Her overreaction reminded me that she was an aging woman who felt her lack of control. I thought about her declared predicament, weighing my own level of involvement. "Shall I speak to the pediatrician?"

Once again I reflected that when a crisis appears, it is always at the wrong moment. This was absolutely the worst time for me to be distracted from Stow's case. However, my generous offer appeared to make Anne more agitated. "No," she said. "No, please, Ellis. I'll talk to the doctor. I mean, just forget about this conversation. Really. I'll take care of it."

Not wishing to disturb her fragile composure, I hailed a cab and after seeing her into it, walked the short distance down Queen to my office.

When I got there, I remembered how the day had begun—with that odd document that had come from Aliana in the middle of the night. She'd asked me what to make of it, but I wondered what her own thoughts were on the matter. I opened the drawer and pulled out the courier's envelope. I reached inside. It was empty.

I phoned Nicky at once. "Did you take a document from my drawer?" I demanded, barely concealing my ire.

"Ellis," he said, immediately angry himself. "Either you trust me or you don't. If you think I'm pulling something in the office when you're not there, why don't you just come out and say what it is?"

I recalled the last time we'd had this conversation. Demanding to know what Nicky was up to was no good. What did I expect? A confession that he was on Ellen's side because he kept making moony eyes at her? If there were sabotage in my ranks, I was not going to get to the root of it by asking possible perpetrators to tell me what they were doing. I made up my mind to watch Nicky more carefully, much as it broke my heart. Besides, I needed him. I couldn't handle the case by myself and there was no one else who could help. "Sorry," I told him. "Forget it."

I was so upset that I completely forgot the neurotic encounter with Anne. In fact, when a "Family Diagnostic Laboratory" called me the next day, I insisted they had the wrong number until they explained that they required me to submit a mouth swab. Not needing any further aggravation, I complied.

As the days went by, I began to realize that my inability to get into Riverside Hospital was a serious stumbling block to Stow's defense. He was no more forthcoming than ever; in fact I seriously considered having him examined to detect mental illness. Perhaps I could put an application before Judge McKenzie requesting that Stow be declared unfit to stand trial. But when I considered the implications of that, the certain ruin of his future, I backed off. Notwithstanding that he was going to be ruined anyway if I failed to defend him successfully, which would ruin me, too.

If I could just see the place where Harpur had died, even the lobby, the corridors or the elevator, maybe I could find one fact I could use to make it seem ridiculous that Stow had been sneaking around there intending to kill his wife. Maybe I could find the witness that Ellen couldn't find—the person who really knew what had happened in that room.

Nicky and I had once again patched up our differences, but I never mentioned Ellen's signature on the trust document again. I didn't ask Aliana, either. Maybe I was embarrassed that it had gone missing before I could figure out what it meant.

There were no further suspicious disturbances in the office, but one night, I decided to hide out in the corridor, after making a rather noisy show of turning off the lights and locking the door. I crouched painfully in the shadows for what seemed like an eternity, before I heard the downstairs door open and slow steps ascend the stairs from the street. Startled out of a half doze, I peeked out to see an old drunk lumber toward the door, shake the handle, then shake it again. Had someone paid a street person to burglarize my premises? I was ready to confront the man when I realized he was headed for the next door in the corridor. He wasn't interested in my office, just in any open door that might afford him shelter. I'd shaken a few doorknobs myself in my bad days. I left the man alone.

The next day, Aliana accosted me on the way from my car to the courthouse. I felt like she was stalking me, but when I took a good look at her, I decided against reprimanding her. I marched down University Avenue, daring her to keep up with me. Of course, she did. She wore slim blue jeans, a tight little purple leather jacket and stiletto heels in a bright shade of green. Her hair, misted by the rain of March, fell in lush waves against her olive-skinned face.

"Amazing endorsement on the front page of the *World!*" she shouted. The roar of rush-hour traffic on University nearly drowned her out. I didn't know what she was talking about, as usual.

"Aliana, I'm a little busy right now—"

"Oh, quit trying to shoo me away as if I were a bug or a groupie. The whole legal world is holding its breath to see whether you'll be a judge again."

"Give me a break. I don't think so."

"Did you even *see* the paper this morning?" She waved her copy in front of my face. I took a step out to cross Dundas. A car honked sharply, forcing me back on the curb.

"You're going to get us killed," I complained.

She ignored me. "You probably don't even know that one of the Supreme Court Justices 'heavily favors' your candidacy."

"What?"

I stopped in the middle of the crowded sidewalk. A well-dressed man bumped me from behind, uttered a profanity and hurried off. I grabbed the paper from Aliana's hand and read it as fast as I could. Much as I liked seeing my name in print, the piece was disappointing. "It's totally meaningless," I told Aliana, shoving the paper back into her hand. "The justice didn't endorse *me* for the judgeship. She just endorsed the Attorney General of Ontario for suggesting me. These people tend to pat each other on the back. This isn't news."

"It is and—"

"And you want to interview me again? Get off it, Aliana. You're becoming a pest. Like I said, I'm busy." We'd reached the courthouse. I hoped I wasn't being too hard on Aliana, but I wished she'd leave me alone. I found her distracting for more reasons than one.

She grabbed my arm. "Ellis, give it up! I'm going to write about you whether you want me to or not. I've written about you for years now. I've made you famous. You might as well cooperate. It would save us both the hassle."

I shook her off, found Nicky and headed into the courtroom, where Ellen was soon regaling the jury with more dramatics.

"By now," she said, "you are beginning to have a clear idea of the scene of this horrendous offense."

I couldn't see her face, but I imagined she wrinkled her nose slightly when she said "horrendous." It was one of her favorite words for anything she didn't like.

"Each officer you've heard," she continued, "has added some small detail to the overall picture of the hospital lobby, the corridors, the vault from which the drugs were stolen, the nursing station, the volunteer lounge and, of course, the unfortunate victim's room."

I rose. McKenzie nodded for me to voice my objection. His immediate response meant that he knew what I was going to say. "Your Honor, no witness has given any indication of ever being in Mrs. Stoughton-Melville's room."

"Ms. Portal?"

"I apologize, Your Honor," Ellen replied snappily. "Several officers," she corrected, with what I thought was annoying care, "have told you what a typical room at Riverside would have been like at the time in question. They've also been able to say that most of the rooms were quite similar." She paused as if she still had something to add, but she thought better of it. It was a weak note on which to end. I glanced at Nicky, almost expecting him to show pity for Ellen. Instead, he winked at me.

Behind me in court at all times, I could feel the strange presence of my client, who said nothing, not to the guards who daily brought him back and forth to his cell, or to Nicky, or to me. I wondered sometimes whether he was asleep. But when I glanced at him in the glass-enclosed prisoner's box, I saw that his eyes were on Ellen, alert, ablaze.

On the second Friday of the trial, Justice McKenzie decided we all needed an afternoon off, which meant, of course, that he needed an afternoon off.

I was grateful for the break because I had promised my grandson I would spend some time with him. When I got home, I found that Ellen's nanny had dropped the boy at our building. Angelo was playing with his cousin Sal. Tootie was minding them, but she was distracted by a lively conversation with her Tamil neighbor, conducted in brutally fractured English and street slang. Angelo was in the process of taking his tiny cousin into custody.

"These are handcuffs, see," he told Sal. Both the children were still sporting brightly colored winter gear, and Angelo appeared to be fiddling with the sleeve of Sal's jacket. As I moved closer, I saw he was tying something around the little girl's wrist. He tried to make a knot, failed, then tossed something away behind him. "Forget it," he said.

I saw a small strip of red blaze against the ground. It was a length of tape, exactly the same red tape that had bound the boxes in my office.

"Where did you find this, Angelo?" I asked.

He looked up as though caught in an illegal act. He was only eight, but I saw adult defiance in the set of his jaw, the levelness of his gaze. "I have rights, Grandpa. I don't have to tell you."

I didn't want to get into a discussion with him about illegal search and seizure of evidence. I was half convinced the little genius could argue such a motion.

"Angelo, *please*. It's really important. Just tell Grandpa where you got this tape."

He shrugged. "It probably got stuck on somebody's shoes or something. I found it on the floor in the apartment."

"My apartment?"

"No, Grandpa. Not your apartment. Sal's. What difference does it make, anyway?"

"I'm not sure," I said honestly. "It just seems funny to see it here."

"Yeah," Angelo answered, no longer interested. "Can we do popcorn and homemade ice cream?"

After spending time with this family, I felt compelled to visit my "other" family.

Down in Tent City, I found an evacuation in full swing. Clearly the situation had worsened since the firebombing I had witnessed. Looking south from the bridge, I could see extensive damage. Shacks and tents were charred, and whole sections of the riverbank had been torched. Pathetic figures shifted through piles of scorched rubble trying to rescue personal belongings.

A narrow file of displaced people wound along the path that led north, like foreign refugees displayed on the evening news. They carried bags and bundles and even some of the support posts from huts. It was a dispiriting sight in a wealthy city. I made my way down the embankment, careful not to push anyone aside in my eagerness to locate Queenie. I found her with a woman about her own age, whose shaky fingers prevented her from tying up a small box. When Queenie tried to help, the woman slapped her hand.

"Let me help," I said, stepping up to the two of them. Queenie looked tired, but a small smile flitted across her features at the sight of me.

She handed me a ball of rough twine. Her hand brushed mine, and the warmth of her fingers filled me with a desire long quiescent.

I knew at that precise moment that she deserved to be taken away from the dirt and grimness of her chosen work, and that I was the one to do the taking. I opened my mouth to utter something personal when someone called out her name in seeming anguish. As if my existence was the least of her concerns, Queenie turned and headed in the direction of that sound. One small glance of approval was all I received before she disappeared into the confused mass of the dispossessed.

Chapter 13

The next day, Saturday, I woke at dawn and headed back to the Tent City site.

It was as though the settlement had never existed. The river lapped the shore's beaten earth where the tents had once stood, but otherwise, there was no trace of any kind of human existence.

It wasn't until I read the *Toronto Daily World* back at the office that I learned the evacuees were thought to have scattered throughout the city, some moving farther north in the valley, others giving in to the prodding of city officials to enter shelters. Many had probably disappeared altogether.

"I don't know how Aliana does it," Nicky said with evident admiration. "She tracked down the Tent City gang, wrote about them *and* about you, too. Women today are ballsy!"

"Yeah, right," I answered. No doubt he meant Ellen, too. I glanced over the piece about me and the judgeship. It seemed general and innocuous, which was a good thing. To be perceived as someone's favorite might give the Attorney General the wrong impression.

"You're going to get this judgeship, Ellis," Nicky said. "You're the man." He raised his Styrofoam cup of coffee in salute. "Thanks," I said. His expression of loyalty was touching, even if it did remind me that the empty courier envelope still sat unexplained in my desk. Maybe the time would come when I could ask him, yet again, why the office never seemed to remain the way I left it, but not this morning. I had to break the news to him that I was going alone to Fernhope. During the week, Stow was kept at the Don Jail, the usual remand facility for unconvicted detainees. On the weekend, the cops took him back up north.

"Stow wants to talk to me alone, Nicky." I gestured around the room. Boxes were scattered here and there, covering two-thirds of my tiny office's floor. "This mess could use some help," I said tentatively.

Nicky surveyed the boxes that had once sat in neat stacks against the wall. Some lids were askew and papers were spilled out onto the floor. "Yeah, a disaster waiting to happen," he said. "Are you sure you haven't been hosting an orgy?"

"Nicky," I asked carefully, "does it seem to you that somebody *has* been in here? Besides us and the orgy attendees, I mean."

I feared he'd get angry, as he'd done on the phone. Instead, he gave me the same look of worried exasperation as when he caught me daydreaming. "I'll do what I can about this mess. I'll even admit that I don't always know exactly where every document in here is all the time."

"You're a solid kid, Nicky," I said. I walked over to the nearest box and straightened a file that was teetering atop a pile. I recognized the file as one I, myself, had left there the day before. "Do what you can, but take some time off, too. All work, etc., you know. I'll see you on Monday."

He nodded, but he didn't look up because he was busy extricating his fingers from a piece of red tape. "Yeah, right, bye . . ." he said absently.

On the drive up to Fernhope, it was hard to keep up my spirits. I kept mentally going over the testimony of Ellen's witnesses thus far. My cross-examinations of all those cops had certainly alienated Ellen. She became frostier by the day. Worse, I might also be alienating the jury. As for whether I was pleasing my client, the question was moot—and mute! Stow had offered no help in his defense, and I was surely wasting my precious weekend in traveling up to prison again. It seemed he had no intention of offering any fact, any opinion, even any genuine interest in his case.

My only comfort was glimpsing the woods of early spring, dappled sun on melting snow, sparkling blackness of clear forest streams no longer bound by ice. Contemplation of rebirth occupied me completely until I reached Fernhope.

As I waited for Stow, I remembered how shocked I had been the previous autumn when I'd first seen him here. Now I could not imagine seeing him anywhere except in custody—in shackles, behind glass walls.

But if I expected Stow to enter the visiting room subdued and meek, I was mistaken. Instead of his usual air of detached mental instability, when he entered the room I could see that he was deeply annoyed. Something or someone was bugging him.

"You know, Portal," he said without preamble, "it's not every day that a man being considered for a judgeship receives a recommendation from a judge of the Supreme

Court." He scowled. "So you should be more careful. Pandering to the media does not advance your cause. Shake loose that reporter who's always on your tail."

This was the Stow of old—arrogant, even imperious. So it was he who—I was forced to this conclusion—had not only put in the good word for me, but had chosen to leak the news to a reporter other than Aliana. Was he controlling the press now, as well as the real estate market—not to mention my career?

"Stow," I said, trying to keep all emotion out of my tone, "why don't you just skip the favors? Because if you're the one who influenced that justice, you're more likely to lose me the judgeship than to win it."

I waited for lightning to strike. His silence was so deep and so long that I could hear crows cawing in the woods beyond the compound.

"Get McPhail off the case" was his only reply. "He's as green as an unripe mango, and he can't keep his thoughts to himself. He's favoring the Crown. Lose him."

"What?"

"Do the cross yourself. I don't like you sitting there doing nothing. I mean, half the time you look like you're asleep. I want you up there alone. Starting Monday."

The man had to be mad. He veered day to day from dazed silence to ramblings to peremptory advice. "Stow, give me a break. Is this behavior of yours an elaborate act to drive me as crazy as you are? If you've suddenly become concerned about the most efficient cross, you've got to cooperate, help me out a little. I can't make a sensible cross without your input." I felt like shaking the man until his teeth rattled. "What really happened in Harpur's room that night?" I practically yelled, but the guards barely looked up.

"All I've heard is a number of police officers describing a hospital," Stow responded. "If you think that's all the Crown has, then you should go for a directed verdict."

I laughed. "I'm supposed to stand up and ask McKenzie to acquit on the basis of the weakness of the Crown case? I don't think so. Besides, there's more to come from Ellen."

Stow didn't challenge my statement. "Her most damaging witness thus far is the one we're going to face Monday morning," I continued, "the expert from the pharmaceutical firm. He's going to describe the trials he conducted, the study that alerted him to the irregularities in Harpur's blood test results . . ."

"Portal, that evidence is useless. The Crown is relying on experimental results gathered more than five years ago." He made that dismissive gesture with his long fingers. The movement infuriated me further.

"Stow," I said, "what are you hiding?" I remembered the document that was missing. "Has your silence got something to do with the fact that the Crown signed a statement regarding Harpur's fortune? Come to think of it, why wasn't that paper part of the original disclosure? I may need to petition Judge McKenzie to find out if anything else hasn't been disclosed."

I thought I saw a change in his expression. Had I surprised him?

"Ellis," he said, after a moment's reflection, "Harpur's money has no part in this. I assure you the Crown has signed no such paper. I instruct you not to seek any further disclosure. Don't forget that whatever else I am, I am still an officer of the court. I know that nothing is missing from this case. Just get that greenhorn off the matter and dump the reporter." He glanced at the guards. "Or all the recommendations in the world will be powerless to save your career."

Before I could react, the guards sprang to life and spirited him away, just as though they were servants eager to do his bidding.

I didn't follow Stow's instructions, not exactly. On Monday, I asked Nicky to sit in the body of the court, behind Stow, rather than at the counsel table at the front. I told him to take careful notes because I was going to be on my own when it came to the cross-examination of Ellen's expert.

"This drug Somatofloran," Ellen said. "What does it do, exactly?"

"Somatofloran is an oxygen-absorption inhibitor," the witness answered. "It slows the absorption of oxygen into the blood."

"For what purpose?"

"In certain patients, the blood absorbs oxygen too rapidly. This causes a sort of internal hyperventilation—just as if the patient were breathing too shallowly and too rapidly. Under such circumstances, the body receives the false signal that it is no longer necessary to breathe because no further oxygen is needed."

"The patient would stop breathing—that is, would suffocate—if there was an overdose of Somatofloran?"

"No. Quite the opposite," the witness said. "Somatofloran is used when the patient's breathing is lazy. It causes the body to compensate for a lack of oxygen by increasing the rate of breathing. The very worst that could happen with an overdose of this drug is that the patient might actually hyperventilate, that is, breathe too rapidly. The patient might then briefly lose consciousness, but his or her body would soon compensate by beginning to seek oxygen again. I mean the resumption of normal breathing, albeit at the usual 'lazy' rate."

Ellen appeared to ponder this information. She was stalling on purpose so that the jury had more time to consider the witness's remarks.

"Let me be certain that I understand this, Doctor," she said. "A person—say Mrs. Stoughton-Melville—is not breathing as efficiently as she should. So she's chosen to take part in the Somatofloran trials. Is that right?"

"Yes."

"Okay. She's given the drug—in the proper dosage, of course—and her breathing becomes easier because the drug increases her rate of breathing. Correct?"

"Correct so far. Yes."

"But somehow she is, let us say, *accidentally* given too much of the drug. The result then is hyperventilation. An undesirable but not fatally dangerous situation, am I right?"

"You are right," the doctor said. I could tell he was beginning to be impatient with the slowness of the questioning. Good. Maybe I could make him even more impatient, make him annoy the jury.

"Bear with me for a moment, Dr. Swan," Ellen said, sounding pleased with her own sensitivity to the needs of the witness as well as the jury. "We just want to make sure we are clear on this. So," she rose slightly on her toes, "if this drug is in itself benign, easing the breathing of patients, and if the sole effect of an overdose is to cause momentary hyperventilation, which, though uncomfortable, is a fairly common and natural occurrence, then how could such a drug be suspected of being used to murder someone?"

It is an old trick of the prosecution to pretend to be puzzled as to how a murder could possibly have taken

207

place, and one that Ellen had mastered. Her witness was primed to tell the jury exactly how my client could have done away with his wife.

"The fact is," Dr. Swan said, "that if the patient had received an excess of Somatofloran, she would have momentarily stopped breathing because her body would have registered a surfeit of oxygen. Under such circumstances, the slightest interference with her regaining control of her breathing would have resulted in the complete inability to resume the natural function."

The doctor didn't look at the jury. Perhaps he could sense that he needed to be clearer. "What I mean is, the patient would have been in such a state that even holding a hand in front of her nose and mouth for a few seconds might have rendered her unable to catch her breath."

"So she would have suffocated without a fight?"

"Yes," the doctor said. "Normally a person puts up a powerful fight when anyone or anything interferes with breathing. An overdose of Somatofloran would have made that struggle impossible."

"I see," Ellen commented, as if she'd finally understood a difficult point. "Thank you for that lucid explanation, Doctor."

I fought the urge to object. Unlike in trials on TV, objections are fairly rare in actual criminal trials, and are perceived as a rude interruption of the opposing counsel's presentation. But it was improper for Ellen to praise her own witness while he was still on the stand.

"There's another area we need to cover, Doctor," she said. "I would like the jury to know why incriminating irregularities were discovered after so long a time."

Now I did spring up. "Objection!" I declared a little too loudly. "Counsel cannot make findings as to the incriminating nature of evidence. Only the jury can do that." I turned slightly so that I could glance at Nicky. He nodded. Stow frowned as if well aware we were not following his specifications. Tough!

"Sustained." McKenzie was not one for elaborating on his decisions.

"I apologize, Your Honor," Ellen said evenly. "Dr. Swan," she continued, "why are we looking at this matter after so long a time has passed?"

The doctor opened the slim leather portfolio he had carried with him to the stand and extracted a single sheet of paper. He appeared to slowly peruse it without a lot of regard for the jury, most of whom were leaning forward in anticipation. Finally he deigned to ask, "Your Honor, may I consult my notes?"

McKenzie nodded without looking at the witness or his papers. "If it will assist, and if counsel has no objection, then by all means."

Dr. Swan adjusted a pair of rimless eyeglasses perched on the end of his long narrow nose. "In a clinical study conducted at Riverside Hospital over a period of three months approximately six years ago, we gave a group of elderly patients a regular course of Somatofloran with the objective of assessing the drug's ability to cure moderate to severe respiratory impairment. Naturally, each patient's results were carefully monitored." He found and held up a second sheet of paper. "This," he said, "is the report on Harpur Stoughton-Melville."

Ellen stepped closer to the witness stand and, not to be undone in dramatic effect, I approached the witness, too. "Dr. Swan," she said, "can you tell the jury what this report says?"

"Well," he answered, "it shows the day-to-day dosage given to Mrs. Stoughton-Melville for the first thirty days of the drug trial."

"And during those days, was there evidence that Mrs. Stoughton-Melville was responding to the drug you administered?"

"Yes," Dr. Swan said, tapping the paper in his hand as though he were sending a short message in code. "For the first thirty days of the trial, Mrs. Stoughton-Melville's body was found to absorb exactly the amount of Somatofloran that we expected for a woman of her age and body weight."

"Okay," Ellen said, moving away from the witness and closer to the center of the room, closer to Stow. She glared at me, and I moved back to my place at the defense table. "So Mrs. Stoughton-Melville was showing no unusual reactions to this drug?"

"Not in the way in which the drug was absorbed."

"In any other way?"

"No."

Ellen jotted something down on a long pad of lined yellow paper. "You said, Dr. Swan, that the drug tests went on for three months, did you not?"

I glanced at the jury. They seemed to be following every word of this.

"Yes, Madame Crown."

"So I assume, then, that there were subsequent reports at intervals during those months?"

"There was one final report at the end of the third month," Dr. Swan said.

"And did Mrs. Stoughton-Melville's report show any abnormalities at that time?"

"No. The report showed the same results as the other report," he answered. "Normal."

Ellen thought about that for a moment. Then she raised herself up on her toes ever so slightly. "Dr. Swan," she said, "you alerted the administrators of Riverside Hospital that you suspected grave irregularities in the toxicology report on the body of Mrs. Stoughton-Melville more than five years after her death. Why would you do such a thing—so long after the fact and especially when your own drug trials showed no irregularities prior to her death?"

The witness adjusted his glasses and also his shoulders. He squared himself and faced Ellen with his body erect, as though to emphasize the importance of what he was about to say. "It was not the results of the initial tests that caused me to suspect that something was amiss," he testified. "Part of this study was to test the long-term effects of patients who took Somatofloran. A significant aspect of that portion of the trial was the assessment of the time it took for the by-products of Somatofloran to completely leave the body. In the early stages of testing, that is, during the trials in which Mrs. Stoughton-Melville was a participant, we had a breakdown product problem."

"I beg your pardon?" Ellen said. "Could you repeat that, please?"

"We had a problem with the length of time it took Somatofloran to break down in the body. Several years later, after a good deal more research and development, we felt we understood the breakdown product problem. But to help us be sure, we decided to go back to our records of the earlier tests in order to compare breakdown and residue times. Of the original sample of patients at Riverside, about 12 percent were deceased. As part of our study, we had asked the hospital to do toxicology tests at the time of death of patients who had been in our sample. The hospital agreed to keep the results of those tests on file. When we studied the file on Mrs. Stoughton-Melville, we noted that at the time of her death, her body contained five times the amount of Somatofloran breakdown products that we would have anticipated."

"I see," Ellen said. "The amount of drug residue you found in her body struck you as unusual?"

"Given the amount of drug administered in our tests, the residue at the time of her death was not just unusual, it was inexplicable."

"Is that why you contacted police, Doctor?"

A smug, self-righteous grin wrinkled the pharmacologist's lips. "We have the highest standards for the tests we conduct," he said, "and we cooperate fully whenever there is any question of the misuse of our products. We felt that there might be a criminal explanation for this unusual result. We felt it our duty . . ."

"Thank you, Doctor," Ellen said, cutting him off before he went one step too far.

I risked a glance at the jury. All but two of them looked puzzled. Either they were confused or else they were still pondering the implications of Dr. Swan's testimony.

But the two who did not look confused knew exactly what the doctor was saying. He was saying that Harpur had been given an overdose of a drug that would not have killed her itself, but would have made it easy to kill her by other means. By the brush of a hand across her face, by the briefest contact of a scarf, a pillow, the edge of a sheet. Even, it seemed, by turning her head so that her mouth and nose made contact with her bed. Clever, effective and impossible to trace. Only the presence of an eyewitness could prove murder here. But where *was* the eyewitness?

"Please remain where you are, Dr. Swan," Ellen concluded. "Mr. Portal may wish to ask you a few questions." She fiddled with her papers, swept them into a pile, resumed her seat. Slowly I rose, testing the feel of my gown against my knees, the way a man who has not swum in a while tests the waves.

I moved to the lectern, adjusted it a bit so that to lean against it would put me in profile to the jury but face-to-face with the witness. I have always been praised for my profile. I did not fiddle with papers. I carried none. What I had to ask Dr. Swan was clear in my mind, and I needed to impress but two members of the jury—the two who understood the implications of Dr. Swan's testimony. Nobody else mattered.

I did not fidget, or clear my throat, or grasp the lectern in my hands, or rise up on the balls of my feet.

"Good morning, Dr. Swan," I said, and I smiled.

The sanctimonious little prig did not smile back. Ellis Portal 1. Witness 0.

"Did I hear correctly that the problem the Somatofloran trials were intended to investigate was the erratic breakdown of the product once it entered the body?"

"It was not erratic exactly, it was . . ."

There was quite a pause. I just stood there waiting.

"It was not as fast or as complete as we finally achieved."

"I see. So at the time Mrs. Stoughton-Melville had Somatofloran administered, there were questions concerning just how long the drug would remain in the body?"

"Yes. The drug remained too long."

"Too long," I repeated, letting the words echo in the large courtroom. "Tell me, Doctor," I asked, "is there a difference between the physiology of the living and of the dead?"

He looked startled. "Of course there is," he answered after a few seconds. "That is the meaning of death itself."

"I understand. So if you are in the business of selling drugs, then it matters to you whether the customer is alive or dead."

"Objection!"

My daughter rose to her feet. I could only see her from behind, but I knew by her posture that she was not angry, but keen.

Judge McKenzie nodded and Ellen sat down.

"Mr. Portal," the judge said, "considering that you have been away from the bar for a period of time, I'm willing to allow some latitude, but I'm sure you recollect that disparaging the reputation of a witness by gratuitous insults will not advance your cause."

I bowed my head in obeisance. Judges need to garner some trial attention, too.

"Pardon me, Dr. Swan," I resumed. "What I meant to ask is simply this: Does the physiology of the body change dramatically at the time of death?"

"Yes, of course," he answered. "Once the heart and brain cease to function, various chemical processes immediately begin to alter the body."

"So that you can't really tell, can you, by examining a cadaver what effect a drug may have had on that person during life?"

"That depends entirely on the chemical substances in question—and, of course, on the condition of the deceased."

"I imagine the condition of the deceased would be rather obvious, wouldn't it?"

There was a titter from several jurors.

"Clearly what I mean," the witness said, "is that variable factors come into play: the pathological reasons for death, the weight of the body. Even the temperature of the room. And also," the doctor added, "the gender and age of the person who has died."

"The age . . ." I said, as if pondering those words. "Tell me, Dr. Swan, what would you say is the average age of patients at Riverside Hospital?"

Ellen sprang to her feet again. "He's asking the witness to speculate, Your Honor."

"Dr. Swan is an expert witness," I retorted. "Surely he can offer an opinion on the average age of his study group."

"That's not the question counsel asked," Ellen replied hotly.

The judge responded, "I do think Mr. Portal is asking for an opinion rather than inviting speculation. Proceed, sir." He nodded toward me, and Ellen sat down. Now she *was* angry. But only a little. Temper ran in my family, but I always felt it was diluted in my children by the calm personality of their mother.

"I can rephrase the question, Your Honor," I said graciously. "Mr. Swan, in the studies you performed—upon the living and upon the recently deceased—approximately what percentage of the patients were elderly?"

"Elderly?" he asked, stalling, as if he weren't sure what "elderly" meant.

"Old, Dr. Swan. What percentage of the population you tested were over sixty-five?"

"Pretty much all of them. That was the whole point of the drug trials. To see whether Somatofloran, when administered in a premeasured syringe, could regulate the breathing of elderly patients with respiratory difficulties and do so without harmful buildup of breakdown residues in the bloodstream."

I heard what the doctor said, but his words skittered across my brain without sinking in because I was stuck on one word. *Syringe.*

I felt my previous trancelike state begin to steal up on me again, and I fought hard to keep my mind on the evidence of the witness. It was as though my brain had split, one half listening to Dr. Swan, the other elsewhere.

Syringes lie scattered on the tile floor. What is this place? Some dive that Queenie and I find ourselves in? Some den of the devil?

"Mr. Portal, please proceed if you are not finished. If you are finished, please sit down."

The judge's words jolted me back to an embarrassed consciousness. "Yes. Yes of course, Your Honor. So, Dr. Swan," I went on, "in your opinion, how likely is it that participants in your study might have died of natural causes shortly after you administered the drug?"

"Elderly people can be expected to die of old age, Mr. Portal. Our study has nothing to do with that fact."

I could see my daughter squirm. She was longing to rise, to suggest that I was misleading the jury because Harpur Stoughton-Melville had not been elderly when she died. But there were no grounds thus far to take exception to my line of questioning. Ellen would just have to squirm until I made my point.

"So it's not really cause for surprise when a resident of Riverside dies, is it?"

"Not particularly."

"Even if they are not old. Harpur Stoughton-Melville wasn't yet sixty, was she?"

"No."

"But she'd been ill for a while, correct?"

"Yes."

"Ill enough to be placed among people who were elderly and in need of constant care, am I right?"

Unable to restrain herself, Ellen rose. "I don't know where this is leading, Your Honor. The questions strike me as irrelevant."

"Focus, Mr. Portal," the judge warned.

"Yes. Okay. So, Dr. Swan, can you tell us what was so surprising about Harpur Stoughton-Melville's death that you had to report it to the authorities? She was incapacitated enough to have been in a hospital for the elderly—before her own time. She had a fatal illness. Five years have passed since her death."

"Yes, but . . ."

"The drug she had been given could not cause death."

"No, but . . ."

"Dr. Swan, do you know what Occam's razor is?"

"I believe I've heard the term," he replied uncomfortably.

"Could you tell the jury what you understand to be the meaning of that phrase?"

"I don't think I can," he said, glancing down at his notes hopelessly.

"Allow me to assist you," I said to the witness. "Occam's razor is a philosophical principle that says that entities must not be needlessly multiplied. Plainly put, Dr. Swan, that means that when there is a simple answer to a question, that answer is most likely to be correct. There is no need to seek complicated and arcane solutions to problems with obvious answers. Now, Doctor, under ordinary circumstances, if a person has a terminal disease and that person dies, what is the most reasonable, I mean the simplest, conclusion you could reach?"

"That the patient died of her illness, but—"

I waited, but he added nothing. "I have one further question, Dr. Swan. Can you please tell this court whether Somatofloran is in use today?"

"No, sir. It's been withdrawn from the market."

As the witness stepped down, McKenzie called the morning break. Ellen accosted me before I got out of the courtroom. She didn't seem to mind that the court staff could hear our conversation. Having once been court staff myself, I trusted them to keep quiet about it.

"What are you trying to prove, Daddy?"

"That should be obvious. That you can't establish the guilt of my client."

"That's not what I mean," she declared in outrage. "You're deliberately misleading that jury. Do you really expect them to believe that Harpur died of natural causes?"

She was really worked up. "Take it easy, little one. Take a break." *Uh-oh. Big mistake!*

"Don't you *dare* call me 'little one,'" she hissed.

"I'll stop calling you 'little one' if you stop standing on your tippie-toes in court."

She shot me a look of pure fury. "Take your own break," she declared and stomped off, letting the huge wooden door of the courtroom bang behind her.

I took a walk to cool off, and when I got back ten minutes later, Ellen seemed to have calmed down, too. The doors to the courtroom were still locked for the break, and we found ourselves alone in the corridor. "You've got to put Stow on the scene if all your witnesses' testimony is going to mean something, Ellen."

"You don't need to give me lessons anymore, Daddy," she answered. "Of *course* I'm about to put Stow there."

"But what or who is the grand slam?" I asked her. "Aren't you obligated to let us know?"

"I don't know what you're talking about," she said. She gave me another of her exasperated you-don't-know-squat looks. Her head held high, her body stiff, she moved toward the high wooden door of the courtroom, suddenly surrounded by her coterie of police officers.

I have made too many mistakes in my life, and it looked now as if my rehabilitation had not taught me better. This case would surely cause irreparable damage between me and my child. How could I have been enjoined to oppose her? *Total folly, Ellis, you dunce.* Somehow, though, I had to honor my commitment without completely losing my daughter's love and respect. I could easily see that her method of constructing her case limited her legally. Because of the rules of full disclosure, no witnesses or exhibits that she hadn't told us about ahead of time could be introduced. The only way she could surprise the jury was by slanting or interpreting the evidence in some unknown manner. I looked around for Nicky to ask him what he thought about all this, but I didn't see him, and I was glad he was nowhere around when the guards escorted Stow into court.

As Ellen's next witness, a middle-aged female hospital administrator, went through the preliminaries of laying her credentials before the court, I studied her tired, serious face. It was vaguely familiar. Had I seen this person before? Her long list of assignments and accomplishments told me nothing. As with most expert and professional witnesses, the more she talked about herself, the more she seemed to disappear. Until she mentioned the dates of her service. Then I knew she'd been there when I, myself, had been a regular visitor of Harpur's.

"Do you keep a list of volunteers who regularly visit Riverside patients?" Ellen asked.

"We have no volunteers," the woman answered. "No one is allowed on hospital grounds except patients and staff. Front-line staff, incidentally, never go home during their shift, which lasts three months. That's because of the isolation regulations."

"That's now. But at the time in question?" Ellen prompted.

"At the time in question, that is, about six years ago— long before 9/11 and SARS—we were not so security-conscious."

"Do you recall procedures for volunteer visitors then?" Ellen asked.

It was evident that the witness was responsible and that she'd given her testimony a lot of thought. "I've checked our records," she said. "At the time that Mrs. Stoughton-Melville died, we employed a reusable-pass system."

Ellen made a great show of writing the phrase down. It was always dramatic to painstakingly make notes if you wanted the jury to pay particular attention. For all I knew, Ellen might have been jotting down a list of groceries to pick up for supper.

The witness continued, "Up until December of 2001, we kept a box of numbered passes on the counter that separated the nursing station from the bank of elevators that ran along the west side of our wing."

I tried to picture the layout. I could, of course, ask to see Ellen's exhibit again, but that wasn't the same as being able to see what the woman was describing from my own memory. I forced myself to listen carefully, remembering how my mind had wandered before.

"How did that pass system work exactly?" Ellen prodded.

"Well, when a visitor came onto the floor—usually just off the elevator—they reached into the box and pulled out a pass. The passes were on a sort of string, and it went around the neck." She made a motion with her hand. "You know," she said, "like the ones they use at conventions."

"I see," Ellen said. "And was there any written record kept of the pass-holders?"

The woman looked a little sheepish. "Well," she answered, "to tell the truth, no. At first we had a book—you know, we used those log books, and when visitors came in, we asked them to write down the number of the pass they'd taken and their name, but sometimes they forgot."

"Will you tell the court what happened to those log books?"

The woman looked surprised, as if this were the first question she'd failed to anticipate. "I—I don't know," she said. "I guess they've been filed away in storage or something. All I remember is that one day they just weren't out anymore."

My turn.

"Are you saying visitors came and went at the hospital without staff knowing who they were?" I began.

"Well, we knew the regulars," the woman answered defensively.

"After six years, Madame, I don't suppose you would remember who any of those visitors might have been?"

She stared at me. "*You were one*," she answered.

Or at least that's what I thought she answered. "What did you say, Madame? Who did . . . ?" I felt my heart begin to pound. I glanced at the jury. They sat motionless, waiting for me to say something more. McKenzie was staring. Ellen, whose back was to me, sat immobile.

"Are you having trouble hearing, Mr. Portal?" the judge asked, not succeeding in masking his impatience.

"I'm sorry, sir," I said, confused. "Might I ask the witness to repeat her answer?"

Pay attention, Ellis. Pay attention.

"You asked whether I remembered who the volunteer visitors were six years ago, and I answered that I remembered a few, but not every one. Sometimes people look familiar—like you. But the only one I remember for sure is the patient's husband, Justice Stoughton-Melville."

"Good," I said, as if a golden opportunity was presenting itself to my client. "He came regularly to see his wife?"

"No," the witness said a little regretfully.

I heard one of the jurors sigh. I hoped that Nicky was behind me taking notes again and that he was writing down *which* juror.

"Can you tell the court why Justice Stoughton-Melville might have been severely limited in his ability to visit his beloved wife?"

The witness smiled. "He had to live in Ottawa because of his duties on the Supreme Court," she said. "But I remember him well because it was a big occasion when he could come. He had a driver and a bodyguard. Sometimes a secretary was with them, too. And I remember I saw him by himself in the lobby the night Mrs. Stoughton-Melville died. I was going to tell him how sorry I was that she was doing so poorly, but the elevator door closed before I could. He seemed really sad. He wasn't in his wife's room when I got there a few minutes later. I never saw him again until the next morning. Then I told him how sorry I was that his wife had died in the night."

"When you saw him that next morning, Madame, what was his reaction to the mention of his wife's death?"

"He was devastated," the woman said quickly and firmly. "He acted like he had lost his best friend."

Chapter 14

"You're looking good up there."

"If you say so, Aliana." Exhausted after the long day of cross-examination, I wasn't up to dealing with the press, especially my private reporter. Prior to 9/11, it had been easy to sneak out of the courthouse and avoid them, but now, getting out was as carefully monitored as getting in. There were only three doors through which one could exit, and only one person at a time through each door. Reporters and TV interviewers waited outside like so many vultures. Not that Aliana needed any assistance in capturing her prey.

She grabbed one of the banker's boxes that I had to carry back to the office and slid it onto the little cart Nicky and I used. Why couldn't she leave me alone, as the other spectators had, including Anne? That one *would* disappear when I needed to know how the tests we'd taken for little Sal had come out.

"Nicky's gone?"

"I thought he deserved a decent evening, so I sent him on his way," I told her. It was none of her business that Nicky had to lie low because of Stow's command.

"Ellis, winning this case is a no-brainer," she insisted, and tagged along to my car. She heaved the banker's box into the trunk like a weightlifter. The same could not be said of me.

"You're as sharp as ever," she persisted. "And a lot cooler."

"Thanks for the help, Aliana. Bye." I rushed to the driver's side. Before I could stop her she had slipped into the front seat, showing quite a bit of leg. She had the slim thighs and shapely calves of a much younger woman. Probably from running up and down the courthouse steps chasing interviewees like me.

"Ellis," she said, "why don't we relax somewhere and just have a little chat?"

"Look, Aliana, I'm not in a position to 'chat' with the media. I think you should get out of the car."

That was too harsh, and I instantly regretted my meanness. I owed Aliana more than I could repay. If it hadn't been for her reporting, there was a good chance I would have been forgotten—just one more loser who couldn't hack it. But she'd been there for me when I'd been down and she'd lifted me up by her attention and, above all, by her excellent writing. Nevertheless, she was a pain in the butt.

"Look," I said, "I've got time to answer a few questions, but I don't want to compromise myself by . . ."

"By being seen alone with me? Don't be ridiculous. This is a public parking space."

So I gave her what I'd hoped would be a short interview, careful to say nothing quotable and not mentioning Stow at all.

But nothing is ever short when Aliana goes into reportorial mode. It was past midnight by the time I had gotten rid of her. "By the way," she said as a sort of parting shot, "your friend Queenie Johnson is up against the wall. The city's cracking down on her clinic. Budget cuts or something. I hear she's got to be out of there by the end of the week." She flounced away. "Bye."

I guess I had it coming. I grabbed something to eat, then drove to the clinic. I saw that the light in Queenie's office was still on. I stopped, ready to park and go up to check on her, but then I thought better of it. Would she be humiliated by this turn of events? Would she resent my interference? I drove away.

The hell with it. It was the middle of the night, and Queenie might be angry, but I stopped the car after a few blocks. I had to know what Queenie was thinking, what she planned to do next.

By the time I got back to the intersection, I was too late. No light shone from the office. The door was locked tight. I saw with poignant dismay a neatly handwritten sign that read, "Thanks for coming to this clinic. It's closed now, but you can find another location to help you by calling the city health department at 647-555-1212." I recognized the large, almost childlike handwriting.

She looks up at me, and I see the embarrassment—no, the fear *in her face. "I don't like people to know I can't do this," she says.*

I shake my head. "There's nothing to be afraid of—ashamed of." I put the pencil between her fingers and cover her hand with my own. Slowly, I guide her as the pencil slides across the page. "There. This is your name," I tell her, "and before the hour is up, you'll be able to write it on your own."

"Doubt it," she answers, pulling away. But I can see that she's eager to learn. I put the pencil between her fingers again. I cover her hand with mine.

I stood on the sidewalk for a few minutes, before it occurred to me that during the hours in which I'd let Aliana stroke my ego, I could have been helping Queenie deal with her crisis. I had betrayed her.

When I got home, despite the hour, I called her at her house. She didn't answer. She didn't answer the next morning, either.

Ellen was the first person I encountered in court that day.

"What's the matter with you? You look lousy. You're not sick, are you? I'm not going up against you if you're not well. I'll ask McKenzie to adjourn."

"Take it easy, little one. I'm fine. Bring 'em on."

Ellen frowned, cocked her head, studied my face. I wished I could reach over and tousle her black curls, as I had done a thousand times over the years. "Thanks for your concern, sweetie," I said, and I winked. She crossed her eyes and grimaced.

Her officer-in-charge caught this exchange and laughed, which must have embarrassed Ellen because she was exceptionally fierce that day, beginning with a painstaking examination of her police fingerprint specialist.

"Five years ago, you were called to Riverside Hospital to investigate a break-in on the third floor in an area colloquially referred to as 'the drug vault.' Is that correct?"

"Yes, ma'am," the expert answered.

"Tell us if you saw anything unusual there. Take your time. We're here to listen."

I rose. "Your Honor," I objected, "I don't think Counsel needs to coach the witness."

"He's right, Ms. Portal," McKenzie warned. "Just ask the questions."

Maybe Ellen scowled. I could only see her back. But her voice sounded gruffer when she carried on. "Tell us what you saw that day."

"May I use my notes?"

I had no objection. The expert thumbed through a small black book. He glanced at a page for a few seconds before he said, "On the night of December 28, I was dispatched to Riverside to check on a reported break-and-enter in the secure area of the third floor, a large walk-in closet commonly called 'the drug vault.' When I arrived on the scene, I found no damage to the closet or the lock. But I did find that several shelves of the vault were in disarray."

"Disarray?"

"Yes. Like somebody had broken open a glass case and extracted a tray of syringes."

"Tray?" Ellen asked. "How did you know it was a tray?"

"It was a prepackaged type of drug. I'd seen packaging like it before. The doses are prepared at the pharm lab ahead of time and packaged a couple dozen to the tray. The whole setup is disposable."

"You say you've seen such packaging before?" Ellen prompted.

"Yes." The officer turned and spoke directly to the jury. Expert police officers often got away with a tactic like that. I didn't like it, but I didn't object. "Unfortunately," he continued, "I get called in on a lot of drug thefts at hospitals. This type of setup is common when a large number of patients receive a standard dose of medication at the same time."

"Can you give us an example of the administration of drugs under such circumstances?" Ellen queried.

"Yes. Sometimes at mental health centers and also at seniors' homes, trays of prepackaged injections are passed out to nurses to give to patients to facilitate falling asleep."

"Are you aware of such a procedure at Riverside Hospital, Officer?"

"Not personally, ma'am, no," the expert answered.

Ellen jotted something down. Several members of the jury watched her, as though wishing they could read what she had written. I wished the same.

"Officer," Ellen resumed, "this missing tray of syringes, was it eventually found intact?"

"No."

"Some syringes had been removed?"

The witness gave the matter a moment's thought. "I don't know about them being removed as such," he said. "The seal on the tray may have broken when the thief took it out of the cabinet. At any rate, I found three full syringes on the floor of the vault."

"How could you tell they were from the tray that was stolen?"

"Because all the trays were numbered and so were all the syringes, and the numbers were keyed to each other."

"And three syringes from the stolen tray had fallen to the floor?"

I was watching Ellen rise almost imperceptibly onto her toes and back down when I thought about that haunting image again. The image of the three syringes left on the floor of the closet. Two dozen minus three? That left twenty-one syringes in my mind's eye that insinuated themselves without my bidding.

But I had never been near the drug vault. If only I could get into Riverside! I didn't even have a clear idea of where that closet was despite the testimony. But now I would get a chance to examine the schematics that Ellen began to introduce. "Your Honor," she said, "this is a schematic of the drug vault on the third floor of Riverside Hospital. May I enter it as an exhibit, then show it to the ladies and gentlemen of the jury?"

The court clerk took the large piece of poster board from Ellen's outstretched hands, pasted onto it a small label and gave the label a good smack with a big rubber stamp. Then she wrestled with the board until she could maneuver it backward over her head and into the waiting hands of the judge.

McKenzie studied the diagram for a few minutes. No emotion registered on his calm face as he studied the picture.

"Proceed."

I moved away from the defense counsel table, closer to the witness. As I did so, I caught a glimpse back into the body of the court. One of the reporters in the first row of the spectators' benches was peering at the diagram through opera glasses.

I moved closer still, not caring whether I obstructed the journalist's sight line, but careful to avoid blocking the view of the jurors or of Stow. I put on my reading glasses and studied the Crown's schematic.

There was the square representing the drug vault. I saw that it lay before a double door through which was an elevator and, farther down the hall and around the corner, the door to the stairwell that I had used to climb to Harpur's room. It was a long hallway. If the thief had indeed been Stow, as Ellen was attempting to prove, it would have taken him some time to go through the doors, past the elevator and up the three flights to Harpur's room carrying a stolen tray of syringes.

Of course, there were other staircases. I thought about the very courthouse in which we now found ourselves, a building with which I was intimately familiar. There was an elevator, a central escalator, a central stairwell and four additional stairwells, one in each corner. The hospital was a larger building. It must have at least as many staircases as the courthouse. So, if Stow had indeed taken the elevator from the lobby to the drug vault as the evidence seemed to suggest, then he had a choice of routes from there to Harpur's room.

"Now, Officer," Ellen said, holding up a red pen, "I want you to mark an X on each and every spot on this schematic that corresponds to where you found fingerprints."

I moved away as the witness stepped down, level with the jury box. He took the pen from Ellen's hand and peered at the schematic myopically. He lifted the pen. He made three careful X's, and then, without a word, he climbed back up onto the witness stand.

"Okay," Ellen said, studying the position of the dramatic red X's. "Okay." She walked away from the schematic. Toward it. Away again.

Meryl Streep at work.

McKenzie watched Ellen intently. Like every judge in the land, he prided himself on his impartiality, but it seemed to me that his favoritism in this trial leaned toward the Crown.

"Will you please tell the jury where these marked locations were?" Ellen said.

"Yes," the witness answered. "The first X, the one on the right side of the drawing, represents a location on a door leading from the drug vault to the central area of the floor near the elevators. The mark beside that indicates the location of fingerprints on the exterior door of the elevator. The remaining X marks three prints very close together inside the vault."

"Did you follow standard procedure in obtaining these prints?" Ellen asked.

The witness seemed to give careful thought to his next words. "Ordinarily," he began, "I would not have bothered to fingerprint doors and elevators, because areas like that have so much traffic that one person's prints are quickly wiped off by the prints of another. Besides, with hundreds of possible prints on every square inch of such a surface, there's not much chance of a match. And unless a culprit is a repeat offender who has been printed before, there's nothing to match the new prints to."

"What was different in this case?" Ellen asked. "You said that ordinarily you wouldn't have checked doors and elevators for prints."

"Here we had three good prints on the wall, door and cabinet in the drug vault. Very clear prints. Once we got them—immediately on our arrival on the scene—we proceeded to dust public areas in the hope of determining how the culprit might have escaped, what route he might have taken out of the hospital. We had no luck. Merely finding matching prints in the public areas told us nothing we could use to apprehend the thief." He paused as if awaiting instructions from Ellen. The Crown witnesses were as groomed as thoroughbreds, as though they had gone through their paces ahead of time.

"Go on, then, sir," Ellen said. "Tell us whether you confined yourself to the fingerprint dusting you conducted immediately after the break-in."

"I didn't," the witness said. "We decided to fingerprint staff who worked near the drug vault to see whether anyone working in or near the drug station that night might have been involved in the theft."

"And?" Ellen let the question hang in the air.

"We found no matches. So we filed the case, set it aside as pretty much unsolvable. It wasn't such a big deal, really, because the drugs that were stolen were not opiates or hallucinogens and therefore had limited value on the street. We more or less let the whole thing drop. Until . . ."

"Until?" Ellen asked, feigning surprised interest.

"Until we heard about Mrs. Stoughton-Melville's case being reopened. We were informed by the hospital that it now suspects she was injected with the same drug that was stolen. It got us to thinking. We checked out a few new angles, took another look at some facts from the old case, re-read some of the old records. On a hunch, I ran the prints I had found five years ago through the computer—I mean those clear prints from the drug vault. This time, I wasn't disappointed."

"What did you find?"

The face of the officer remained as it had been, polite, immobile. "I found that the prints matched those of Supreme Court Justice John Stoughton-Melville."

Perhaps I imagined the sound, but I thought I heard one or two of the jurors gasp.

"The prints of the Supreme Court Justice were on file?" Ellen asked, again in the tone of feigned surprise that indicated to me that she had been paying attention in advocacy class. "Why would that be?"

"Because of a routine background check now required of all appointees to the court."

"But Justice Stoughton-Melville had already been appointed at the time of his wife's death," Ellen pointed out.

"The checks were done after 9/11. Retroactive," the witness explained.

I wished Nicky could be in the courtroom. We were ready for this. We'd known from the start that it was coming. Ellen went on with the examination, but I just sat back and listened. I had my angle ready. When her questioning of the witness ended, I rose and slowly approached the man.

"Sir," I began, "you have told the jury that you found three fingerprints that you believe might match those of the accused before the court . . ."

"Not *might* match," the witness interrupted. "*Do* match."

"Perhaps, sir," I said, "you would be so good as to let me finish my question?"

"Sorry." To my surprise the witness blushed. Not good. More than half the jurors were women, and their sympathy toward the handsome young man thus embarrassed was obvious.

I nodded indulgently at his apology. "So," I repeated, "in your opinion, then, you found three fingerprints inside the drug vault at Riverside Hospital that appear to match some computer-generated representations of the fingerprints of my client?"

The witness, perhaps to spare himself further cause for blushing, answered right away with a simple yes.

"Thank you," I told him. "Now, could you please tell the jury again whether you found a print of three different fingers or three prints of the same finger?"

"I don't think I said, but it was three different fingers," he replied.

Giving the impression that this information was of great importance to my case, I stood still long enough to seem to ponder, to calculate. "Is it true, sir, that there are about ten areas on any given print that must match before you can offer an opinion that a print is from a particular person?"

"Yes."

"Okay. Let's look at some numbers. John Stoughton-Melville is blessed with the continued possession of the number of digits he had when he was born, am I right?"

"What?"

"He has ten fingers."

"Of course."

"So," I said, maintaining eye contact with the witness, "ten times ten equals one hundred."

"One hundred?"

"Yes. You have about thirty points of comparison from which you have concluded that my client was present in the drug vault?"

"I suppose, but . . ."

I interrupted the witness quickly. "As compared to one hundred points of comparison for both hands?"

"Yes. A hundred points of comparison could identify both hands."

"Then what you actually have here is a 30 percent chance of the fingerprints being those of John Stoughton-Melville?"

"Not exactly." The witness looked startled, as if he felt he had neglected some crucial piece of testimony.

"Well, you must agree, sir," I went on, "that you have relatively few matching points when you consider how many points it is possible to match overall?"

"We had enough to make the comparison," he persisted.

"Enough to make a comparison, yes. But to make an identification?" I shook my head ever so slightly. Before the witness could react, I said, "Thank you. Now let's move on to another area." I reached down and picked up a thick sheaf of notes that Nicky had prepared. "You said that you reviewed some of the evidence from five years ago. Is that correct?"

"Yes."

"Did you suspect that a homicide had been committed at the time the original fingerprints were collected?" I asked, "—all those years ago?"

"No. As I said, we were looking into a theft, not a murder."

"Exactly at what point did you make the connection between the fingerprints in the drug vault and the death of my client's wife? I mean in your own mind, sir."

The witness gave the matter a moment's deep consideration. "Recently," he firmly answered, "at about the same time as the results of the drug test were made known."

"Don't you find that rather strange, sir?" I asked. "Rather coincidental? You have drug tests suddenly appearing to show that Mrs. Stoughton-Melville was murdered five years ago. And then, lo, and behold—again after lying buried for five years—three perfect prints show up that just happen to belong to Mrs. Stoughton-Melville's husband! I call that quite a coincidence, don't you?"

"It's only a coincidence if the two events are not really connected," the witness replied.

"Oh, really?" I said, lightly mocking. "If the events were 'not really connected,' as you put it, then we really have no case at all, do we?"

"But they *are* connected."

"The death of Mrs. Stoughton-Melville and the missing drugs are connected? You're absolutely sure of that, even five years after the fact, five years in which nothing was done to find the real killer of Mrs. Stoughton-Melville?"

"I'm absolutely s-s-sure," the witness answered. But the stutter made him sound less certain.

I shook my head again. "Five years is a long time, sir, and a mere one-third chance of being right is the same thing as a two-thirds chance of being wrong, isn't it?"

"I don't know," the witness said, now licking his lips.

Which is where I ended my questioning. It's always good to get an expert to say those three words if he or she is testifying against a person you are trying to prove has done nothing wrong.

Though it was strictly against the rules, I followed my client when court was done for the day—right down into the sweat-smelling concrete bowels of the courthouse. I knew every staircase in the place. Besides, the guard escorting Stow that afternoon knew me.

"Tomorrow I've got to let His Honor know, Stow. I've got to tell the court whether we are going to call witnesses in your defense. I've snowed them with tricks as long as I can, but the end has come."

He smirked, but remained silent.

"You've got to instruct me," I persisted. A second guard joined the first and together they bolted Stow's shackles to the floor of the van that would speed him back to jail. "You've got to tell me what happened on that night."

"I didn't kill her," he said, and he signaled the driver as if he were in the backseat of a limo and the man was his chauffeur.

Later, I tried yet again to figure out Stow's behavior. I replayed my own actions in my mind over and over. What had I seen that fateful day? No one in Harpur's room. I remembered that it had been daylight when I'd arrived. I remembered seeing the children at play in the park beyond Harpur's window. I remembered sitting with her until it got dark. I remembered leaving her asleep, all traces of her sorrowful condition wiped clean by the smoothing blanket of slumber.

And then I remembered when I had seen the syringes spilled on the floor.

Chapter 15

Queenie's house was on a little cul-de-sac. I hesitated for an instant, framing in my mind the one question I had to get Queenie to answer. Then, I walked up to the brightly painted wooden door and pressed my finger to the bell.

And pressed.

When she finally came, it was clear that I'd awakened her. Surprise at seeing me caused her to rub her eyes sleepily.

"Queenie," I said, almost throwing myself into her arms, one hand poised on the door, one on the doorjamb, "thank God you're here."

She stared at me. "I wasn't missing," she finally said.

I moved toward her, but we didn't make contact because she spun around and led me down the short hallway into her small living room. When she flicked on the light, I saw the room was piled high with boxes.

"Why didn't you tell me they were closing the clinic? And why didn't you answer my phone calls last night?" I asked.

"It was no big deal." She shrugged. "And I was out." She pointed toward the one piece of furniture not covered with boxes, an armchair. I sank into it.

While she was making tea, I glanced around. Happy as I was to see that she was okay, I had something else just as urgent on my mind. "Queenie," I said when she came back, "I don't want to upset you the way I've done before, but I have to be straight. I came at this hour of the night because I need your help. I'm not going to beat around the bush."

"I'll help you if I can and if I want to." She pointed at the box on which she'd rested the tea tray and some sandwiches. "Eat something. You look like you need to."

I shook my head.

"Well, you *must* be in trouble if you're saying no to food." She pushed the tray away. "Okay, then. I'm listening."

I leaned closer to her. She smelled of the warmth of her bed. "Queenie," I said, "Stow is using me. All during this trial, he has refused to do or say anything in his own defense. Nicky and I have constructed the entire case simply from studying Ellen's disclosure—the material she gave us to show what she intended to prove against Stow."

Queenie nodded.

"The whole time," I went on, "I've wondered whether there was something that Ellen was holding back, some secret witness. That's illegal, but a really clever lawyer can find ways to spring something on the defense, especially if that something has been obvious all along. I have heard it said that the best way to hide a leaf is on a tree."

Queenie thought over that figure of speech and seemed to approve. "I think Ellen's secret witness has been in court all along. Every day," I said.

Queenie seemed interested in this assumption, moving closer to me, putting her warm hand on my cold one, encouraging me to continue.

"Today we had a witness who made me remember something I'd forgotten—something that could change this case entirely."

"What did you remember?"

I looked again around the room of the house that Stow had made possible for Queenie. "The time will come when I can tell you everything," I told her. I didn't add, *And you can tell me everything, too.* "But right now, about this one favor. I want you to call Riverside Hospital to determine whether there is anybody in quarantine. Whether there's anybody contagious or in any other way a danger to public health. Please, Queenie, I can't do this without you."

"Your Honor, nobody is allowed in Riverside except doctors or . . ."

"Exactly. One phone call, that's all I'm asking."

She raised her eyes, and it was as though I could read a thousand questions there. I admired her for not asking even one of them. She sighed, not something she usually did, and left the room.

After an eternity, she returned. I had heard no phone, no voices. I was so intent on her message that I didn't notice at first she was carrying a small package. "Your Honor," she said, "I don't know what you're up to, and I hope I don't find out. But I have the answer to your question, and then we're going to forget the whole thing. Deal?"

"Deal," I said, half grateful, half afraid.

"There is nobody contagious or quarantined in Riverside right now. If somebody breaches security, they will get arrested, but they won't get sick or spread a disease."

"Thank you, Queenie," I whispered. I leaned toward her and kissed her hair. She pulled away and pressed the parcel into my hand.

Later, in the car, I opened it. It was a surgical mask, a green plastic disposable gown and an envelope. I opened the envelope. Inside was Queenie's nurse ID, an electronic badge.

Northeast of the former Tent City encampment, on the edge of the Don valley, Riverside Hospital loomed like a fortified redoubt. If I hadn't known from past experience how to sneak up the steep valley walls and into the wooded area adjacent to the hospital parking lot, I would have been unable to breach the security of the hospital. City police officers with their cruisers blocked the main entrance off Gerrard Street. Armed contract-guards were closing off the paved path that led from Broadview past the Don Jail and across the front of Riverside. From the parking lot at the rear I could see the white isolation tents glowing in the cold night air. Lit from within, they looked almost festive, as if patients were awaiting guests for a lawn party instead of death.

From the shadows beneath the trees on the western side of the building, I watched the action near the tents. Several people I took to be front-line nurses and doctors were silhouetted against the white walls of each of the four tents. They seemed to be communicating at close quarters with their patients. Clearly, Queenie had been correct that there were no contagious cases in the hospital.

I watched and waited for the better part of two hours. It was almost dawn. I couldn't see my watch, but I didn't need it. I had lived in the valley as a vagrant for five long years. I could tell time by the way the moonlight fell on the water, by the sounds of the wildlife as foxes and raccoons scurried away from coming daylight and cardinals and jays sang its approach.

I was less successful at judging the coming and going of humans, because I was caught by surprise when the shift-change of non-front-line workers began. Secretaries, maintenance workers, nurses who dealt with records instead of people, all the workers who had no contact with patients in the facility. These people came and went on a regular schedule, though they had to be gowned and masked the same as nurses and doctors.

I slipped out of my jacket and donned the gown and the mask just in time to join the long line of males and females who moved toward a metal door beyond the fourth tent. When I finally got to the front of the line, I flashed my pass, like everyone else. I passed through without incident.

The long line proceeded down a corridor with a number of doors. I wasn't sure where I was, but I guessed that we were headed east, toward what had been the outer wall and the eastern stairwell in the old days. I guessed that that stairwell must lead to the quarantine area now. As we passed each door, a number of workers peeled off, until I alone was left at the end of the hall. In a matter of seconds, I was accosted by a guard. Not being able to do anything else, I flashed Queenie's pass again. "Special duty," I mumbled into my mask.

"Hold it up, please," the guard insisted.

If I were caught, I faced ninety days' quarantine followed by arrest. Without any hope of contacting Nicky on a daily basis, and with Stow's refusal to let Nicky represent him, our case would be declared a mistrial. All our work would be for naught. Plus there'd be no possibility of my returning to the courtroom, or to the law. I'd escaped the consequences of criminal behavior already in my life. I couldn't afford another misstep.

"If you are medical, why are you entering from a non-secure area?" the guard asked.

"Public health informed me there are no quarantines," I answered. "They said it would be okay to . . ."

"Can you step back, please?" he interrupted.

I did as he said. I stepped back. He pulled a black metal device from a loop on his belt. But it wasn't a weapon. It was some sort of communication tool. He pressed a button and held the thing to his ear.

I tried to look around without moving too much. My only escape route was the long corridor back toward the door to the parking lot. That door would be harder to get out of than into, if I knew anything about detention, which I certainly did.

In front of me, the door to the eastern stairwell beckoned, but between it and me stood the dragon.

Until the guard realized his communication device wasn't working. In an automatic gesture, he held the thing up and shook it. He only moved an inch or so, but suddenly I knew I could get by him.

I grabbed the door, pulled it open, jamming him behind it. I sprinted up the stairs as fast as my sixty-year-old legs could pump. My heart began to pound, my ears rushing with the roar of my own blood, I didn't realize at first that the stairwell was ringing with the pulsating screech of an alarm.

I'm running up the stairs. I reach Harpur's floor. I turn the corner. An old lady is down the hall, but she has nothing to do with me. I don't really see her. Or anybody. Because all I can think of is

Harpur. I feel a slight bump. I hear something fall and skitter across the floor. I glance down. A dozen or so syringes are scattered there. Half are full—blue. Half are empty—clear. I mumble a swift apology to the orderly who has bent down to pick them up.

I hurry to Harpur. I stay with her for a little while. I feel overwhelming relief. She has forgotten. She does not ask me again to help her to die. All she asks for is a drink of water. But when I come back with it, she has pulled the sheet up over her lower face, as if she were cold. I want to pull the blanket up, too, but she is so deeply asleep that I don't want to risk disturbing her by touching anything. It pleases me to see her so still, so peaceful.

After a little while, I leave her. I hand back my volunteer badge. I head for the elevator. All I'm thinking when I walk out of the hospital is that they've finally turned off those stupid Christmas carols.

I staggered, hit my hip against the stair rail and almost lost my balance. I could hear footsteps charging up the stairs behind me. Unless I found a hiding place this instant, Stow's case and my career were dead in the water. Unlike in the old days, every room and closet would be locked. It was hard to run up the stairs when it seemed there was no escape.

I reached a landing and grasped at the door handle. By some miracle, just inside was a cart with a box full of surgical masks. I jostled the cart hard enough for the masks to tip onto the floor. I leaned down to pick them up, believing hopelessly that my pursuers might think I was an orderly picking up supplies knocked over by a just-passing intruder. My fingers shook as I toyed with the objects on the floor. So when the pursuing footsteps ringing in the stairwell grew more and more distant, I clutched the cart for support while reminding myself that I had to breathe. *Inhale. Exhale. In. Out.*

Chapter 16

"Daddy, it's 5 a.m. What's the matter? Are you ready to concede?"

"Ellen, please, I know it's early. I need to talk. Just you and me."

In the background, I heard my son-in-law, Brad, protesting. But I didn't hear Ellen answer him. She was thinking—thinking, I was sure, about the perils of two opposing counsel meeting in secret to discuss the case.

"Where are you now?" she finally said.

"Downtown. I could come over there."

"No. I don't want to wake Angelo. Is there someplace else? Someplace where nobody from court is likely to see us?"

"Ellen, it *is* 5 a.m. Who but us would be out and about? And it's not that dangerous!"

I could almost hear her brain cells firing. "If anybody sees us together," she replied, stifling a yawn, "there could be a mistrial. This is my first case as a Senior Crown, Daddy, and . . ."

"And mine since I appeared there as a criminal? Look, Ellen, we're father and daughter. Who would think anything about our talking to each other?"

"At five in the morning?"

"All right," I retorted. "Make it 6:30. I must talk to you before court opens. There's a doughnut shop on the northwest corner of King and Church."

"Right." I thought she had hung up, but she added, "This isn't about the DNA tests, is it? Did you send that sample Mom asked you for?"

"No. Yes. I mean I did send the sample, but this is about something different."

"Okay, Dad. I'll be there if it means so much that you roust me from my warm, cozy bed."

The need to talk to my daughter occupied all my thoughts as I walked south and west toward our meeting place. The city was waking up. *Our* coffee shop would be open. Queenie's and mine. Hadn't we pulled all-nighters there when we were on the skids, making one doughnut between us last for hours?

Now that I could recollect the image of the syringes on the floor and the "orderly" picking them up the night Harpur had died, I felt I was destined to go down in flames. The most inattentive security guard was a mere blunderer compared with me. Was I under an obligation to disclose what I had recalled to the police? Was I guilty of obstruction of justice if I failed to do so?

And what would I say to Stow? He had tricked me—of that, I was sure. Disclosing this new evidence would force me to remove myself from his case. I would look like a fool. But I'd look even more a fool when I revealed that I'd suddenly recalled the presence of my client coming out of his wife's room. I was a witness. And not just a witness suddenly remembering important evidence, but the accused's counsel.

How was I to deal with Stow's lies about his presence at Riverside that night, about the drugs and about accidentally encountering me? Clients lied to their lawyers, sad but true, but to hide the fact that one's lawyer was an eyewitness to one's misdeed? And now I was on my way to spill the beans to my daughter. Nicky was right, I thought. I should get a life.

Day broke on one of those fresh April mornings with the sky a milky blue and the clouds translucent, high and scudding. I was admiring the view when I saw Ellen walking west on King Street toward me.

"Why in here, Daddy?" she said when we entered the doughnut shop, wrinkling her nose in distaste. I wanted to tell her to shape up and act like a lady because I didn't want to disrespect my old hangout. This was one of the few places in the redone and newly chic neighborhood that still gave decent treatment to the street's few remaining down-and-outs. "I would have thought they'd torn this dump down by now."

"Take it easy, Ellen. I like this place. It's where Queenie and I always meet."

"How is she?" Ellen asked, glancing around as if she expected to see Queenie in the flesh. "Back on the skids?"

"Watch your tongue, Ellen. I've had enough."

"Oooh, so defensive!"

I needed to keep cool. "I'm not sure exactly how Queenie is at the moment," I said evenly, "but as soon as I straighten up this mess, I intend to find out."

"Mess? You're in a mess?" She reached across the table and grabbed my hand. The strength of her grip surprised me.

247

"I think so," I said. "But let me just tell you . . ."

"Daddy, if you've discovered something that changes the course of the trial, the proper way to handle any new evidence is to get your client into court and lay it all out before the judge. Since you know this as well as I, I can only assume there is some extraordinary circumstance to make you reluctant to obey the rules. You're not going to ask me to assist you in breaching the court's accepted procedure, are you?"

Despite my fear over what I had discovered, I had to smile. My kid was as big a prig as I.

"So, let's speak only hypothetically at the moment," she continued. "You postulate a certain scenario, and then ask me what I would think if such a scenario were real."

I took a deep breath and plunged into the chaos. "Suppose," I said, "that a lawyer were defending a client that he did not know for sure was innocent."

"Daddy," she said with a mocking little laugh, "that's your only issue?"

"No. Suppose that this lawyer begins to suspect that his client is hiding information that would alter the direction of the case."

Ellen was silent for a moment. "Do you remember the Millerene tapes?" she asked.

"I think so. Millerene and her brother were charged with torturing, then murdering teenaged girls—and videotaping themselves while they were doing it. The police searched for the tapes, but never found them. During the trial, the male accused turned the tapes over to his defense lawyer, who kept them."

"Yes, something like that. But my point is, as I recall, the lawyer was found not guilty of obstructing justice."

"Which would mean?"

"That his primary duty lay with his client—with mounting a fair and full defense. I believe that under the law a lawyer is not obligated to reveal information that would damage his client's case, but I'd need to check before you can quote me on it. In any event, what we are—I mean *would be*—dealing with here is known as the difference between moral and legal guilt. Defense counsel need not concern herself with whether her client is morally guilty—that is, whether he has really done the deed—she only needs to know whether the client is legally guilty—that is, whether the case against the client can be proven by the Crown. And of course, what is not known or accepted by the jury as fact does not exist."

I persisted. This would put her knickers in a twist. "What if a lawyer found out that his client had hired him to prevent said lawyer from giving testimony?"

"What?" Ellen looked as alarmed as I had expected.

I hastened to add, "Theoretically, of course."

She answered slowly, as if she had suddenly discovered her law training to be lacking. "I don't know. I never heard of such a thing."

"Keeping this case hypothetical," I said, "here's an imagined scenario. A man commits a crime. He believes no one is a witness, but coincidentally, someone does see him, or at least sees something that would lead any reasonable person to conclude that he has just committed a crime. However, the culprit is not sure how much the witness actually did see and, more importantly, he does not know how much the witness realized he was seeing."

"I don't get it. Was the so-called witness blind?"

"No. Suppose he was in a hurry, or just distracted and depressed. How many times do we notice some act, but are unaware of its significance and therefore forget it immediately?"

Ellen nodded. "Once, Jeffrey and I were talking about our youth and all the things we did. I was shocked to discover that he remembered more about my behavior than I remembered myself. We discussed it, and Jeffrey pointed out that I'm not calm like him and Mom. I'm nervous and always in a hurry—like you used to be, Daddy. Jeffrey said I couldn't remember things because I was always in such a rush that half the time I didn't even notice what was going on. Is that what you mean?"

"That's the general idea."

"But this hypothetical killer, he knows the witness has seen him?"

"I didn't say killer—just a criminal. The only thing the criminal knows for sure is that another person was with him at the scene of the crime. If he tries to ask the witness what he knows, he risks bringing the incident back to the witness's mind, an incident that might remain forgotten otherwise."

"So," Ellen said, "he has to find some way of stopping the witness from testifying, without allowing the witness to know why—or even that he is being stopped."

"Yes," I answered.

"It's like a crime novel," Ellen said, shaking her head.

"In a novel, it's easy," I commented. "The killer just kills the potential witness."

"But you said we're not necessarily talking about a killer."

I realized with pride that my daughter was a quick observer of inaccuracy, a necessary trait for a lawyer.

"Right. A criminal."

"A criminal who knows that a lawyer can never testify against his own client."

"And in this particular case," I added, "an accused aware that for his lawyer to be taken off the case would cause irreparable damage."

Ellen studied me. I was sure she got the picture. That Stow had tricked me. That I had seen something that convinced me of my client's guilt.

"Daddy, how sure are you about what you've learned?"

I couldn't answer that question.

"I really need a coffee," Ellen said. She got up, and I glanced outside. The spring sun was growing warm. The faces of the crowd heading to work showed their delight in the unexpected heat of the morning. I thought about Queenie's people hiding away in the valley. Spring is mercy after six months of cold.

I glanced at the counter, waiting for Ellen to finish there. She paid for two extra-large coffees and doughnuts with a credit card she fished from the pocket of her coat. She set down the tray with the food and the receipt on the little table. I could see that she'd made a decision about giving me advice.

"Listen to me, Daddy, and pay attention." Again her haughtiness put me off. "I've called all my witnesses, citizens who know what they've seen and can swear to it. No way would I jeopardize the Crown's case by calling a new witness who may or may not have seen something, may or may not remember something, may or may not know the significance of anything seen and may or may not be jeopardizing himself by testifying. It's useless, and I don't want to hear one more word about it. Understood?"

I sure did understand. She was letting me off the hook.

"Sweetheart," I said, "don't put your case at risk to help me."

She glared at me. "One: don't call me sweetheart. Two: my case is strong enough already. Three: get a grip. You're starting to lose it. Four: don't call me again until this case is done. Got all that? I hope so, because now, since you dragged me here before the cock crowed, you should hear my news."

I managed to get out, "You're pregnant again? You're giving little Angelo a sister?"

"The way Mom gave me Jeffrey?" she said. Her face turned red. There are a lot of blushers in this world, but Ellen had never been one of them.

"You are pregnant, aren't you? Oh, sweetie, that's some good news for a change."

"Daddy," she said, gulping down half of the big coffee. "This isn't about me. It's about Mom."

"She sees me in court every day. She can talk to me anytime she wants."

Ellen shook her head. She stood and pushed in her chair. "Privately. She's finding court hard to take. She's not coming again."

"Is this about those tests on Sal?" I asked in alarm. "What do you know about that?"

Ellen didn't hang around to answer my question, but was out the door before I could stop her.

"Hey—" I shouted after her, jumping up from the table. "What the devil? That's not even civil to your old man. And you forgot your credit card receipt." She waved her hand in a gesture of dismissal and disappeared into the crowd. I glanced at the slip of paper. At the bottom was her signature. Something about it struck me as odd. I remembered an old trick from forensic science. I turned the receipt upside down and studied the signature again.

Why had I been so sure that I knew Ellen's signature? The writing on the slip looked something like the "Portal" signature I'd seen on the financial information, at the pharmaceutical company, on the document from Stow's trust company. But it was not the same. I sank back onto the rickety chair. The Portal who'd signed all those documents hadn't been Ellen. The writing was neat and precise. But upside down, I could see the slant was different, the loop of the P not as round. Who had signed those documents?

Each time I'd checked on a piece of disclosure, I had assumed that Ellen had been there before me, that I had been following her paper trail. But no. Someone had been following *mine.*

I turned the receipt right side up, then upside down again, and studied the signature. Another thing I remembered from forensics was that people from the same family often have remarkably similar styles of writing. Suddenly I knew who had tampered with the boxes in my office, who had left the lights on and trailed red tape home on his shoes.

Jeffrey Portal, my son.

But why? Was Jeffrey working with Ellen, an accomplice in her bout with me? More likely, in his quiet and incomprehensible way, my son was checking on me, the way you check on someone you fear cannot properly do his job. I blushed as red as Ellen at that thought. I did not need anyone following me about to prevent fatal errors.

Or did I?

I was still rattled an hour later when I met Nicky outside the courthouse. "I got into Riverside last night," I managed to tell him.

"No way!" He actually backed away from me, though I could tell it was involuntary.

"Way, my boy. I had Queenie do some investigating first. There's nobody contagious. Hasn't been for months. Just a few people in the isolation tents for control purposes."

He studied me for a moment before he stepped closer. "So?" he finally asked.

"I'm not sure. I need some time."

"We're asking for an adjournment?" His face was a study in disbelief.

"You can use a day off, son."

Nicky said, "I don't want a day off. I like sneaking around pretending I'm off the case. Plus McKenzie's going to go ballistic."

He was right. "Mr. Portal," the judge bellowed, eyeing me up and down for effect, "why have you not informed the court earlier of your decision not to call a defense witness today? You should have properly let the court know yesterday at the completion of the Crown's case that you require additional time. The jurors have all arrived to do their duty. Your conduct is an insult to the good people of this city."

"I apologize, Your Honor." I raised my eyes to the bench but was careful not to make eye contact with the judge. "Your Honor, sir, I am deeply cognizant of the inconvenience I am causing the court on behalf of my client and would under no circumstances occasion such inconvenience unless I was sure I could not fully conduct my client's defense without this brief delay." Then I added as an afterthought, "I only discovered the need for it last night after court had closed."

This little speech seemed to attract the attention of the media in the body of the court. I could hear pens scratching and handheld electronic devices clicking. The sounds made me wonder why I'd not seen Aliana in court since our last interview in my car.

"Lovely rhetoric, Portal," McKenzie said snidely. "Quite reminds me that you used to be a remarkable lawyer."

There had been a time when such an insult would have caused me to throw a few punches, but age, experience and a distaste for drawing blood had made me immune to such comments.

"Yes, Your Honor."

McKenzie sighed, as if he and his golf game wouldn't love a day off. "Very well," he said, "you can have your adjournment."

He turned to the deputy who sat at his right hand, a faithful civil servant always capable of paying attention to the judge and working complex crossword puzzles simultaneously. "Deputy, please ask the jury to come in so that I can dismiss them properly."

To the court clerk he said, "This court will adjourn until 10 a.m. tomorrow morning, by which time Mr. Portal and Mr. Stoughton-Melville shall have made up their minds as to the wisdom of asserting their right to remain silent."

I did not use my extra time trying to get any information from Stow. I did not use it to find my son and ask him why he was signing important legal papers. I did not use it to learn what was ailing Anne or Sal.

I used it to look for Queenie. For the first time in our long friendship I could not do without her company.

I went first to have a look at the clinic. It had only been a week or so since the operation had been shut down, but already a "For Rent" sign had been posted on the front window. Storefronts with offices above went fast on Queen Street. Queenie's clinic would soon be replaced, probably by something far more upscale, another antique shop or art gallery.

I decided to explore the valley, check a few likely spots for Queenie's clients to have holed up. I turned away from the clinic and headed back to my car. I was just about to unlock the door when a ragged man rounded the corner, raised his hand and shouted a slurred greeting in my direction.

"Hey, you there. Yo!" he called.

Having been a beggar myself, I'm not a man who flees the needy. "Yes?" I answered, reaching for the spare change in my pocket.

The man came nearer. When he was about ten or twelve feet away, he stopped. Just what I needed! Johnny Dirt. A smile cracked his filthy face, showing his stained and broken teeth. "Sir!" he cried. "Your Honor!"

After several weeks of bowing and scraping to Justice McKenzie, I had almost forgotten that in this other world, the world of the derelict citizens of the back streets, there were those who remembered my former reputation.

He eyed my hand in my pocket. I withdrew it quickly. I didn't want to look like I was reaching for a weapon. Even in my lowest days when I had had to defend myself from ruffians on a regular basis, I had never been armed, not even with a piece of sharpened metal or a rock.

"That's right, Your Honor," Johnny said. "You take that hand out of your pocket. You don't gotta give no money to me. You give enough to us all, and I'm grateful."

"I'm not sure what you mean, Johnny." Was the man drunk?

"I changed my mind about you when I seen how you helped down at Tent City," he replied. "In the winter when we was freezin' our butts off down there and you was takin' the trouble to teach us stuff . . . Made me wish I could do something for you—like pay you back."

"No need," I said, "unless you'd like to tell me where Queenie is today."

"Sure, man. She's down in the valley, north of the viaduct between Bloor and the Pottery Road Bridge," he blurted. "You could find her behind the willow trees where them boards from the old factory are stickin' out of the ground, but don't tell nobody I'm the one who told you. She's got rules and I respect them."

"Thanks, Johnny," I replied. "I'm glad we're not enemies anymore." I stuck out my hand for him to shake.

"Don't push it, man," he said, turning away.

About a mile north of the bridge at Queen Street, the Bloor Viaduct, a high multiple-arched bridge of weathered metal that was one of the most beautiful structures in the city, had been recently fenced with metal poles and mesh to prevent would-be suicides from jumping into the valley below. I negotiated a secret path down into the ravine underneath the bridge. A blue jay screeched in the trees, but the loudest sound was the rush of the Don River swollen by spring rain and the runoff of melted snow.

Late purple crocuses and early wild daffodils swayed in the slight breeze that bent the new grass in which they danced. Ordinarily, the sweet peace of the valley was as calming to me as a drug. Today, it seemed, I could not be calmed.

When I got near the location that I thought Johnny Dirt had meant, I stepped off to the side of the path. Behind a tall stand of spindly, leafless trees, I could see the flash of metal—traffic on the Don Valley Parkway. On the other side of the path, the trees were much denser. Years' worth of sumac made a thick barrier between the path and the river, which was not visible, though I knew where it lay not only from previous experience but also because of the line of stately weeping willows that marked its eastern bank. Near the base of several of the

257

willows, a decayed row of ancient wooden planks rotted at leisure in the mud.

I stood still and listened. I heard a cardinal, a red-winged blackbird, the faint and distant whiz of cars. I heard, too, as I always can, the sound of the great heart of the city—a pulsation composed of all the sounds made by four million people intent upon living their ordinary lives. I heard the soft breath of a river breeze rustling the grass and the flowers. I heard the river itself. And I heard, faintly audible between me and the water, Queenie's voice. "There," she said, "is that better?"

Yes, I wanted to say. *Yes. Yes.*

The dense sumac branches were no barrier. I wove my way through them in a way I had learned from a feral dog. On the pebbles of a narrow beach made by the river in its meandering, a woman lay on a ragged blanket. Bending over her patient was Queenie, her dark silver hair catching the sunlight from the deep green waters. Queenie had a white cloth in her hand, mopping the forehead of the other woman.

The patient sighed, reached up to touch Queenie's hand. Queenie nodded, took the cloth away, rose and stepped closer to the water, which bubbled over a riffle of concealed rocks. With the agility of a younger woman, Queenie stooped toward the river and dipped the cloth into it, swirling it in the sparkling water, splashing a little on herself. She wore a light jacket, jeans and hiking boots, and also her nurse's smock, as pristine and white as the cloth she now wrung out and replaced on the head of the woman.

"Okay," she said, "I'll come back later." She packed a few things into a small medical bag and stood, brushing the dust of the pebbled beach from her jeans. Then she saw me. "I'll just check on a few of the others," she told her patient. She walked a little way down the bank of the river, the sun off the water dappling her lithe body as she moved among the willows. I followed closely on her heels. I stumbled over pebbles to get nearer. I let the bare stalks of last summer's wild grass slap my legs, the twigs of willows scratch my face. It seemed that now nothing could distract me, slow me. The time had come for me to admit that Queenie and I were beyond friendship. I caught up with her and grabbed her, perhaps a little too roughly. She didn't protest, simply turned and found her way into my arms. As if we had practiced the moves all our lives, our lips met, cautiously at first and then deeply, my tongue exploring the recesses of her mouth. Without reservation, she pressed her small body into mine.

I grabbed the rich thickness of her hair, hair I already knew the heft of. She pulled away and put her cheek on mine. It was cool and comforting, but with a suggestion of inner heat that stirred me.

"I like this," she said, emitting a ripple of laughter that was as soft as the sound of the river kissing its stony shore.

"Queenie, I love you," I said, hoping my legs would not give way. "Can you think kindly of the old fool who should have said this a long time ago?"

And the few brief moments we seemed to spend there beside the Don became an entire afternoon, where two lovers in a pebbly Eden hardly noticed the sun sinking behind the shallow bank and the green waters turning black.

When the sky's azure finally relented into purple, I stroked her face and said, "It's been so long since I've been with a woman, my love, that I was afraid I wouldn't know what to do."

We had moved from the beach into a sheltered area where snow still lingered under willow branches that shaded the underbrush from full sun. Anyone else our age would have thought of catching cold or worse lying on the cold earth of the spring forest. But not us. Queenie and I were used to far worse. I thought of the irony of two old ex-bums coming together at last in an environment far from silk sheets and soft mattresses.

Queenie jumped to her feet and pulled on her smock and jeans. "Good Lord, you haven't forgotten one thing. You made *me* forget what I'm here for. Look at the time. I've got people I have to see down here. Come with me." She reached down and pulled me up. "You know all those people who disappeared when Tent City was burned?"

"Yes."

"Well," she said, "I'm still helping them out. It's going to get dark pretty soon. You have to come along. So let's go." As if I would consider another alternative!

As the light faded, Queenie and I made our way from camp to camp in the valley, searching out the displaced and the dispossessed. I held the flashlight; she told me where she wanted to go. We visited the ill and the lonely, those who sheltered beneath the trees and those who hid in caves behind the narrow expanses of pebbled beach. We found the old curled under tattered blankets, and the young stretched out beneath the northern stars with nothing to protect them. We listened to woes and laughed at jokes and shared stories.

When we finished, the sky over the eastern rim was just beginning to turn from indigo to pink.

"I'll take you home, Queenie," I said. "It's been a long night."

"I need to walk," she replied. "To think about things." Her face was tired, her body was stooped. She was wary now, sad and almost, I thought, defeated. But she kissed me on the cheek before she walked away.

In my car, staring in the mirror at my bleary eyes and gray stubble, I wondered if I'd lost my mind again. Yesterday had been spent more productively than any I'd spent in ten years, but today was supposed to be *my* day in court, the day when I must produce witnesses for the defense or suffer the infamy of defeat.

Lucky at love, unlucky at cards . . . Maybe I should have spent the previous day working in my office.

Or not.

Chapter 17

I was foggy-brained by the time I got to the courthouse, so exhausted that I almost missed Nicky waving at me from the doorway.

"Stow left a message with Security that he needs to see you before you go in," Nicky said, sounding scared. Without comment, I made my way on foot through Security and down to the cells.

Despite Ellen's insistence that my remembrance of the syringe incident was irrelevant, I felt that I must inform Stow. In the few moments I had before I confronted him, I decided that the quickest way to accuse him of being a liar was to immediately remove myself from his case and take the consequences. But before I had a chance to utter a word, Stow, as always, trumped me.

In the parking garage beneath the courthouse, a cavernous, complex, concrete labyrinth that seemed to stretch in every direction, I fought for breath because of the exhaust fumes of three prisoner vans that lumbered by. The fourth van came to a stop in front of me near the short driveway between the judges' parking area and the fortified steel garage door that led to the unloading dock of the cells. A side door slid open, and a guard motioned me to enter.

I sidled in beside Stow onto the wire-mesh seat of the van. He signaled to the guard to unlock the shackles that bound his ankles to a loop on the floor. I was astonished when the guard complied. This was my first experience with a prisoner van that did not smell of sweat, urine or disinfectant. Indeed, the only odor was a faint one of Stow's cologne. Outside, the garage was a cacophony of slamming doors, trampling feet and the grinding of gears on the metal door that separated judges from prisoners, but inside the van, it was as still as a church.

"Ellis," and here Stow clutched my wrinkled jacket in excitement, "I tried to have you reached all yesterday. I wanted you to know that your appointment is a fait accompli."

I was astonished at his gall.

"Don't sit there looking stupid, Portal. As soon as this trial is over—whatever the result—the announcement will be made. You will become a judge again."

To say I was angry is to underestimate my revulsion. The man—even in a prison van, indicted for murder—knew how to put me on the defensive and make me inarticulate with rage. "St-Stow, I know you take consummate pleasure in be-bedeviling me, but not any . . ."

He seemed to hear nothing I was saying. "I'm taking the stand. Today."

"What?"

"Tell McKenzie I'm ready to talk."

"You *are* crazy. We're not prepared. One way or another, you're determined that we lose this case, unless, that is, we plead complete and total insanity then and now."

"It's almost ten o'clock. Let's not keep the judge waiting, Ellis. You look like you slept in a tree last night, but you're still working for me, and I'm telling you that in eight minutes, I'm going to testify."

Before I could reply to these words, which I considered the bombast of a seriously deranged man, the rear door of the van slammed open and two guards took Stow off for processing. I felt as helpless as a baby, no sleep for twenty-four hours, dirty and bedraggled, unable to bring Stow down from his hysteria and at a loss to deal with it.

I gowned quickly, hoping to have a brief word with Nicky, but at the door of the courtroom I was surprised by my ex-wife. She looked, as usual, the picture of a Toronto society matron, but even her exceptional poise and exquisite grooming couldn't hide a certain air of being distraught. Something was amiss. Sal?

"Ellis, we need to talk."

"Anne," I said, glancing at my watch, "I can't possibly talk now. Unless it's about Sal, and even so . . ."

A look I hadn't seen in twelve years crossed Anne's face. The look she used to give me when I made a promise to her that had no chance of being fulfilled.

"I will talk to you later, Anne," I said more assertively, and I gave her hand a brief squeeze. I felt like everyone was coming at me at once.

"Grandpa," I heard a voice pipe up. It was Angelo, arriving with his uncle Jeffrey.

"Why are you all here today?" I asked. "Why isn't this child in school?"

"We want to see who's going to win," Angelo said. "Mommy said it's almost over. She said the judge might talk. Plus, if a judge wants to talk in court, he can. For as long as he wants. Is that true, Grandpa?"

My ire rose by the minute. Why had Ellen allowed the family to come? Whatever happened, the day would not provide pleasant listening. Did my daughter want her little son to witness the grim closing addresses to the jury? Today might well be the day that Ellen would remind the twelve exactly how, in her submission, the evidence proved that Stow had murdered his wife.

"Well, Grandpa, is it true or not? Can a judge talk as long as he wants? Can he say whatever he feels like saying?"

The child was, in fact, pretty much correct. A judge could filibuster in court to his heart's content, unless he feared that a higher court, the Court of Appeals, might reverse him or render what he said ridiculous by a ruling of its own.

Was Angelo reflecting something Ellen had said about the case? And if so, to which judge was he referring? To McKenzie? To Stow? Or to me?

I motioned for Nicky to sit beside me. What was Stow going to do about it—fire me? Nicky didn't hesitate. He plunked down his files and began a flow of words. "I tried to get you all day yesterday and all night, too. Where were you?"

"I was out," I whispered.

"Didn't you have your cell phone? How could you be incommunicado at a time like . . ."

The loud knock of the deputy interrupted us. The court sprang to its feet as McKenzie climbed the few steps to his seat.

A fresh pile of folders sat on the desk in front of Nicky, and, as the clerk officially opened court for the day, I tried to take one. I needed a clue as to what he'd been working on since court had adjourned. Good thing one of us had been working. Nicky didn't take the hint, only straightened the files self-consciously and laid his hands on top of them.

"Mr. Portal," McKenzie began the moment the deputy had poured his water, "have you reached a decision about defense witnesses?"

I hesitated. What a mess—my first trial finding me so unprepared, so open to condemnation. But like any good lawyer, I decided to bluff.

"Your Honor," I began, "my client has indicated to me his intention that I mount a defense on his behalf. We will be calling . . ."

"Just a moment," the judge said. "I don't think I want you to lay out your plan in the absence of the jury. Deputy," he said to the man at his right, "instruct the matron to bring them in."

In the few minutes it took for the jury to arrive, I finally was able to have a whispered conference with Nicky.

"Tell him we have three witnesses," Nicky told me, still protecting his notes.

"But who?"

"Just tell him three. Trust me, Ellis, it's the best we can do. I'll explain as soon as I can."

"The jury is present, Your Honor," the clerk announced.

The twelve looked eager, excited, their faces fresh and their eyes bright. In just a few hours, they would look haggard, puffy-faced and dazed. Mood swings were part of the game.

"Good morning, ladies and gentlemen," McKenzie began. "As you will no doubt recall, the case for the Crown has now been fully put before you. The time has come for the accused to answer this case, if he so chooses. He is under no obligation to do so, and, should he choose not to respond to the allegations of the Crown, that choice is not to be construed as reflective of guilt. It is the onus of the Crown to prove to you beyond a reasonable doubt that the accused committed the act for which he has been brought before the court. He may, if he elects to do so, provide full answer and defense."

McKenzie turned from the jury and leveled his gaze upon me. "Mr. Portal . . ."

My opening address in Stow's defense would have to be generic. The jury knew as much as I did about what was going on in my client's mind, and had as little to gauge his guilt or lack of it.

I rose; I walked slowly to a position directly in front of the jury box. There was a little collapsible shelf hidden in the decorative wood paneling on the front of the box. I treasured it as a useful prop for manipulating the thoughts and feelings of the jurors.

I carefully ran my fingers along the molding at the top edge of the paneling, feeling for the small brass knob that would release the shelf.

As I did this, the jury studied me, those in the front row only inches from my face. I was certainly not as good to look at as Ellen. But human beings, sociable creatures that they are, equate intimacy with familiarity and familiarity with trustworthiness. Just by allowing the jury to be this close, I was already beginning to gain a psychological advantage.

I released the catch and extended the shelf. On it, I placed a single sheet of paper. From a short distance away and upside down, it appeared to be a succinct outline of a brief address. From a shorter distance and right side up, it could actually be seen as a list of the day's selection of luncheon dishes in the Barristers' Dining Room. All the jury knew was that I respected their time by planning my remarks and keeping them short.

"Ladies and gentlemen," I started, "I do not have an extensive opening statement to make to you. I intend to let my client's case unfold before you in a logical, I might almost say natural, fashion. You will hear three witnesses in defense of the innocent man who has sat here all these days listening to false charges against his honor, his integrity and—most ignominiously—against the great love he bore for his wife. You will hear from each of these witnesses exactly how Supreme Court Justice John Stoughton-Melville tended to the woman he loved. You will hear of his devotion, which began decades ago when Harpur Stoughton-Melville was a beauty and a legal genius in sui juris, that is, in her own right. And you will see, as these witnesses have seen, that Justice Stoughton-Melville did not waver in his love and his devotion despite the passage of years and the devastation wrought by a cruel and unrelenting disease."

I paused, scanned the faces of the men and women before whom I stood. This close, I could tell that several jurors had already made up their minds. These jurors did not look open, inquisitive, curious. Indeed, they looked determined, as if they had heard all they wanted to hear. Had Ellen convinced them, so that they were simply marking time, waiting to find Stow guilty?

"Ladies and gentlemen, I have but a single thought to put before you, and a single request. All I want you to think about is whether a man who so loved his wife"—I pointed to Stow—"whether that man could kill her. And all I want to ask of you is that you listen to his defense."

I might have added, *I'll be all ears myself.*

I sat down, signaled to Nicky to take over and surreptitiously wiped my brow on my gown.

The first witness was a Ms. Myra DeCosta, chief supervisor of the nurses who tended to Harpur during the final days of her life. Nicky's examination-in-chief lasted half an hour. DeCosta was a pleasantly plump woman with a rosy complexion and a matronly manner. Nicky, handsome, tall and lean in his black robe, black vest, gray legal-stripe trousers and white linen shirt with tabbed collar, looked like a nineteenth-century print of an English barrister. His examination was akin to a polite son asking questions of his cooperative mother. The image Nicky tried to convey of Stow was that of a husband who would spare no effort in the service of his beloved wife.

"Did Judge Stoughton-Melville visit often?" Nicky asked.

"Oh yes, Mr. McPhail."

"Did you actually see them together—Mr. and Mrs. Stoughton-Melville, I mean?"

"All the time. He would come by private plane and limo very early in the morning, and he stayed until very late at night. Sometimes he even had a bed brought in so he could stay overnight with her."

"Did you ever see Justice Stoughton-Melville express any impatience with his wife? Any shortness of temper?"

The woman gravely shook her gray-haired head. "No, sir," she answered. "Never."

"Thank you, madame," Nicky told her, turning the floor over to Ellen.

"Ms. DeCosta," Ellen said, "you've been a nurse for a long time, haven't you?"

"Yes," the witness answered. Her smiling manner had given way to frostiness.

"How long?"

"Over thirty years," the woman answered.

"And in that time you've had the opportunity to observe quite a range of human behavior, have you not?"

The witness eyed Ellen warily. "I guess you could say that," she answered after a pause.

"And," Ellen went on, "you've noticed, I imagine, that visitors and family members can sometimes act one way toward a patient when being watched and quite another way when they think they aren't being watched. Correct?"

While the witness thought about that, I sneaked a look at the jury. A couple of them were paying very close attention to the witness's obvious struggle to find the right words.

At last the witness spoke. "You know, Miss," she said, "having a beloved family member suffer from a lingering and incurable illness is one of the hardest things a family can face. Of course, people sometimes lose their temper. Of course they act rude once in a while, or speak sharply. Nobody likes to see that, but everybody understands. It doesn't mean anything."

"Oh, I see," said Ellen. "Nine times out of ten, when a family member loses patience with an ill, elderly relative, no harm comes of it. Is that what you're saying?"

"Yes," the witness responded, "I am."

"So then, one time out of ten, that is, 10 percent of the time, one of the patients in your care is seriously, shall we way inconvenienced by the impatience or anger of a visitor?"

The witness looked genuinely surprised. I hoped the jury noticed that surprise. I could not risk looking over to them again. I kept my eyes lowered as the witness soldiered on.

"That's not what I meant at all," she said. "I never in my whole career had a visitor harm one of my patients—or call them names or yell at them, either. Never."

"But you can't know, can you, what a visitor might do to a patient when you're not looking?"

I could see Nicky tapping his long white fingers on his notes. If Ellen could get this witness to admit that even once in a while relatives of patients might lose control when faced with certain frustrations, all Nicky's work with the witness would be nullified.

But Nurse DeCosta was made of sterner stuff. "Listen, Miss," she said, "I don't know what you're trying to get me to say, but I'm telling you right now, I've seen Justice Stoughton-Melville early in the morning, and in the middle of the day, and at night when I've been the only nurse on duty, and I never—I say never—saw him treat his wife in any way that I wouldn't like to be treated my own self."

"No further questions."

The Crown fared no better with the next witness, the recruiter of volunteers, who had, he said, personally screened most of the nonprofessional caregivers who had worked to make Harpur's last days as comfortable as possible. "They were all wonderful," he said, "including Mr. Portal there."

"Mr. Portal?" Ellen asked. "Mr. Portal visited Mrs. Stoughton-Melville?"

I cringed. What was Ellen doing now? If she had a notion to incriminate me in the case, I might as well give up on my rehabilitation and take to the valley again. Suddenly, the idea had great appeal.

"Mr. Portal knew Mrs. Stoughton-Melville's husband very well," the witness replied. "They went to law school together, I believe."

Ellen nodded and let the statement pass. I glanced at McKenzie. He had the look of a man who had considered making a statement but decided against it.

This witness, like the previous one, had so many good things to say about Stow's kindness and devotion that Ellen wisely kept her cross-examination short. When she finished, it was 11:15, time for morning break.

I made a great show of studying my notes as the jury and the judge left the courtroom. All members of the public were ushered out also, and no one remained in the courtroom except for the accused, his guards and the defense. I crossed the few steps between my counsel table and the prisoner's dock.

I leaned down and put my ear to Stow's lips. I was surprised when he said, "Thanks for seeing me through this, Portal. I'm ready now. Put me on and don't ask a litany of inconsequential and misleading questions. I want you to ask me one thing and one thing only."

As much as I had longed for instruction from Stow all these weeks, I now deeply resented his sudden decision to take over the case. When I knew he was a guilty sham? However, when I heard the question itself, I realized we might get out of this alive, with both our reputations intact. "Just ask me what happened the night I lost my wife."

The judge returned, then Ellen, then the jury. In the body of the court, the reporters sat with pens and various small electronic devices at the ready. Aliana was still missing, but my family—Anne, looking pale, apprehensive and fragile, Ellen's husband, Angelo, Tootie and Jeffrey—sat together like a resolute cheering squad. Exactly which team they were rooting for remained to be seen.

Near the rear door sat two beefy officers from the federal prison, Stow's usual escorts on the trip up from and back to Fernhope. Weird. I had never seen them in the courtroom before.

An air of hushed expectancy suffused the court. Even the brush of the hem of my robe against the counsel table seemed to echo in the huge room.

"I call Mr. John Stoughton-Melville to the stand," I stated, marveling at the authoritative and sonorous voice

I was able to muster in the midst of counsel's greatest fear, putting a witness on the stand whose answers are unknown to him. I heard the door to the prisoner's box unlatched by one of the guards. And Stow's step as he climbed down onto the broadloom that covered the floor of this court-room from the bar to the bench. A guard poured him a drink of water, then stepped back while my client swore on the Bible to tell the truth before God and the court.

"Good morning, Mr. Stoughton-Melville," I said, but Stow said nothing in return. For one anguished moment, it occurred to me that he had changed his faulty mind again and decided to continue as he had begun, by refusing to talk. McKenzie would not hesitate to let both of us have a piece of his mind, and on the record, too. Contempt charges would follow.

Weakly, I began my questioning.

"We've heard a lot of testimony over the past few days, Mr. Stoughton-Melville, and during that time, you have had to listen to the allegations against you without having the opportunity to say anything about those allegations."

He glared at me as if saying, "Get to the point, you fool." I intended to do as he had instructed, to ask the one simple question, but I needed an introduction, a lead-in to make the transition.

"But now, sir," I told him, "the time has come to state your own case, to tell the jury the real meaning of the evidence they have heard, the real events of December 26, the real reason Harpur Blane Stoughton-Melville died."

At the mention of Harpur's name, I noticed a small shift in Stow's demeanor, his face momentarily softening. But quickly it regained its harsh immobility.

"Are you prepared to do that now, sir? Prepared to tell us exactly what happened the night your wife died?"

Slowly Stow nodded. I glanced at the jury. A few were looking at the floor, embarrassed. Others seemed prepared to leap from their seats.

"Mr. Stoughton-Melville," I said more assertively, "I want you to begin at the beginning. Tell us firstly whether you visited Harpur Stoughton-Melville, your wife, on the day she died."

"Yes."

His voice was soft now, like that of an old or defeated man. I could sense the jurors leaning closer almost as one.

"Speak up, please."

Again he glared at me. I couldn't see how treating me with a lack of respect would improve his position in the eyes of the jury, but I gave him a big smile back. He looked a little surprised.

"Yes," he said strongly. "Yes. I did visit my wife on the last day of her life."

"Did you go directly to her room when you entered Riverside Hospital that day?"

"No."

Now it was I who was surprised. I struggled not to show it.

"Okay," I said, "please tell the ladies and gentlemen of the jury exactly where you went before you entered Harpur's room."

I remembered now what little Angelo had said about a judge being able to speak however long he wanted to speak in court. Let Stow talk, I thought. There's nothing else you can do anyway.

"I parked the car just as the Crown's witness said I did," Stow began. "It was a rental car because my own was under repair. That day was the day after Christmas." He looked up, and I could swear he looked straight at Anne.

"Harpur always loved Christmas," he said. "It meant little to me, but I knew that the Christmas of which I speak would be her last, so when in one of her lucid moments she asked for our traditional forty-foot tree, our golden ornaments to be put up as they had always been, I made sure her wishes were met.

"But she was not at home on Christmas morning. In fact, she was taken to Riverside for the last time a few days before Christmas Eve, and she never saw our home again.

"I left Ottawa specifically to be with her—closed up my office there and left word that I would be detained indefinitely in Toronto. On the day in question, I entered the lobby of Riverside Hospital early in the afternoon. I had a purpose—almost, you might say, a mission."

He paused, and his eyes took on the opaque glaze of ice. "You see," he went on, "I had made Harpur a promise." He lifted his hand. In the bright light of the courtroom, I saw again the same gold ring that I wore myself. "Long ago," Stow said, pointing to the ring, "I swore on this ring that my wife could ask a favor of me and that I would not deny it, no matter how grave. At the beginning of her illness, when she was still nearly in full possession of her faculties, she exacted that promise from me. She made me promise that I would make sure that she died with dignity."

Stow stopped. The silence in the courtroom was so intense, so complete, that it was unmarred by anyone drawing a breath.

"On the day after Christmas," he resumed, "I went to Riverside Hospital with the express purpose of carrying out that promise. I had thought about the matter long and hard during the empty hours in which I sat in the home that Harpur and I had made together, the home in which we had lived for nearly forty years. I decided that my life meant nothing to me if Harpur could not share it. I decided to lay everything I was and everything I had on the line. I decided there was only one way in which I could keep my promise. Daily, Harpur had become less and less the woman I loved. Gone was the fire, the defiance, the will stronger than I'd encountered in anyone else. Gone was her ability to understand in an instant the most complex concepts, the most compelling ideas. And gone, too, was her remarkable beauty, a footnote to her tragedy." ·

I listened to this slick speech with disgust. I had never heard Stow sound so personal, so . . . perhaps the term was *intimate*. He was leading toward some sort of self-incriminating admission, which could prove fatal to his defense. Every listener except me was spellbound, including McKenzie himself.

Stow continued, "I knew that Harpur was receiving a great deal of medication. It had been explained to me, but I remembered only a little of what I had been told. One thing I did remember, however, was that she sometimes received a drug that made it easier for her to breathe—and also easier to stop her from breathing under certain circumstances. I also knew that the drug was kept under lock and key in the drug repository on the floor beneath Harpur's floor. I knew this because Harpur herself had told me." He stopped again and drew in a ragged breath that ended in a sound halfway between a sigh and a sob. I looked toward the jury box. All twelve were riveted.

"In her more lucid moments, Harpur told me that the door to the vault was sometimes left open for brief periods during the change of nursing shifts. I realized that Harpur had made it her business to know these facts. On the afternoon of December 26, unfortunately, Harpur herself

277

was no longer in control. It was time to fulfill my promise to her . . ."

"Stow—" I interrupted. I had to stop him. I could not allow my client to make an admission of guilt, a confession. Especially under circumstances in which he appeared distraught. "Stow, please wait . . ."

He was so wound up nothing could stop him.

"I went to the drug vault. I stole a tray of syringes. I wanted to do as Harpur had asked. I wanted to end her misery, and then my own. I grabbed the drugs and made for the stairs. Nobody saw me in the stairwell. I didn't know that there were other stairwells and that someone might be approaching Harpur's room from another direction." He shook his head. "No, I didn't even think about that at all, because I was hurrying, my intensity at its peak. But just as I reached Harpur's door, someone—a man—crashed into me, scattering the syringes. I saw in an instant that the man was Ellis Portal and assumed that he recognized me.

"But he didn't say anything. He was so deep in thought that he didn't seem to see me at all. His sudden presence on the scene, however, caused me to lose my nerve. I left the syringes and I fled. When I learned that Harpur had indeed died that night, I realized that Ellis Portal had the same reasons to put Harpur to death as I. Five of us made the same promise to each other." Stow spoke directly to me now, his voice strong and vindictive. "You always loved her, loved her as much as I . . ."

The jury gasped. So did the body of the court. Ellen rose, but she sat down again as though no objection occurred to her. McKenzie was scratching his head, as though he was searching for a precedent for this situation. Nicky had turned pale.

I should have known. I should have seen it coming. I should have realized that Stow would try to pin Harpur's death on me, the Italian bricklayer's boy who had risen above his station not once, but twice.

In those frozen moments, I stood in awe of my enemy. Yes, I had loved Harpur. A man loves many things he can't have. Or can't keep. Like my law career, my honor, my reputation, my naive belief that the past was behind me, done and gone, and that I finally had a future as a decent, ordinary man. Finally, I had no defense against Stow. I *was* in Harpur's room the night she died. Someone had phoned. Someone had heard my voice. For all I knew, I was the last person to see her alive. The police had found those syringes. No one's fingerprints could be proved to be on them. No one's fingerprints could be proved to be absent.

When the silence was finally broken, it was still Stow who spoke. It took me awhile to hear him. And awhile after that to understand.

"But I knew then that Ellis would never kill Harpur," Stow said. "I realized that Ellis Portal was different from me in every way."

What? Stow seemed almost in a trance. To interrupt him now seemed downright dangerous.

"Yes, my counsel, Ellis Portal, is a man of dignity, of ambition. He is a survivor. But he is not a man with the courage, the sheer guts, to kill the thing he loves, even from feelings of mercy. Knowing him, he would have just talked to Harpur . . ." He glared at me. "Maybe he tried to talk her to death."

One member of the jury smiled as if this were a joke, as if *I* were a joke.

"But running into him," Stow went on, "when I was planning a dreadful act stopped my hand. Ellis Portal did not have the courage to put Harpur out of her misery. And I knew that I couldn't, either. A sudden conviction told me that what I was going to do was wrong. I realized I had no right to take her life. I realized that I was as cowardly as Ellis Portal. I had no part in my wife's death, and I will forever mourn the loss of the only woman I've ever loved in my long and miserable life."

Stow's voice sank to a whisper and he wiped his eyes. McKenzie, for once in his life, was struck dumb, and the sound of weeping began to insinuate itself into the stillness. Stow had chosen the wrong profession. He was a tragedian, a great actor. The only dry eye in the house was my own. Trumped again!

Ellen didn't even attempt a cross-examination. No legal formalities seemed necessary to the jury. They returned with their verdict within the hour.

"Not guilty."

Chapter 18

A week later, I met Stow approaching me on Bay Street. I was so used to seeing him shackled or in a glass box that my first thought was of an escaped lion coming for my throat. We stood face-to-face across the street with a red light between us. Stow made a slight gesture that I understood to mean that he would remain and I must cross.

The lion was wary. But I did as he bid. Whenever had I not?

"No hard feelings?" was the first thing he said. I thought he was going to clap me on the shoulder. He hesitated before adding, "And we have honored Harpur's memory in a fit and worthy manner. You've lived up to your promise to me and to the law."

I lost it completely, realizing finally how much I hated him. Nearby was a small park on the corner of Hagerman and Bay. I grabbed Stow by the lapels of his silk suit and dragged him a few feet into the bushes that shielded the park and its resident druggies from the view of passersby.

"You son of a bitch," I yelled. "You've always been a liar and a schemer, especially toward me! So I'm gutless, am I?"

His tailor-made was soiling from my sweating palms. He tried to push my hands off him. Around us, the druggies perked up and started to pay attention.

"You knew I was the only witness in this case! You decided to screw me one last time!"

"Ellis, please, stop," he said feebly, waving his hands and gasping for breath as I pushed him to the ground and tried to ram my knee into his stomach. My leg slipped, and my shin hit the dirt with a sharp pain. I kept at it anyway.

"Why did you do it, Stow?" I pulled at his lapels again. The silk began to come apart beneath my fingers.

"Ellis," he said, still gasping, but making no attempt to push me off. "Everything I said in court was true."

"Need help, man?" A fellow who resembled Johnny Dirt was looking us over.

"Get lost," I snarled.

"Let me up," pleaded Stow. "My suit . . ."

I got off him but, still holding his lapels, I hauled him to a nearby bench, shoving away two sleeping bums.

"Give me a minute to explain," Stow begged. "When Pipperpharmat got the test results about Harpur, I informed them that I was going to instruct my arm's-length counsel to initiate a class-action suit on the part of her estate and of others who'd been part of the drug trials. Counsel came back with the information that Pipperpharmat would countersue, and that I stood a strong chance of losing Harpur's estate. So—"

"So you engineered a dramatic criminal trial to forestall the suit?"

Stow didn't answer. He didn't have to.

"But what if it hadn't worked? What if the jury had found you guilty?"

He didn't have to answer that, either. If the jury had found him guilty, he would have appealed and claimed that *I* was the killer. Me, the once and future object of his scorn.

"You really are a low-down mother, Stow."

"And you really are a good lawyer, Portal."

For a moment, we just sat there staring at each other. Until we realized we had nothing more to say to each other. We dusted ourselves off and walked up Bay. We caught separate cabs. We never spoke again.

Suddenly I was the darling of the press, for the first time in over a decade. Reporters followed me; they e-mailed, faxed, phoned and lay in wait outside my door. Years before, when I had been the youngest and most controversial judge in the Provincial Court of Ontario, they had hounded me similarly. I had forgotten how much I had loved that attention and also how much I eventually came to hate it.

At first, Aliana was not among the admiring throng. She had given me up as a lost cause. She wrote a searing article for the *World*, suggesting that Stow and I had cooked up the whole murder case in order to, in her words, "grab the fame of sports stars or rock bands."

In the following days, however, she took a new tack and wrote a flattering little profile of me. She said she had never found me gutless, but "dogged and determined." At the end was a short paragraph written by the editor, thanking Aliana for all her years of insightful journalism and wishing her well on her return to the Middle East.

Later that week, Anne and I met. She, like everybody else, seemed to need absolution. She spoke in a rush.

"There's no easy way to tell you this, but before I begin, I want to ask for forgiveness. I know you're not a man who goes to church often—"

"I seem to have repented," I joked, remembering the Red Mass, the christening . . .

She didn't smile. "Ellis, those DNA tests for Sal?"

"Yes?"

"The sample from Jeffrey showed my DNA, but not yours."

With that absurdly brief sentence, my ex-wife informed me that Jeffrey was not my son.

I stared out the window. In the deep shadows of the forests of the ravine, the white trillium was beginning to unfurl its three petals, its dark green leaves. In the distance, the newly verdant boughs of an old apple orchard awaited blossoms and then fruit. "Every spring," my mother used to say, "everything changes." I was thinking about how right she'd always been when I heard a knock on my apartment door.

"Can I come in?"

Did Jeffrey expect me to say no? *No, because you are not my son. No, because for some reason you broke into my office and read my files and stole a document. No, because you've trespassed on my investigation and my life.*

"Of course."

"I guess you know about the result of the DNA tests," he began awkwardly.

"I heard your daughter's just fine, thank God. Was there anything else?"

The pain in his face shamed me for torturing him. What had happened was no fault of his. "Sit down." I gestured toward my living room, and Jeffrey took a seat near the door.

"Can I get you something to drink?"

He answered, "Water," and I went to the kitchen. When I opened the cupboard for a glass, I knocked one off the shelf into the sink. It crashed and shattered. Jeffrey came running.

"I'm okay, Jeffrey."

"Dad—"

"You don't need to tell me how long you've known that I'm not your natural father. Or how you found out. Or what knowing has done to the relationship with your mother and sister—half sister. That is, I assume Ellen *is* related to me in some way."

"Dad, please."

"I knew long ago, but refused to consider the evidence. Was it when I realized—the day I watched you being born—that you bore no resemblance to my family? Or the first day of kindergarten when your teacher initially refused to let you come home with me? Then there was . . ."

I turned my back to him, stood still for a moment. Then I went back to the window. Over the valley, a hawk circled, effortlessly gliding on the currents rising from the ravine. Watching it, I regained composure. "I loved you then and love you now as if you were my natural son."

He answered softly, "I'm sorry about ransacking the office. Are you going to charge me with B & E?" He brightened a bit with his small joke. "After all, it *was* because of the money."

"What money?"

"Harpur's money. My father put her estate into a numbered account in my name."

"Jeffrey, weren't you worried that you yourself would be a suspect in Harpur's death?"

"No, Dad, no! I followed you around because I had to know for certain that my father didn't kill his wife. I had to make sure her money wasn't blood money."

Jeffrey's blond hair lay only slightly mussed on his fair brow. His blue eyes held my gaze, his slender body sat poised, his long-fingered hands folded on his knees. Never had he looked less like my flesh and blood. Never had he seemed more like my child.

"Son," I said, "your sister is a fine lawyer, and she put together a strong case. Despite all her efforts, the Crown was unable to prove that your father killed anyone. You may have all sorts of theories as to what really happened that night, but if you have any respect for the law, you have to accept that John Stoughton-Melville is not guilty of premeditated homicide."

"Do you really believe that?"

"My life in the law would be a mockery if I didn't." I watched as the young man I loved gave a tentative smile, as if the assurance of my words had relieved him of a terrible burden.

I took Nicky to visit Queenie in her small house on the old narrow street at the bottom of the city. He was hanging around me like a dog that thinks his master will soon leave on a long journey. I think he was still recovering from our narrow squeak in the case. "Ellis," he commented as we drove through the city, "your daughter is brilliant. She gave us a great fight! Are you ever going to tell her so?"

I shook my head in an emphatic no, and squeezed the car into a space at the end of the street, where the houses gave onto a little park. I wondered if my decision to bring Nicky to see Queenie demonstrated my desire to avoid further commitment.

When Queenie opened her door, it was immediately clear that I didn't need Nicky as a buffer. Outlined in the wooden frame of the door, shaded by the cool darkness of her hallway, Queenie was a raven-haired girl. Lost in the mists of memory was the abuse we'd both put ourselves through together, the nights we'd huddled drunkenly against the cold of the city and the cold of our despair, the mornings we'd spent walking the streets in the heat of summer. All I could think of was tomorrow.

She stepped into the sun, and I saw a woman in the fullness of her years, a woman of wisdom and strength.

I introduced Nicky, who sized up the situation in an instant and shook Queenie's hand with the ardor of pupil to master.

"I need exercise. Nice-looking park down the street," he said quickly. "Good to see you, Mrs. Johnson." And before either Queenie or I could exclaim, he was off and out of sight.

"Nicky wanted to tell you a few things about how he helped me win the case, but I guess he's shy." I laughed, a ripple of happiness flowing over me.

"You better come in."

Before we had gone two steps, I grabbed her. "I love you, and I want you to marry me."

I felt her hold her breath, but otherwise she remained silent and unmoving against me. The warmth of her, the dusky scent of her skin. I breathed deeply even if she would not.

"Look," she said, "before I make any promises, I got to tell you that Stow told me a secret—as a way to get me to help him. He said that you were the only person who could win his case and that winning would make sure that your son would have his rightful fortune. He—"

"Queenie," I interrupted, "Jeffrey and I have been strangers most of our lives. In the last couple of years, since he came to live and work in our apartment building, since he married Tootie and had my granddaughter, Jeffrey and I have had a relationship as friends and business partners that we could never manage as father and son. But since this trial . . ."

Queenie waited for me to compose myself. "All his life," I went on, "I looked at Jeffrey as an incomprehensible alien, a puzzle, an enigma. But now that puzzle is solved. He is another man's natural son. I accept that. But he's my boy, too. We've made our peace."

"What about *our* peace?" she asked.

"It's in the bag," I said lightly. And when she smiled, I pressed on. "Think about it, Queenie. Say you'll be my wife."

She did think about it. Four days later, she called me. "Yes, Your Hon—I mean, Ellis, yes I will."

But before we became legal, Queenie and I had a project to complete. Which is why she and I, accompanied and assisted by Johnny Dirt, grunting and complaining throughout, sought out every homeless person we could find in the valley to offer them a chance at a new home.

"They ain't gonna go for this," Johnny had insisted when I showed him the map.

"It may be remote from downtown," I conceded, "but it's close to major suburban streets, and it's close to me."

"Why would you want a bunch of bums livin' right under your nose?" Johnny asked with a skepticism honed by a lifetime spent at the bottom of the barrel.

"Because I like them, and because you're my kind of guy."

"Yeah, and I'm the Lord Mayor of London."

Eventually he got into the spirit and helped Queenie and me round up almost fifty homeless and assist them in discarding belongings they didn't need and packing up the remainder. Finally, on a cool morning in mid-June, we all met at the Bloor Viaduct and wound our way up into the wilderness of our chosen ravine. When we arrived, we forded the shallow Don and set up a new Tent City, whose denizens I could guarantee permanent habitation. "Because nobody could find it if they tried," Johnny said with satisfaction.

And because Jeffrey and I owned the land.

June turned to full summer, and summer slid into August. My "victory" in gaining an acquittal for Stow meant I had gained some prospective clients, too. When a courier brought news from the Attorney General that I'd been appointed the Judge of Orphans, I was pleased, but remembered the price I'd pay in giving up my law practice yet again.

At Michaelmas in the autumn of the year, it was time once again for the Red Mass.

The judge's deputy assigned to me carefully adjusted the red sash that crossed my new black silk robe. "You look splendid, sir," he said.

"You sure do!"

I turned at the familiar voice. It was Ellen Portal, chief Crown prosecutor, mother of Angelo, my daughter. I hugged her. "You're a good sport," I said, and hugged her again. "Nicky McPhail is taking over my practice. He says if he ever comes up against you again, he's going to concede on the spot. He thinks you're a genius. Way smarter than your old man."

"I am," she said. "Smart enough never to be in the same courtroom with you again. Promise you'll recuse yourself."

"I promise," I said. She stood on her tiptoes and kissed my cheek. I took her arm and together we walked toward the door of the great cathedral. She left me in the company of my fellow judges.

Soon we entered in stately procession. I glanced ahead to see where Queenie was sitting. Ellen and Angelo were on one side of my wife and Nicky and Ellen's husband on the other. Jeffrey and Tootie sat at the end of the pew. Ellen and Tootie were whispering to each other, perhaps about Tootie's hat, which resembled a large, burnt-black marshmallow.

The row behind was full of our homeless friends from the valley, and everyone was clean and appropriately dressed. My heart swelled with pride.

Anne sat a distance away, not with the family but with the spouses of some of the most senior-ranking judges in the court. Her future with Stow seemed assured. *Forgive us . . . . as we forgive.*

My thoughts of the turmoil of the years were distracted by the roll call of judges.

"Supreme Court Justice John Stoughton-Melville," I heard.

Slowly, his head as elevated as his position, Stow turned away from the head of the procession and took his seat in the first row. He was wearing his ring, the one he had bestowed on five of us so long ago, conferring loyalty to our friendship. All our debts to each other had been paid. Justice may be balanced, but it is also blind.

I walked on. Then I heard my name. "His Honor, Judge Ellis Portal."

It was enough.